black box

First Volume of the Save the World, Complex Series

**Gary "Chris" Christopherson
University Park, Maryland
Nelson, Wisconsin**

ISBN 978-1-4357-0464-0

Library of Congress Control Number: 2007909680

Copyright (Gary "Chris" Christopherson) 2007
All Rights Reserved

black box

DEDICATION

Irene and Lynn, nurturing and inspiring parents.

Plato and Hegel, philosophical parents to conversionism, anticonversionism, and their synthesis.

ACKNOWLEDGEMENT

My deep appreciation to Dr. Patricia Haeuser, friend and editor, whose support, applying warm reality with a contagious appetite for good science fiction, made this better science fiction.

My thanks to Heather Blain for her careful and thoughtful help with the final editing of black box.

CONTENTS

Book 1 – The Black Box

Prologue	8
Chapter 1 – Discovery	12
Chapter 2 -- Recovery	21
Chapter 3 -- Safe Haven	35
Chapter 4 -- First Revelation	47
Chapter 5 -- Near Conversion	56
Chapter 6 – Frustration	65
Chapter 7 -- First Conversion	79
Chapter 8 -- Experimentation	92
Chapter 9 -- Personal Conversion	109
Chapter 10 -- Anticonversionists	124
Chapter 11 -- Weapon	139
Chapter 12 -- Conversionists	156
Chapter 13 -- Probe	170
Chapter 14 -- Loss	181
Epilogue	196

Book 2 – Save the World, Complex

Prologue	204
Chapter 1 -- Search	207
Chapter 2 -- Note	218
Chapter 3 -- Capture	224
Chapter 4 -- Alive	232
Chapter 5 -- Restore	235
Chapter 6 -- Modify	243
Chapter 7 -- Miscode	254
Chapter 8 -- Devil's Hand	266
Chapter 9 -- Banned	272
Chapter 10 -- Personal Code	275
Chapter 11 -- Redemption	287
Chapter 12 -- Conveyance	296
Chapter 13 -- Mission	305
Epilogue	316

Book One: Black Box

black box

Prologue

South American jungle, the distant past.

"At a time in the distant past, there is one and it is me."

Through the warm, moist jungle, many rich images dance and complex sounds reverberate. At times, the images clash, sending forth messages of chaos, conflict and disharmony. Breaking through that shallow view of discordant images and sounds, a deeper, truer view reveals a living tapestry weaving together sounds, colors, threads and objects of every shape, size and material. Essential to this living tapestry are harmony and disharmony, order and chaos, and conflict and peace. As the morning sun rises, it sheds revealing light on the true nature of the jungle, potentially on life itself. As the jungle animals emerge for the day, each has its own individuality; each comes together and contributes to life's diverse and powerful tapestry.

As I appear, I know there are momentary pauses as unfamiliar sights and sounds enter many animals' perceptual space. At this moment, there is unmistakable silence. I am the cause; I am the disruptive force; I am the focus of attention. The creatures around me engage their most acute senses to uncover the mystery that I am. I am a new creature to them. I am not the usual creature of the jungle, though others living in the jungle bear some similarity. Still, life in the jungle is disrupted by me, a new face and a new shape.

In my silent coming, the jungle animals are confused. To them, I appeared with more stealth than other creatures in the jungle. It is as if I appeared out of nowhere. As I now move through the jungle, it is clear to them that I am quiet in my movements, but I move loudly when compared with many who live in the jungle. Stealth does not alone explain my unannounced coming.

Those animals nearest to me watch me closely. They see that I move easily and smoothly on just two legs. They see my features. I am different. I seem only to have hair on the top of my upright body and then only in certain spots. I have hair on my face, just like some of them.

And then there is the object I hold. It is a simple object that might look too perfect even for nature at its best. It is as dark as the darkest stones hidden in the deepest caves. They might see that the corners are as sharp as their sharpest rocks and the sides are straight, unlike almost anything in their experience. If they could look closely, they would see no scratches or other marks on this strange dark object.

For a few moments, I pause to consider all the life around and take some pleasure and pride in its diversity

black box

and perfection. But enough! I am here today for another purpose, a purpose requiring quick and careful attention. I stop by a mound of earth in a small clearing, drop to the ground and dig a large hole in the mound. I gather up stones for my task and, within the large hole, arrange the stones to create a small, stone-lined enclosure.

The jungle animals watch me closely and I have their full attention. I need to stay focused. I need to keep moving.

I pick up the dark object and touch it carefully. It changes. No longer is it just a dark object. It now has a life of its own. To the creatures observing me, "scratches" might seem to dance across the object. As they dance, the stones in the earthen mound change, lose the look of individual stones, and take on the semblance like a stone chamber. I check the object again; I touch it one last time. It goes dark again. As I bend down, I place the object in the stone chamber and cover them both with earth.

I feel relief that the task is done. I feel relief that the creatures observing my work care little about the object buried in the ground. I confused the jungle animals with my sudden appearance. I am sure that some are curious about the mound and what it holds, but that curiosity probably lasts for only for a few moments. Life elsewhere in the jungle demands their attention. Their very survival demands their attention. Survival is what they care about; survival is what they will quickly return their attention to. My dark object in its strange stone chamber and I are of little consequence to them. We are quickly forgotten in the coming of other mysteries of sight and sound.

As I stand and turn, I contemplate all the nature around me and feel good about the helpful, guiding role I have played.

In an instant, I am gone. No trace remains of me in that jungle other than the freshly dug earth on the mound in the clearing.

black box

Chapter 1. Discovery

South American jungle

As Ti Ching [1] wades through the tangled jungle underbrush, she keeps wondering if all this work is worthwhile. Maybe it is just too late. No. That is far too defeatist, she chastises herself. Even with all the destructive forces attacking the jungle in the 20th century, some good can come from preserving what's left

---

[1] Ti was born in the United States, ten years after her Chinese parents migrated from Hong Kong. In a few months, she will turn 30, though she looks young for her age. She wears her black hair cut just above her shoulders and softly brushed back from her face. Her round, black framed glasses set off the round shape of her face. Her friends and co-workers often call her cute even though she hates it. She hates being seen as effervescent as well, but knows she exudes effervescence. Neither is terribly helpful in her being taken seriously as a professional.

Her profession, a civil engineer, is a critical part of her. She received her civil engineering degree from the University of Wisconsin, specializing in environmental restoration. She has learned much from studying the work of the Army Corps of Engineers and is determined to avoid repeating many of its mistakes.

and trying to reconstruct some of what has been lost. Sure, the jungle remains threatened. On the other hand, the problem is catching people's attention and turning that attention towards restoration. She pauses and reminds herself not to become too optimistic or to pessimistic. She has to maintain the right balance and stay focused.

Given the amount of damage done to the South American jungle, she's decided to apply those lessons in a place where human beings have been and continue to be extraordinarily destructive. Having worked in the jungle for several years, she is now viewed by her peers as a jungle restoration expert, someone who is making a positive contribution to an enormous, unending undertaking.

Emerging from the trees, Ti comes upon a small clearing, leans down with her hands on her knees, and pauses to catch her breath. She's tired and hot and the sweat keeps running off her forehead into her glasses. There's still a long way and only a couple of hours to go before she reaches the relative comfort of her base camp. Her last two weeks of life deep in the jungle have been difficult. Fortunately, for Ti, the difficulty is easily countered by the jungle's stunning beauty and never-ending diversity.

Breathing hard and sweating profusely, thinking wearily of the remaining miles ahead, Ti stops in the clearing. This is the one last opportunity for a brief respite before the final trek back to base camp. She removes her glasses, wipes the sweat off her face and shoulders, and cleans her glasses with a dry strip of her shirt sleeve. Looking for a place to sit, she spots a small earthen mound just ahead of her and walks over to it.

Seating herself upon the earthen mound in the clearing's center, she tries to imagine what secrets the jungle still holds and she has been just too busy to

black box

discover. The next trip is going to be different, she tells herself. Next trip, she'll take time to stop and absorb all that nature is willing to share. No more "running" through the jungle with tunnel vision. Here is nature in all its glory in front of and all around her; just look around at the stunning beauty in this isolated clearing. Very likely, Ti is the only human being who has ever stepped foot here.

As she takes a moment and scans the clearing, the mid-day sun's rays bounce off the edge of a piece of smooth, grayish stone partially hidden in the earthen mound on which she sits. Hit with the brief flash, Ti squints her eyes so that she can see the object more clearly. "Far too smooth and sharp to be in a place like this," she thinks.

Quickly, she takes out her knife and gets down on her knees. Carefully, she removes earth from around the stone. The more she digs, the more it is clear that something unusual is buried in this mound. Her excitement builds. Now she uses both hands and digs as fast as she can.

As she digs further, the dimensions of the stone become apparent, about three inches by one foot by one and one-half feet. She stops, drops backward to sit on the ground in front of the stone and drops her head onto her arms.

"Too bad it's this big," she says in frustration as she thinks about the long hike still awaiting her. "No way am I going to be able to carry a big, heavy stone like this out by myself. But there's no way am I leaving it behind."

She resumes her excavation. Finally, enough earth is removed for her to try to move the stone. She applies all her strength to moving the stone. To her surprise and relief, the stone moves easily and is much lighter by far than she expected for a stone this big. In fact, it's too light. Ti thinks it must be hollow.

This observation is soon verified as she looks over the stone carefully and sees what appears to be a sliding panel.

She slides the panel open. As she does, she sees that the stone chamber is unique in several ways. She takes a mental inventory: its sides are wafer-thin. It has the appearance of stone, but has the flexibility and resilience of metal. Commensurate with the thinness of the material is its great lightness. She gently weighs the object in her hands. It's feel like about 10 pounds.

But to her great surprise, there is more. Much more. The chamber is not empty. Her pulse beats rapidly.

Inside the chamber is an object as unusual as the chamber itself. There's a solid black object of nearly the same dimensions as the stone chamber. She carefully removes the black object from the chamber.

"Amazing!" she thinks, "there are absolutely no markings at all. Not even the slightest scratch or blemish! From everything I can see, it is a perfectly formed black stone, glass or metal object and it is apparently solid."

"But that doesn't make sense. It is far too light to be solid!"

"I have a stone chamber that is too light and its walls too resilient for stone," she says to herself.. "This is very strange. It looks like and feels like stone, yet it doesn't look like an object that is cut or carved by technology that I know of."

"The black object seems to be the same. It appears hollow as well or to be some super-lightweight metal alloy or glass. But unlike the stone chamber, there is absolutely no sign that it can be opened."

Ti is perplexed. She has two objects that make no sense in either the jungle or in civilization. Even so, she has a "find". She jumps up and starts dancing around the clearing.

black box

After a few minutes of uninhibited joy, a more immediate concern hits her. She stops cold. Time has escaped her. She's been here for more than an hour. If she doesn't move quickly, she won't make it back to base camp before dark and the next stretch of jungle isn't the friendliest place to be after dark.

Her mind drives forward another thought: she's got to get her find back to civilization as quickly as possible.

She hesitates. "Do I have the right to remove something that has probably been part of the jungle for a very long time?" She's often referred to herself as a 'jungle preservationist'. Her life is dedicated to preserving the jungle, not stripping it. "But surely, these objects could not have anything to do with the jungle or "preserving" the jungle," she argues out loud. "But then again, why were they here? What is their purpose? And how did they get to a spot that supposedly no other human being has ever visited?"

She shakes the soil off her hands and gets up. She's got to get moving and make it to base camp before dark.

During the journey back, her mind weighs what she is going to do with her find. She's here under a U.S. government grant and she feels some obligation to turn her find over to the government. However, she's not totally comfortable with that course of action. Her experience with government and how it responds to unknowns, especially where there appears to be an 'intelligence' associated with it is far from a positive one.

Ti tosses around the idea of treating the object as an archeological find and turning it over to a scientific institution, like a university or the Smithsonian Institution. Yeah. The Smithsonian. She could compromise and send the object to the Smithsonian, but let the government know that they have it. The idea of turning it over to the Smithsonian gives her a bit more comfort. Still, she has to be concerned about my government grant and the people who she reports to. She can't afford to get them upset and lose the grant. Then she'd really be finished here. After all, the government agency is trying to do some good in the jungles of the world and deserves some credit for that. Still …..

Suddenly she loses her balance, falls down hard and bruises her knee badly. Shocking herself back to the immediacy of a painful reality, she realizes that if she does not focus on where she is going right now, both she and the objects might never see civilization again.

She quickly reminds herself, "Jungles are not forgiving to fools or those with minds lost elsewhere."

She renews her trek, a bit bruised and limping badly.

With about an hour to spare, Ti limps back into her base camp, empty at the moment, and resolves to let her internal debate rest. Unfortunately, sleep tonight is not going to be an easy goal to achieve. She has too many thoughts and too many questions.

Having tossed and turned for most of the night, Ti awakens abruptly at dawn.

"What am I going to do? Since I'm the one who removed the chamber and object from the jungle, I'm now responsible for what happens next."

"Oh my god! What if I get it wrong?

"Okay. Okay. Think. I can do this. Fortunately, I have over a week over figure this out before civilization returns in the form of the supply helicopter."

With her digital recorder in hand and the tools available in the camp, Ti proceeds to discover what she can about the two objects. She suspects the black object

black box

is probably the most important, but the least penetrable. She'll have to be careful to not destroy it as she's conducting her tests.

Ti decides to focus her attention on the stone chamber first. As she looks over the object and its stone chamber, she narrates constantly into a tape recorder, keeping a detailed description of all that she sees.

Her first discovery is that the stone chamber is made of stone like that commonly found in the area in which she discovered the earthen mound and its holdings. But the fabrication of the stone chamber is a whole other thing.

"The stone itself is not uncommon," she says into the recorder. "However, in its current form as a stone chamber, it has apparently acquired properties that go far beyond the original stone upon which it is based. No stone could be so thin and yet not be at all fragile."

"I'm confused here," she mumbles. "I don't get it."

"Though the chamber is hollow as if carved or cut, that explanation doesn't seem to make sense. The stone chamber has all the characteristics of being formed molecule by molecule and, in that formation, of being reformulated so that the stone acquires the additional characteristics of the most high-tech of metals. But, as strong it is, I don't think it's indestructible."

After Ti conducts several tests with mechanical cutting tools and gas torches, it's clear that the stone chamber can be cut, though not easily. If the tests with the torch are any indicator, a higher temperature torch or a laser will do the job.

With all her tests, she still believes that the chamber is made of stone, but, no ordinary stone. Somehow, it has been formed into shapes and is as indestructible as any modern metal available.

Impatient, she turns her attention from the

chamber to the black object. Somehow, she thinks this is not going to yield that much information. With a great amount of care, she conducts similar tests on the black object as she had on the stone chamber, but here she tries to exercise a bit more care, since she does not want to destroy the object.

After some time, she pauses, sits down on the workbench and puts her chin on her knees. She sighs with a bit of relief and resignation. She holds the tape recorder close to her mouth. "Apparently, I don't need to worry about damaging the black object. No matter what carving, cutting or chipping tool I employ, there are absolutely no signs of any impact. I'm beginning to suspect that this object is much more than just a perfectly formed black stone, glass or metal box with no other use. This is no natural object; this was crafted with great skill and knowledge.

Someone went through an awful lot of trouble to make this dark object. Someone took extraordinary steps to leave it in a place that no human being is ever expected to visit."

Exhausting the tools available and her own analytic skills, she now knows as much as she is going to know without outside help. She has to make a decision about what to do next. Not fully trusting either the U.S. government or the scientific institutions by themselves, she decides to notify both and send the chamber and black object to the Smithsonian via the supply helicopter due tomorrow morning.

Since she's got a small amount of leave time available, she'll ride along to the airport and make sure that the two objects get on the next available flight to D.C. Once she does that, her mission is complete and she can return to her work in the jungle."

But it's going to be incredibly hard giving up these objects and returning back to her regular work here.

black box

She's been so excited about her work here. But now she's been bitten by this new find. She's got so many questions and no answers. She doesn't want to let this go.

"But I must," she says with unhappy resignation.

As the day wears on, she makes the calls. The government officials are somewhat curious, but are more so skeptical. To them, the find is not terribly important. Give it to the Smithsonian, they tell her. As far as they see it, it will write off as some archeological find that will end up at the Smithsonian anyway.

On the other hand, the Smithsonian officials have much more than a passing interest. They, as does she, realize that the objects just do not fit in the area of the jungle in which she found them. Someone, for some inexplicable reason, went way out of his or her way to place the objects there. What these objects are is a tantalizing question to the officials. If she did what she says she did, these objects do not make a lot of sense in terms of what they are or where they were.

The arrangements are simple. She is to deliver the objects to the airport and place them on a plane bound for the U.S. The plane is to arrive at Washington Dulles Airport late the next day. The two objects will be marked for pick-up by Smithsonian Institution officials and their government escorts.

The next day, Ti watches the plane take off. She is not happy. She pouts. She wants to be on the plane and be there for whatever happens next. Frustrated, she turns away, kicks the dirt, and admits her misery, "I'm torn," she mutters. As important as her work here is, she fears she's making the wrong choice. She should have gone along. She should be part of the discoveries yet to happen. She fears that the black object and its mysteries will impact the world in ways she can't even begin to fathom and she fears most that she'll not be there to be part of what happens next.

Chapter 2. Recovery

Dulles Airport, Washington, D.C.; late the next day.

      In the early evening of the next day the plane with Ti's parcel lands at Washington's Dulles Airport.

      Inside the sweeping main terminal at Dulles stands the restless reception committee made up of a government official and a Smithsonian scientist. They are anxious. They check their watches frequently. They are not quite sure what they are about to receive. They have Ti's description of the chamber and the black object therein. Beyond that, they know little. What they do know is they have a good hour, if everything goes well, to wait as the plane's arrival is delayed by the custom's clearance process and baggage unloading.

      As he paces back and forth anxiously, Dr. Joseph Form,[2] a forty-three year old scientist at the Smithsonian

---

[2]   Joseph has been a scientist with the Smithsonian for nearly a

black box

Institutions, tries to contain his rising anticipation of the engineer's find. If Ti Ching is right, the find defied explanation.

As he waits, his mind wanders back to his childhood. "I have to admit that even as a child I was a bit unstoppable when faced with what some would see as the seemingly great unknowns. I must have dissembled dozens of old clocks and radios in search of 'great truths.' I had to quickly re-assemble some of the newer ones at the demand of my family who saw the need to tell time or hear music as greater. In my biased view, my contribution to discovering truth far outweighs my failures in the pragmatic reconstruction of household items. My family didn't quite see it the same way, but perseverance has served me well."

But he went beyond mechanical object in his early truth discovery phase. Many chemical concoctions, primarily made up of discarded household products, were mixed and tested on all kinds of inanimate and, somewhat regrettably, animate objects.

He reflects, "One of the earliest measures of my 'judgment' is that I was always wise enough to stay away from tests on my family's household pets. Not that I wasn't somewhat interested, but the risk was far too great.

---

decade now since graduating from the University of New Mexico with his doctorate. He is well-respected and has a reputation for a thorough knowledge of South American artifacts. His is an unyielding scientific curiosity for almost any seemingly unsolvable puzzle. He hopes that this little puzzle proves to be a worthy challenge.

Joseph is a man of moderate build standing about five foot nine with black medium length hair. He is a Native American raised in the Four Corners area of the Southwestern United States. His family wasn't terribly poor but didn't have much extra beyond the necessities and Joseph was left to find his own entertainment in his imagination and in the world around him.

If I couldn't always put the family clock back together, I suspected I just might have greater difficulty resuscitating the family cat or dog."

Beginning in high school and continuing through today, science fiction novels have been his addiction. In them, he searches for and critiques the mistakes of science fiction writers who not only cannot foresee future science, but do not even understand current science. In these novels, he searches for the creative thoughts that might suggest paths for current and future scientists. Science fiction always pushes his imagination and challenges him, as a scientist, to translate some of that fiction into non-fiction.

So far, he has done little beyond reading science fiction.

He sinks down into the waiting area chair, his hands cupped under his chin, and muses, "My work at the Smithsonian is great, but it is more of a look back than a look forward. I spend more time cataloguing past achievements of others than making my own contributions. I'm a stuck and not particularly happy about it. My interest in future science hasn't waned a bit. I just can't get traction. Can't find the path. I just can't seem to get myself into a situation where those interests and skills are needed by anyone. I just need a little push. I need the right challenge. Maybe, just maybe, this is it."

"Sure it's a "historical find," he thought, "but, according to Ti, it seems to be something more. My gut tells me that this find might just have more future value."

He looks over at Maria, sees her fingers thumping the arms of her chair, and senses that she has a whole different perspective on the "find."

Beside Joseph, his government escort, Maria Mendez[3], is quickly losing interest. An attractive

---

[3] At the age of thirty-four, her career is a pressure-laden one.

black box

Hispanic woman of about five foot seven or eight with long, black hair, a doe-like face, and dark piercing eyes, Maria is an intense woman. She talks very, very fast. She has absolutely no tolerance, except for the things occupying her fast track. Increasingly, she is feeling assured that the parcel is no more than the artifacts of just one more "lost civilization."

"I know my impatience is beginning to show too much," Maria says to herself, "I can see it in Dr. Form's face. I know I keep checking my watch. I wish this assignment were over. Still, I'll wait. It's my duty to do so. But I don't have to be happy about it."

"Many of the boys saw me as a threat to them," she realizes, thinking back to her childhood. "Over time,

---

Having moved among a number of different government agencies over her ten-year career, she has acquired the reputation of a strong-willed, hard-working trouble-shooter. Her career is built on her ability to fix things and solve difficult, complex problems. Politically she is astute, though politics is something she carefully avoids. To her, it doesn't matter much who is in the White House, her role is to "fix and solve." It doesn't matter to her much who breaks what gets broken or who creates the problem in need of solving. In doing what she needs to do, she is widely known as an expert on "getting it done," "taking no 'prisoners," and "bending the rules." Breaking the rules is a whole other thing. Oh yes, have no doubt that she knows how, but she knows what happens when government officials break certain rules.

When Maria's family came to the United States several decades ago, they just barely made their way into the American middle-class. Still, Maria remembers all the troubles her family faced and all the rules and promises that were broken. Government is often not a friend to her family and other families like them. She grew up in the barrio in Los Angeles and even thrived in it. With nurturing from her parents and her own natural talents, Maria took to the streets aggressively. She was never someone who tolerated fools. She was as street-smart as a person could be. Her survival skills kept her out of drugs, barely, and kept her alive. Staying alive and healthy had been a challenge.

I got by that as I emerged as a 'valuable asset' to them. That asset is based on the fact that I could take care of almost anything. If someone got in trouble, I could help him or her talk his or her way out of trouble. If something weren't working in the community, I led the battle to get it working again. I had to be as tough as the streets forced me to be."

"But, I never forget what is important. I care deeply about my parents. I care deeply about my community. Fair warning to anyone who tries to hurt either."

Though a loyal public servant now, she distrusts what motivates many federal government officials. That's why she does what she does, to make a positive difference in a difficult environment. As frustrating as that can sometimes be, she knows she must be strong and bear the frustration. Often, doing what she has to do while still being true to the moral values of her family and herself is very, very hard. But she isn't about to stop now. She still cares deeply about her community, only now it is much larger community.

By pre-arrangement, the parcel is arriving as a special handling shipment with a Smithsonian tag. Since the flight first stopped in Miami, the parcel is to clear customs there. As Joseph and Maria move through the concourse to the baggage area, the announcement comes that the luggage from the South American flight will be arriving at carousel one. A West Coast flight has also just arrived with its luggage directed toward the adjacent carousel two.

As they unload the plane's luggage, the regular baggage crew is feeling a little harried and anxious. When the usual crew is there, the luggage generally

black box

arrives at the baggage area close to the same time as the passengers. Unfortunately, today one of the regulars is unexpectedly out for the day and the temporary replacement is helpful, but unfamiliar with the routine of unloading the large jets. To compound the problem, he spends a little too much time keeping a watch out for some special parcel. Fortunately, the parcel is found and the replacement handler with the beard is making sure it gets delivered to the rightful owner.

After the plane is unloaded and the luggage is on the way, the regular baggage crew proceeds to the next jet while the replacement worker drives the special parcel to the main terminal and the baggage area. Along the way, the replacement worker makes a brief stop to pick up some luggage from the West Coast flight also just arriving. Only a small portion of that flight's luggage is unloaded as most of the passengers are proceeding directly to Europe. One bag is separated from the rest and placed next to the parcel from the South American flight.

As the replacement baggage handler drives between the planes, he has the look of a man wrestling with a difficult dilemma. He questions himself, "Is this really the right time? Have the circumstances of this time provided the right people? Are they ready? Maybe I should wait a bit longer. I could just disappear with the objects. A little more mystery would be added, but it would be quickly forgotten."

"No, an accidental occurrence, combined with my own actions, has created this situation. I still believe that the time is finally right for proceeding. I hope that I am not wrong in proceeding to the next step. If I am wrong, there will need to be a lot of mid-course corrections for them and me. I have to trust that they are ready for this journey."

"The consequences of this 'black box' intervention will not be small. So much is at stake. This is no longer the time for doubt. There is no time to waste. Now is the time to make my move and shepherd what happens after that."

In an unlighted and little used part of the airport, he stops and quickly scans the area to make sure he is not seen. He opens the two bags. Recognizing the two familiar objects, he opens the stone chamber and extracts the dark object. To him, this is a "black box." As he touches the dark object, it comes to life just as it had many, many years ago in the jungle and many times before that. He touches the box's top a number of times. Suddenly, the stone chamber begins to change into a somewhat cruder stone chamber more likely to have been carved during an early civilization. Turning his attention to his second task, he first piles together several souvenirs from the West Coast flight's luggage. Then he again touches the black box. The souvenirs disappear. A new dark object is formed, virtually identical to the original black box except that it appears as if carved by humans at an earlier time. The re-formed stone chamber and the newly formed black box are placed back in Ti's Smithsonian parcel. After a few more touches, the original black box goes dormant. He then places the original black box in the bag from the West Coast flight.

"Now, I must get the original black box to the couple," he thinks as he drives toward the baggage area with Ti's parcel and the luggage. "In the meantime, by leaving the re-formed stone chamber and its contents to the scientists and the government, I give them something to spend their time on and buy critical time for the couple's work and my own. Under the Smithsonian and government's scrutiny, the new stone chamber and the new dark object have little importance in their own right. But, I've little doubt that their scrutiny will quickly turn to what is most important, how the two objects came to be what they are."

black box

The replacement worker quickly returns to his route and reaches the terminal's baggage area. Time grows short as the time comes for unloading the baggage onto the carousels. Realizing the growing impatience of the passengers inside the terminal, he and the carousel crew hurriedly place the luggage on the conveyor belts and send them on their way. At the last moment, one bag is snatched from the second conveyor and held aside.

"I just can't seem to shake these doubts," the baggage handler mutters under his breath, shaking his head "I need to see the couple myself before I can hand over the black box. If I could just arrange to meet them face-to-face for even a few moments, then I would know for sure."

Inside the terminal, the official reception committee clearly is losing its patience. Maria, expecting little from this episode, wants it over with. This is a waste of her time. Other more important tasks await her back at the office.

For Joseph, it is like being a kid at Christmas; he paces nervously and thinks excitedly. "A package with my name on it is about to arrive from the jungles of South America. In that package is the potential promise of a career-making find. If it only lives even halfway up to Ti's description, it's a major discovery. Who knows, maybe it will be the discovery of the century. Okay, settle down! Let's be a bit smarter about all this. Let's be a bit more realistic."

"Do you have any clues as to what these objects were doing in the middle of the jungle? Maria asks him, trying to make conversation. "Any idea as to what they are?"

"Not a clue," Joseph replies. "Makes no sense

given what Ti told us. This is an area that we thought had not been touched by humans until Ti's crew helicoptered into it."

"I just keep wondering why I'm here," Maria complains, increasingly impatient with the long delay. "You know that you all will just take it back your lab, decide it has some known or unknown historical value, and put it on display. End of story. It really doesn't have anything to do my agency's work."

"What the hell am I doing here? Why am I wasting my time," she says angrily, again thumping her fingers on the chair's arms.

"Chill!" Joseph says, impatient with the situation, but more so with Maria. "Listen, I don't know what we have here. Ti's story is a little muddled and a bit unbelievable. But there may be something here."

"Try to relax just a bit," he goes on. "Maybe you'll be pleasantly surprised. Maybe this is the long-lost answer to all the government's and your problems. In one sweep, budget deficits disappear. War ends. Hunger is gone. Political corruption becomes a thing of the past. Just think of the possibilities."

"Ah, but then there would be no more broken programs to fix and no more national problems to solve," he suggests, mocking her a little. "What would all the government problem solvers do? They would all be out of jobs! You would be out of a job!"

"Then again, if I were you, I would not worry too much about that possibility," he says more softly, trying to back away from the remark he just made. "They are most likely just a couple of useless objects dropped from a plane by someone to lighten a planeload of drugs. If that's the case, then neither of us will have an interest in this 'find.' Who knows? Let's have a little patience. We'll find out in a few minutes. Then you can leave and you and I will never, ever have to wait together again."

black box

"Maria, sometimes we just waste our time. I do it a lot. Maybe I am doing it again. Maybe this is just your turn."

Maria gives him an intense look of unhappiness with her dark eyes.

Finally, the carousel begins to move and bags begin appearing. Maria and Joseph move toward the carousel to watch for the engineer's parcel.

A few yards away, a second carousel comes to life and bags from the West Coast flight arrive. About 50 people are waiting, some with family and friends. Everyone is in a hurry. Off to one side is a married couple, Taj Curie and Jason Kalder, just returning from a week driving the upper West Coast. Exhausted from the trip and the flight back, they are thinking only of getting their bags and grabbing a cab back home. The bags come round and the tags are matched, except for one. One bag is missing: the couple's. Frustrated and tired, they walk over to the lost luggage counter and begin describing their luggage.

What makes their frustration worse is that their whole trip was fraught with problems in its final days. First, their vacation was cut short by two days due to some foul-up with their credit cards that left them short of money to move around. But that wasn't all. When they checked in with the airline, they found their plane reservations were messed up and they were booked on today's flight, leaving a day earlier than they planned. The airline told them it couldn't make the change without an additional charge. Without credit cards, they were pretty much forced to go on the earlier flight.

Everything seemed to be pushing them toward coming in on this particular flight. Now, one of their pieces of luggage is missing.

Over by the other carousel, Maria and Joseph spot Ti's parcel, pull it off, and check the tag. Everything matches. Even Maria shows some excitement as Joseph's anticipation rubs off on her. They immediately go to a quiet area of the terminal and open the parcel.

"Okay, okay," she admits. "Let's get the bag open and see what we've got here. If it's going to save the world and put me out of work, then we better not waste any time and find out now and how."

Inside, they find the note from Ti describing what she found, how she found it and where. Ti wants them to keep her informed on their progress with the dark object and its stone chamber.

Carefully, they unwrap the stone chamber and open it. Everything is there just as Ti described it. Well, almost everything. Something doesn't seem quite right.

As Joseph carefully looks over the two objects, he feels uneasy..

"Ti was pretty accurate in her description," he tells Maria. She is right on another point as well. These objects don't make any sense being in the jungle where she found them. But, then again, in some ways, these objects don't make any sense either."

"What do you mean they don't make sense?" Maria asks, leaning over his shoulder to get closer to the objects.

Joseph points to the engineer's description, "If you remember, Ti was emphatic about how perfect these two objects are. That is a major reason as to why she believed they were totally out of place in the jungle. But look at these two objects."

Maria shakes her head. "I'm not sure I know what

black box

you mean. They look pretty perfect to me.

"That is exactly the problem," Joseph says as he turns the objects over in his hands. "They're almost perfect, but nowhere nearly as perfect as Ti described. She is very clear that there were no blemishes or scratches on either object. She said she experimented with trying to scratch or cut the stone chamber. But she had little or no impact according to her report. She said we saw at most a small blemish on the stone chamber where the torch had been applied over a considerable period of time."

"I get it," Maria cuts in. "These objects have many scratches and all the markings of being carved. None of that fits with what Ti described. It as if they're not the same as the objects she worked on in the jungle. Yet, they're so close to what she described."

Now they both agree. The two objects look less perfect than they expected, but maybe that is just an unrealistic expectation. They both re-read Ti's note Before buying into this whole arrangement, Ti's reputation and credentials were checked thoroughly. She is highly thought of as an engineer, though early in her career. Somehow, something doesn't quite fit. The only consensus they have is that the two objects aren't perfect enough to fit Ti's description.

"I am beginning to feel that we have a problem here," says Jason as he returns the two objects to the bag. "It's nothing we can resolve here and now. But something's wrong here."

"You're absolutely right," Maria responds. "Somebody seems to be playing games and I want to know who and why. I don't like being played."

"Joseph, you were almost rid of me," she tells him as she gives him a smile. "Too bad. Now, you have a full partner in this little expedition."

And with that, they decide that the Smithsonian

labs should be their next destination.

Before Jason and Taj finish with Ms. Link, the airline's claims person, the replacement baggage handler appears. He comes up to them to apologize for the missing luggage.

"We are short of staff tonight and I mistakenly placed your bag on the wrong cart," he tells them. "Unfortunately, it's already left on another flight. But I've already made arrangements to get it back here by early tomorrow morning. I will personally take responsibility for getting the missing bag to you directly. Again, I am deeply, deeply sorry."

Trying to assure the somewhat distraught baggage handler and wanting to make sure that an innocent mistake didn't get the handler into trouble, Jason waves away the forms the claims person is filling out. "Listen. We're fine. Tired, but fine. Just arrange to have the bag delivered to our home tomorrow and that will take care of the whole thing. We don't want anyone to get into trouble over something so minor. Even if we did, we really don't have the energy."

Taj, too, had had enough but was out of steam. "Most of what's in bag are dirty clothes and inexpensive souvenirs, not something we will need tonight," she adds wearily. "Right now I just want to go home and crawl into bed."

Again the baggage handler apologizes profusely. He assures Taj and Jason, as well as the claims person, that he knows where the luggage is and that he will deliver it to their home himself the next day.

Not looking to make a major problem out of a minor one, Ms. Link, the claims processor, nods and puts down her pen. "That's all I really need to know. If all of

black box

you are comfortable with this, let's let it go at that and we won't complete the processing for the missing luggage. Just give your names, address and phone number to him and that should take care of it. I'll hold onto this partially completed slip for a couple of days and then toss it. If there are any problems, give me a call."

Jason and Taj provide their names and addresses to the baggage handler and leave for the long cab ride back to suburban Maryland.

After they depart, the baggage handler stands by himself in the now quiet baggage area.

"The die is cast," he thinks nervously. "I just hope that I bought enough time for events to develop as they should."

As he contemplates the events of the past few days, he is not sure that he was as successful as he hoped. The scientist and government escort looked too concerned. And his first encounter with the couple raised no concerns, but did little to relieve his own uneasiness.

He strokes his beard with his left hand and thinks of how he will be relinquishing so much control once this journey begins. So many mistakes will be made by so many people. But that is the price of progress. Human progress doesn't occur without mistakes and even without some conflict. It's the nature of humans; it's the nature of progress.

Chapter 3. Safe Haven

Maryland suburbs; the next day, Saturday.
Smithsonian Labs; through the night and next day, Saturday.

In the early light of a warm Saturday morning, somehow the frustration and the weariness had worn off for the Maryland couple, Taj and Jason. Soon their missing luggage would be delivered and they could begin to get their lives back in order after the trip.

Living in a comfortable suburb of Washington with older homes and pleasant people, had proven to be a good choice for Jason and Taj. They have relatively easy access to work in downtown Washington and the comfort of a small amount of green space and peace.

Jason and Taj[4] are married and both 35 years old.

---

[4] Taj received her doctoral degree in political science and moved directly into politics and government service, even though her greater strength is in research. In coming to Washington, her first position was a low visibility position with a Congressional research arm. Recently, she was hired as a senior-level Congressional

black box

They came to Washington a few years ago in search of public service careers. Taj is a senior staffer and Jason is a member of a health-care think tank.

Theirs has not been an easy marriage of 15 years, but it works. As a couple, they play to well to other's relative strengths and do their best to shore up each other's weaknesses. It is a partnership and, as much as any couple's, the partnership serves them well. They also know any relationship is always a challenge. Always there is the balancing act between each's need to be an individual and their common need for each other. It means a lot of work. It means some compromise. But it also means big payoffs when it works. So far, they have no major regrets. They both feel ready for the future no matter what it brings.

About noon, the doorbell rings. The dog, Amber, an eighty-pound Golden Retriever, barks. These two sounds always come together. After separating Amber from the door, Taj opens it and recognizes the baggage handler from last night. To her relief, the missing luggage is in hand and seems to have survived being lost. As Jason comes to the door, he takes the suitcase from the man and sets it aside in the entrance hallway and offers

---

committee staffer and sees herself on the first real step toward a political career.

Jason took a somewhat different route. With a business degree in hand, he started out in the business world and then quickly moved into the public policy world. Having spent much of his early career developing private sector health delivery systems, his later career shifted toward government human service programs. He now works with a privately-supported, policy "think tank" focusing on improving federal programs.

for the man to come inside and cool off.

With a relieved expression on his face, the baggage handler tells them they are extremely kind. This is his last delivery and a cold drink will be greatly appreciated. Taj takes him out to the glassed, air-conditioned porch while Jason gets the sodas.

The baggage handler thanks them again and again for not getting angry last night about the luggage mix-up.

"Trust me, we might not have been so nice if we had had the energy to get mad," Taj laughs as she hands him one of the sodas Jason has brought out onto the porch. "Sadly, we are not always that nice. But, frankly, we were much angrier about the mix-up with the credit cards and the return flight reservations. That one screw-up caused us to lose two whole days our vacation."

Strange, thinks Jason. The baggage handler is so into apologies that he seems to be even apologizing for that mix-up as well.

As they sit in the air-conditioned porch, most of the conversation keeps going back to Taj and Jason and their relationship. With some gentle prodding by the baggage handler, Taj tells about her childhood and about being raised in a rural middle class family that had made sure she was college bound on the first day after high school graduation.

"Much as I like to think that this whole education thing was all my doing, I still sometimes feel the imprint of my family's hands on my back. But things got worse. I met this guy. His pushing left the deepest imprints. Even with my Ph.D., he does not stop. Sometimes I think he is pushing me more now than even back then," Taj says as she gives Jason a look of mock sternness. "Some people just don't know when to back off."

'Yes, I've grown a bit through it all. But at what a price!" she complains loudly.

"What a price you paid!" Jason laughs. "What

about me? Do you have any idea what it was like to be around during those doctoral dissertation days? It was very scary. I feared for my life and had to escape to work every chance I had. When I was cornered at home, I'd slip down into my workshop and pray for deliverance. Luckily, my prayers were answered and a doctorate was delivered."

Smiling at the back-handed kidding going on between them, the baggage handler looks them both over. Taj is a very attractive petite woman with fine facial features, brown eyes, and shoulder-length brown hair. She's healthy and fit, but clearly no major league athlete.

As a couple, Jason marvels at all the wheels that he is sure are turning inside Taj's brain. Taj is always "Here I am 'off to the races' while tries to carefully reason through what is going on here. Jason shows more, though not complete, restraint. To some extent, because of Jason, Taj is allowed the privilege of letting her curious side run free. Jason is always there as a 'check and balance,' not stopping Taj, but making sure she never gets so far out of hand as to hurt herself or anyone else.

The baggage handler points to a science fiction book lying near Taj. "Is science fiction an interest of yours?" He asks.

"It's always drawn me!" Taj responds. " In its best forms, it reaches far out beyond today and poses questions about the world, about how we got here and where we are going. As Jason knows all too well, my curiosity about the future can at times be quite intolerable. I am always trying to out guess the futurist types as to what the world will be like fifty and even a thousand years from now."

"But it is not just trying to guess the future," she goes on. "The real fun in thinking about the future is to think about innovative ways to tackle the problems we are and will be facing. How do we handle the increasing impact people are having on a fragile environment? What political structures will work in a world where technology plays an increasingly powerful role? How will we get around in a world where most of the traditional energy sources are either exhausted or too expensive?"

As he listens to her, the baggage handler thinks that he recognizes the telltale signs of two great attributes, her great curiosity about the world and her creativity in dealing with that world. Both are critical to her being chosen for this journey to come. All these observations are not new to him, but he had felt a great need for a face-to-face confirmation. He has it and sits back, happy.

In Jason, the baggage handler also finds much that he likes and much that is essential to what is facing the three of them. Jason, like Taj, is likable and reasonably good looking person. He has a Midwestern complexion that reddens at the mildest embarrassment or excitement. His hair fine brown hair is styled to cover parts of his forehead and ears. Taller than his wife, Jason is in decent physical shape, but again no athlete. Unlike her, he came out of an urban environment, a large city on the East Coast. But he also came from a middle class family who was determined that college and the resulting career was the destinations of choice.

"Fortunately for everyone, science fiction is common ground for the two of us," Jason interjects. "For both of us, there is the intrigue of the new way of thinking or the new technology that 'saves the world.' A lot of science fiction is also about how these two aspects can bring about a 'losing of the world.''

"But Taj and I approach science fiction a bit differently. For me, it is the interaction among the people that is key. Good science fiction not only shows me the

black box

wondrous technology of the future, but shows me people. The future should be about people growing. People progressing through time are the vitality of science fiction as they are the vitality of the future."

"If you focus on the people of good science fiction, you can see their struggles and the systems that support them in achieving higher planes of existence. In some ways, that is kind of what my career is about, trying to design these support systems and organizational structures that help people to grow. Contrary to the views of my colleagues, these systems and structures only help us make our way and I would like to think, eliminate, the human plagues of hunger, homelessness, and poor health." Jason stopped for a moment. "That's not a small achievement by any measure."

The baggage handler nods, thinking back to when Taj and Jason were being chosen and why. "Neither of these two people is extraordinary by any measure, but they are good people working hard at their careers and at their lives together," he says to himself. "They are growing quickly as persons. They care deeply for each other. In many ways, Taj and Jason seem to be two people who were a good match at the start who are working hard to be a great match. In fact, all three of us seem to be a good match for dealing with what is now our joined futures."

Finishing his soda, the baggage handler gets up to thank them for the drink and the conversation. "Who knows? Maybe we will meet again and we'll talk some more," he says, stroking his beard. "I would like that very much."

Walking toward the door, he realizes he made the right choice. Taj and Jason are two people are capable of handling much more than ordinary circumstances and now the time has come for him to let them and the black box alone together for a short while.

He's anxious, but the black box is safe as long as they have it. The journey begins.

Somehow, it all seems very natural. All seems very comfortable.

The baggage handler was a very bright, nice person. Jason and Taj had enjoyed their conversations, even if it had lasted a long time. The handler's interest in them seemed genuine. Later, they both have relatively little recollection of what they talked about, except that it was almost all about them. They realize they learned virtually nothing about the baggage handler.

In downtown Washington at the Smithsonian labs, a very different set of events transpired throughout Friday night and into Saturday morning.

From Maria's perspective, she was initially relieved to see what she expected: interesting artifacts. She just wanted to get this "escort" business over with, so that she could get on with real challenges. But with the questions raised by Joseph at the airport, she is now engaged but still, sees little relevance of this find to her current work. She does not need this type of distraction. South American artifacts and the mysteries surrounding them do not help carry you to high government posts, more power and greater prestige. She needed that before her career would be a success.

As Maria watches from the other side of worktable, Joseph works to discover what he could about the two objects. At first, Joseph is severely disappointed as the two objects do not appear to be either that perfect or that old.

black box

Archaeologically, the find just does not seem to be that significant. The more Joseph examines the two objects, the more he is convinced that they are not very old. First, he compares the objects to archeological artifacts found in South America. Nothing is even remotely close to what he has here. Then, he expands his search using the Smithsonian's computerized data retrieval system. He sighs as his search comes up with nothing.

"It's not that stone chambers and glass-like objects have not been found before," he says to Maria as he scrolls through the Smithsonian database. "But no objects like these quite fit in with what we found previously. In part, my conclusion draws from my first impressions about the likely age of the two objects, that is, they just do not seem that old."

But Joseph's not ready to give up based on first impressions. He tries various dating techniques to determine the approximate age of the objects in front of him. None of the tests or his observations suggests any degree of antiquity. In fact, his guess is that these objects are no more than a few years old, maybe less.

"Damn it," he says, slamming the mouse down on the table, "these just might be a few days old."

"Maria," he says, exasperated. "there is no solid evidence that these two objects are crafted by some artisan in some distant past. These look more like objects fabricated in some high tech shop." Joseph taps his pen on the table as he goes back over his notes of the two objects. "Then again, the scratches don't look like the markings left by an artisan, but rather like the markings left by a fabrication process trying to reproduce the artisan's markings. Maybe these are just some cheap reproductions that somehow got left in the jungle. But that doesn't make sense either."

Joseph goes back to the notes they made during

their previous telephone conversations with Ti Ching and to her note enclosed with the two objects. Through all of her comments is one recurrent theme, that the objects are perfect. These scratches were apparently not there when the engineer found the two objects.

Joseph and Maria exchange glances. Something is just not right here. They both feel it.

As morning breaks, the first beams of sunlight break through the lab windows and Joseph stops his work. He is tired and frustrated. Maria comes over to him with fresh cups of coffee to listen to him rehash the night's work in detail.

Once Joseph finishes, Maria gets up, stretches, and starts pacing around the desk, and says to Joseph with an agitated voice.

"Look," she tells him, "I admit that I have not had much interest in this project from the beginning. I was dragged into this. All I wanted to do is to get it over with and leave you all with this nifty little archeological find."

"But now it's hitting me in the face. Something happened here. Either we have an elaborate hoax or a major something we have yet to figure out. Maybe it's both. One thing is for sure, we've been had and I, for one, don't like being had."

"Nor do I," echoes Jason. "If we have been had, the next questions are by whom and why. One way or another, we are going to get both questions answered by somebody and soon. Even if it's just a hoax, I want to know how they did it in the time between the find and delivery here in Washington."

Maria grabs the telephone beside Joseph's worktable and immediately tries to track down Ti in South America. Several days of continuous rain had limited the engineer's movement and she is still reachable at the base camp. Maria sets up the videoconference.

black box

As Ti joins the videoconference, they see an attractive young woman with a bouncing, effervescent personality. She's excited and wants to know everything they learned, but quickly realizes they have few answers and are looking to her for help.

"Ti," Joseph asks, "can you tell us again your observations? We have your report, but we'd like to double-check everything."

"Sure," Ti says as she turns to her computer, adjusts her glasses, and pushes her hair back way from her face. She clicks open a file of her notes while she talks, pausing every so often to jog her memory.

"Let me go back over what I remember about the two objects and my finding them. Our crew is focusing our attention on untouched jungle, so when I found the two objects in the earthen mound, my sense was that they had been there for quite some time. I can't be sure on that point because the jungle is quite adept at quickly covering up any human intrusion."

"The objects themselves again seemed remarkable for their being in that part of the jungle. Neither native South Americans nor outside explorers have been in this area for as long as we know. Frankly, I thought I was the first to touch that particular piece of ground. "

, "Tell us more about the two objects themselves," Joseph interjects impatiently.

Ti smiles brightly before continuing. "What I was struck most by was how 'perfect' they were. Neither object had a scratch or a blemish anywhere. The stone chamber is a perfectly formed rectangular box, from what I could tell. The dark object inside is also a perfectly formed, rectangular box or solid. I couldn't tell which. Neither object shows any signs of being cut, scratched or blemished in any way. In the case of the stone chamber, that seems particularly unusual, since if it's stone, it would have had to be cut or carved or something like that. I can't figure out how this could be done."

Joseph and Maria nod, then tell her that her description and the two objects in Washington do not seem to quite match. In general, these objects resemble the objects she describes. They're the same dimensions and the same weight. But they're just not as perfect as her description.

Ti frowns. "I don't get it," she says.

They go back over the tests to which she had subjected the two objects and what little impact had been made on the two objects.

Joseph suggests that they repeat her simplest test over videoconference, seeing whether or not the stone chamber can be chipped.

When they strike it with a hammer and chisel, the stone chamber not only chips but chips easily. Just what one would expect given its appearance.

"Something is very, very wrong here." Ti says uneasily. "I did a bit more than a little subtle chipping. After achieving no impact, I got overly enthusiastic. Not too surprising if you knew me. I went after the stone chamber with a vengeance and struck the stone chamber hard with heavy hammers and chisels. Again, the chisels made no impact. Only with my highest temperature torch was I able to make even the slightest hint of a blemish in the stone chamber. Even that may have just been the residue from the torch."

With some reluctance, Ti, Maria, and Joseph agree that a similar test should be performed on the stone chamber only. Setting aside the dark object, Joseph strikes the stone chamber hard. Just as would ordinary stone, the chamber disintegrates.

Unless Ti is lying, something changed between the jungle and Washington. Either the objects had their character changed or they were switched.

black box

  With that, Joseph and Maria tell Ti that they are going to investigate this further. They will do their best to keep her informed. If she thinks of anything else about the two objects or the circumstances surrounding her finding them, she should call them immediately.
  As the videoconference ends, Joseph tells Maria, "I am going to put my Smithsonian people to work on the former possibility, that is that the objects have had their character changed. They'll try to ascertain whether or not these are the same objects somehow transformed. But, Maria, I'm not sure whether or not they will be able to make that determination with any great degree of certainty."

  Shortly after Maria leaves, Joseph calls together his people and explains what is facing them. As they are about to begin their tasks, he pauses for a moment to meet a new lab researcher named George William who had just joined the Smithsonian staff that week and is assigned to the lab in which Joseph works. Joseph remarks how he and George might become known as the "Smith Brothers" since both have full beards.

  Maria takes the lead in the outside world. She and her people will trace the parcel from Ti's putting it on the plane until she and Joseph took it off the baggage carousel at Dulles airport. Maria makes her calls and launches a government investigation.

Chapter 4. First Revelation

Maryland suburbs; later that same day, Saturday.

After the baggage handler has left, Jason takes the luggage upstairs to unpack. Upon opening the suitcase, he immediately sees that some of their souvenirs, which were on top, are missing. As he starts to dig through the suitcase searching for the souvenirs, he finds another surprise. One new thing, an object of some kind, has been added to the suitcase. The object is black, glasslike, and probably solid, but has no other distinguishing characteristics. When he picks it up, it turns out to be much lighter than he thought it would be. As he looks it over, he notes that is shaped like a black "box." He tries to find a way to open it but can find no surface break of any kind that might suggest that it could be opened.

"Taj!" he yells. "Taj, I think you better come up here. Something got screwed up with our suitcase!"

Taj runs up the stairs, followed by their black cat, G, and Golden Retriever, Amber. Observing the speed with which the three of them moved, it's hard to tell who is more interested, Taj or the animals.

"Okay, what's wrong?" she says as she walks into

black box

the room. She sees the black object in Jason's hands. "What's that thing?"

"Beats me," he replies, handing it to her. "All I know is that we're missing a bunch of souvenirs and we are now the proud owners of whatever that is. But look at it. It's kind of strange."

"How so?" Taj asks.

"When I first saw it, I thought it was a solid object made of glass," he explains. "But that can't be the case. It's too light. But it can't be a box either; there's no opening or cover. Maybe it's just a hollow chunk of glass."

As Taj turns it over, she also is surprised at how light in weight it is. She holds it up to the beside lamp, but no light shows through it, even at its narrowest points.

A bit unnerved by this intrusion into their luggage and their lives, they decide to take the box downstairs to the living room for a closer examination. Once downstairs, they will try to figure out what it is.

Taj rotates the object as she sits on the couple's leather couch. There's no variation in the black coloring she can see that might suggest an opening or any way of accessing the object.

Meanwhile, Jason runs down to the basement workshop and gets a tape measure. When he comes back, Taj holds the black object as Jason takes the measurements. The object's dimensions are three inches by one foot by one and one-half feet.

"Jason, my best guess is that it weighs about 5 pounds," Taj says. "But I don't get it," she says with a perplexed look on her face. "What is this black thing? Is it just some worthless piece of black glass or is it something more?"

"And, by the way, where are our souvenirs?" she says, looking up from the couch. "I would guess that the souvenirs were thrown away to make space for the object, but why? And why give it to us?"

"If you're looking to me for the answers, forget it," Jason retorts. "I don't have a clue. But I'm also not ready to throw it away until we figure this out or get some answers from somebody."

Confused over what they have and how it got into their luggage, they decide to try to reach the baggage claim office and possibly the baggage handler that delivered the luggage. Taj makes the call. Fortunately, she gets the same claims person that they spoke to the day before. She lays out the situation and describes the black object they found in their suitcase.

"Unfortunately," the claims person responds, "I probably know less than you do. Since everything seemed to have worked out between you and the baggage handler, I don't have any records other than the slip from yesterday. No baggage claim was ever formally filed. Nothing in the airline records show that it was reported found by the baggage handler."

"Do you happen to know the baggage handler that was there yesterday with us all?" Taj asks. "Did you know he delivered the missing luggage to us today?"

"Again, I have no record of the luggage being found or delivered. As for the baggage handler, I'm afraid I can't help you," the claims person tells Taj. "I didn't recognize the baggage handler, but that's not terribly unusual. There were a number of new people who came on board in the past few weeks. Let me see what I can find out. I'll get back to you after I make a couple of calls."

About a half hour later, the claims person calls back, "Listen, I checked with the crews and some

black box

remember the new baggage handler vaguely. No one got a good look at him and no one remembers hearing his name. I checked with personnel, but they show no record of a new person coming on board yesterday or within the past week. They're concerned with how he got the identification he needed to get access to the tarmac and the baggage. We're now investigating the security breach."

"Why don't the two of you hold on to the black object for now," Ms. Link suggests. "No one reported it missing. There is no reason yet for you to come all the way back to the airport to bring back something that no one may even want. It may have just been planted to buy a thief time enough to get away with your souvenirs."

" Just in case," she goes on, "I'll file a report on the black object as well as a claim for the souvenirs that were removed from your luggage. As soon as I hear something on either account, I'll call the two of you right away. But don't wait by the phone. There isn't much hope in hearing much about either."

Taj and Jason look at each other trying to figure out what to do next. They're uneasy.

"Most of the day is shot already," Taj shrugs. "What do you say we spend the rest of it on trying to pick apart this black box? I'm getting a bit curious about this little black box."

"A bit curious?" Jason responds, his voice warm, but sarcastic. "I don't know if you have looked at your hands over these past minutes. I have. You haven't put the black box down. Your hands have been giving it a total work over like you're trying to find some secret switch to activate some secret compartment."

"Figuring out the black box is about to be our

Saturday night's entertainment," Jason announces. "Let's crack a bottle of wine and have at it. Maybe some wine will help loosen up our minds as we delve into this."

Jason goes to get the wine while Taj continues to mull over this the box in her living room. While her interest has clearly been piqued, not so the animals' interest. They both lay a respectful distance from the couch and settle into what is likely to be another routine evening.

Jason returns with the wine, handing hands her a glass and filling both her and his glass. Sipping her wine, Taj makes some disconnected remark about how warm the weather is. Jason agrees, and notes that tomorrow they have to get their lives in order from the vacation before their return to work on Monday.

This chit-chat is not working for either of them. Jason sets the wine bottle down on the coffee table and sits down beside Taj.

"This is just as painful as Christmas Eve as a child and waiting for my turn to open presents," Jason sighs.

They pick up their wine glasses again. After a calm and slow sip, they exchange glances. With that as the cue, they both put down their wine glasses.

Simultaneously and impulsively, they grab for the black box. As fate would have it, their hands grab hold of the black box's four corners. Something happens. Slowly, out of the object's blackness emerges a set of lights. Initially, the lights appear to be only symbols, not recognizable by either of them. Jason and Taj get very still.

"I strongly suggest that we not move until we get some better clues," Jason says softly. "I don't know about you, but this is almost like holding onto a live hand grenade, only there we would know what would happen and what to do. No grenade pin to reinsert here."

black box

Taj nods in agreement, her body locked in place.

They continue to check over the box. After a few moments, they both look at the letters next to each of the lights. The letters, some of them forming words, are in English, a fortunate coincidence.

Both of them exhale. Fortunate or not, they are glad to have survived for a few more moments.

, "I think this is going to be it for us," Jason whispers jokingly. "The black box is plotting its revenge for our having touched it without permission."

Taj laughs, but only half-heartedly.

They continue not to move. Their hands remain fixed to the object's four corners. A minute or two passes and nothing more happens. Now comes the dilemma for them. No more clues seem to be coming. The "black box" is leaving it to them to make the next call.

"Look here," Taj says, once again impatient, "If we're gonna die, we're gonna die. The prospect of dying from starvation and being found with this stupid box in our hands doesn't exactly appeal to me. So far the box has been pretty harmless. I say, let's take a chance. On the count of one, we'll place it back on the floor; on the count of two, we'll both remove our hands."

Taj gives him a good-natured glare. "Jason, assuming that your feeble head nod is a sign of agreement, here we go."

"One," she counts and they place the box on the floor.

"Two."

On cue, they both remove their hands from the box.

Looking at the lit, but otherwise dormant box on the floor, Jason exhales uneasily, "Ah yes, I believe that we survived either a destructive device of fiendish design or a pretty harmless piece of glass. For the sake of our reputations, I think I fear more that it might be the latter."

They both glance at the windows, relieved that no one has seen their antics. Thinking about how stupid they must have looked for those few brief moments as they sat in fear of moving, they start to laugh

As they catch their breath from laughing, neither is exactly sure what happened or how, except that it seemed to have started when they both grabbed at and held onto the black box at the same time.

"Enough of this fear and trepidation stuff," Jason tells Taj. "Let's let our curiosity carry both of us. Especially you who was born with extra curiosity genes."

"As I see it the box is giving us some clues," says Taj, only mildly amused. "It's up to us to figure out what is being revealed and what it means for solving the mystery of this 'black box' as I suggest we call it. The box is still lit with lights and letters. Let's try and figure out what they mean."

Slowly they look over the lights and the letters. The letters and lights are lined up on the left hand side of the box. From top to bottom, they read "e," "record," "m to e," "e to m," and "verify." In the case of the letter "e," the light is positioned after the letter. For the rest of the letters and words, the lights are positioned before the letters.

"Maybe this is some type of audio or video recording device," Jason suggests as he slides off the couch to the floor. "There's a 'record' light. Maybe 'e' is some type of power level light that shows the batteries are up to power or just the box has been turned on."

"But that doesn't make a lot of sense since there are no hook-ups for wires, no microphones, and no speakers," Taj says back, having seated herself on the floor to better look over Jason's shoulder at the box. "I guess it could be some type of remote control device, like

black box

the remote for a television. Still the letters and words don't fit in with that type of device. Well, maybe the word 'verify' does. Maybe 'verify' has something to do with making sure that you are recording what you really want. But what do these 'e to m' and 'm to e' letters mean?"

They pause from their inspection for a few minutes and sip more wine. The phone rings out in the kitchen. Jason goes to answer it.

It turns out to be a phone call from one of their friends. Jason talks on and on. Impatiently thumping her fingers on the floor, Taj stares at the black box. Every molecule in her body wants to go to the box and start pressing everything that even remotely looks like it could be pressed.

Taj's patience is within seconds of running out as she hears Jason hang up the phone. As Jason comes back into the room, Taj reaches for the black box. Before she can get to it, the box goes dark.

"Damn," she says under her breath. Jason mutters something distinctly similar.

"Why did it have to go dark now? I was just going to pick it back up," Taj asks angrily. And you! Why did you take so long. You should have hung up earlier. In fact, you should never have answered the phone in the first place. Now we have to start all over."

Both of them have lost any patience that remains. Trying to re-activate the box, each picks it up and tries pressing it in many different places, including the top corners and the approximate spots where the lights and words had appeared. Each of them in turn tries various combinations. Nothing happens. Nothing they do re-activates the black box.

Taj speaks first. "Jason, I'm really sorry. I know you had to answer the phone. Our friends wanted to know whether or not we made it back all right from the trip. Still, that doesn't make me any less upset about you staying on the phone when we've got this to deal with." She motions towards the box. "I'm just re-focusing my energy back on this damnable thing."

"Trust me, you're not the only one who wants to tear open the box and find out what's inside," he says. "My Swiss army knife is sitting in my pocket poised to peal it open like a tin can. But neither of us is representing the height of reason right now and this black box might really be important. Let's finish the wine, let the black box rest, and call it a night."

"I don't want to agree," says Taj, getting up to go upstairs, "but I do. A good night's sleep will do more for us than this bottle of wine. Tomorrow, we'll join these two feeble brains and together we'll discover every secret there is worth knowing about this black box."

Slowly, they turn off the lights and walk upstairs, Amber and G following. They get ready for bed and give each other a badly needed hug. They kiss good night and begin what is not going to be their most restful night's sleep.

Chapter 5. Near Conversion

Maryland suburbs; early the next day, Sunday.

As Jason rolls over, he hears Taj taking a shower and singing "Don't Stop Thinking About Tomorrow". Not great singing, but the usual early morning type, the kind of singing he has come to know and tolerate. This morning Taj sings with more enthusiasm than normal. He knows already what kind of day this is going to be.

Down at the foot of the bed are two sets of eyes wide watching him. As he's awake now, Amber and G show increasing signs of impatience over his lethargy. Amber starts a low whine while G stretches and paces the bed.

"Okay, okay. I get it. Time to get up," he says to the two of them.

As he looks outside, he contemplates the day and thinks about the black box. In too many ways, the experience with the black box is taking on too much of the character of a roller coaster. There was the anxiety about touching the box in the first place. Then there were the ups and downs, the thrills and frustrations, and the curiosity and fear. All that hit last night. As he faced today, again the roller coaster feeling hits. But just like when he gets off the roller coaster at the amusement park, he always runs as fast as he can to get back in line. Now that he's awake, he wants to get back at the box as soon as possible. Knowing Taj as he does, he's not surprised to find her already up."

The shower shuts off and Taj calls out from behind the bathroom door with impatience., "Are you up yet? C'mon. Move it. Move it."

As she towels her hair she shouts again through the door. "We have the great unknown to deal with today, not to mention animal and people feeding, house cleaning, clothes washing, and food shopping."

Jason shakes himself awake. He suspects that neither of them slept well in spite of their both being bone tired.

Resolved to do first things first, they feed the animals and themselves. They consume the Sunday paper. Not surprisingly, they cast periodic glances at the black box still occupying center stage in the living room floor.

"It's time for some fun!" Taj says enthusiastically once the tasks of Sunday morning are behind them. "It's time for the black box. Let's move it! Everybody human or not get into the living room."

Doing his best to keep up with her, Jason jumps up and runs into the living room, Amber and G, not wanting to miss the excitement, right behind him. Too slow. Taj already has the box in hand.

But she stops and waits for everyone else to be ready.

Before she can try to activate the box, Jason puts his hands over hers to stop her. "Given our missteps and failures of last night, let's join these two feeble brains and try to reconstruct how we triggered the box's activity in

black box

the first place. Why did it work when we initially picked up? Why didn't it work when we picked it up later? What was different?"

"As best I can recollect," Taj says, thinking back over the night's foggy recollections and somewhat regretting the wine they drank. "It happened when we both picked up the box at the same time. Later, when we tried to re-activate the box, it was always each of us individually. I don't think we ever tried the two-person approach a second time."

With that observation in mind, they both reach down and pick it up at exactly the same moment. Nothing happens.

"Well that really worked well," says Jason sarcastically but then quickly changes tone as he realizes this is not the right attitude. "Still, it probably is the right start. Let's try other combinations of our four hands picking up and holding the black box."

They try several other combinations. Nothing happens.

"Wait a minute, we got lucky last night when we first picked up the box," Jason points out. "We're obviously not being lucky this morning. So, if we can't get lucky, let's try to be smart."

"This 'hit and miss' touching of or picking up of the box is not the best way to solve this problem. With creativity and a bit of careful reasoning, we ought to be able to figure this out."

"You're absolutely right," Taj muses. "Who ever made this box would not want it to be triggered every time somebody accidentally picked up the box. If this black box isn't meant to be activated accidentally, then the triggering mechanism must be some kind of systematic touching of parts of the box."

"You're right!" Jason smiles at Taj, feeling like they're getting somewhere. "We just happened to get lucky last night. So what did we do when we got lucky?"

With that as a guide, Jason walks them back through the events of last night, reconstructing key moments.

"We sat down and drank some wine. Then we both grabbed at the box at the same time before we picked it up. Our first contact was not picking up the box. Our first contact was when we initially touched its top."

"Just before we picked it up," he continues, pacing the room, "we both realized that we had touched the box and looked at each other with our fingers resting on the box's top. If I remember right, the first lights were already on by the time we actually looked at the box and before we actually picked it up."

"Thinking this through in 'slow motion', I think you're right," Taj agrees. All this happened over the space of a few seconds, but I think that was the order."

"Let's suppose that this box has a 'safety and verification' check built in, sort of like the firing of nuclear missiles. Needs two people and two keys," Jason continues. "If this was really designed so that two people, meaning four hands, are required for activation, then various we should try 'four hands with fingers' combinations."

They nod and place the black box between them and begin different "four hands" approaches. After about the third attempt, they both touch the top four corners of the box simultaneously.

The box comes to life and the lights emerge. They now know the first secret of the black box, how to activate it.

"Hey, what a team!" shouts Taj, pulling Jason up to dance around the floor with her. But before he can lead them in a second round, Taj loses her light-hearted attitude and pulls him down on the floor. "Enough fooling around," she says sternly. "These lights won't stay

black box

on forever."

Knowing what they learned from last night, there seems to be a time limit as to how long the lights remain illuminated before the box goes dark. They think the limit is about 10 minutes. This time they are less concerned about the time limit. This time they know how to activate the box.

"Okay, oh great and curious one," Jason chides Taj. "We got a little luckier and we're a little smarter. Now what do we do? We never quite got around to figuring this part out. There is the lit box. There are the lights. So what happens? Do we press them? If so, what do we press -- the lights or the letters?"

With this, even Taj is hesitant. "You know, I'm not feeling real comfortable with the prospect of going the next step," Taj says, moving around the box, considering what kinds of destruction might be contained inside. "Last night's analogy to a nuclear missile firing is sobering."

"I don't know what the box can do or why we were given it.. Yet I'd never forgive us if we didn't continue." She smiles at him. "You wouldn't forgive us, either. I say let's experiment."

"In this case, I think you'd agree that appropriate haste means taking it slowly and carefully," Jason points out.

Their discussion of how to proceed continues for only so long, about ten minutes. About that time, the box goes dark. They note the elapsed time.

They are both ready to take the risk. They have their strategy. They agree on how to proceed. They are both ready to act. They are ready to reactivate the box. They are ready to follow through to wherever the black box will take them.

Each of them again places two fingers of each hand on the box. They place them so that all four of top corners are touched simultaneously and the sequence reactivates the black box. This time, they are ready to touch the lighted areas.

By now Amber, the golden retriever, is bored to death and sleeps somewhat fitfully on the other side of the room. G is more interested and rubs himself up against the coffee table facing the black box.

"Okay, we're ready," announces Jason. "Just as we decided, we are going to press the lights in the same sequence that they appear on the panel and see what happens. We flipped a coin and you won the questionable privilege of pressing the first light. After you touch the first light and we see what happens over the next few seconds, the next light is mine. Agreed?"

"Agreed," Taj responds, giving a mock salute.

Taj reaches down and touches the first lighted area, the one marked "e." Nothing happens. She also presses the letter "e" itself. Still nothing happens.

"Wait a minute here," she says with indignation. "Nothing happened. I've been cheated. Do these letters and lights do anything?"

"I want a real light to push that does something," she whines.

"Fine," Jason reluctantly agrees, "I'm not sure if I'm really doing you a favor."

Taj presses the area marked "record." The record light brightens considerably. In a moment, the "m to e" light becomes brighter.

"Now that's more like it," exclaims Taj. "Okay, your turn. Let's see you do as well."

Under his breath, Jason mutters something about the total unfairness of one person having two turns. He also mutters something about "Russian roulette."

"What was that?" asks Taj.

"Nothing," says Jason. Not wanting to lose his turn, he proceeds to press the "m to e" light. Within a few

black box

moments, the "e" light flickers. Seconds later, the "e to m" light brightens.

"All right!" he shouts. "One light pressed and two more lights respond. Let's see you beat that."

"Big deal!" she replies. "So far all we have are a bunch of lights; the box still hasn't done anything. No music. No video. No destruction of the world as we know it. Nothing."

"But it's my turn. This will make it all happen. Mine will be the light pressing to end all light pressing." Taj says as she moves closer to the box. She quickly reaches over and presses the "e to m" light. This time the black box responds with more than just lights.

To their utter amazement, a second black cat appears right next to their G. Both cats are frozen in place. Both appear equally real. They seem to be identical in every respect.

Jason and Taj are in a state of shock. G is like a child to them. The fear of losing that child is an almost overwhelming emotion. Neither moves They don't know whether or not to press the next light, which is now blinking brightly as well.

"What do we do?" asks Taj nervously. "What do I do? My god, what have I done. There are two cats. They both are real. Aren't they?"

"I don't know," Jason replies, his voice shaking. He pauses to calm himself before he speaks again. "Without directions, we don't know if the next light results in having two cats, losing the first, losing the second, or losing them all. The next light is 'verify.' 'Verify' what?"

Seconds pass. They are both frozen in indecision like the two cats frozen by the black box. After what seems an eternity to them, but more likely only a minute, the "verify" light stops blinking.

Before they have time to act, the second cat

disappears. Like the spell has been broken, their G starts moving around as if nothing had happened. He comes to both of them, leans his body into each of them and begins to purr. He saunters away.

While G may not have suffered any ill effects, Jason and Taj have. Taj runs over to G and hugs him so tightly that he scratches and scrambles out of her hands.

Jason lays on the floor, shaking his head, "That was real, there were two cats. That was no video image, not even a hologram. Those were two real cats."

"How did it do that?" He says to no one in particular.

They're scared, more scared than they've ever been before. And what about the appearing, then disappearing, cat that was apparently a virtual clone of theirs?

"This is no audio or video recorder," Taj says slowly, thinking out loud. "It's something quite different. It deals in real objects. There were two cats there for those few moments. Suppose you would have gone ahead and pressed the 'verify' light? Would we have lost G? What about that second cat? I don't know about you, but it looked not just real, it looked like an exact duplicate of our G. I was just kidding when I said this box could do big-time kinds of things. No more. This box is serious stuff."

The black box goes dim again. This time, the dimming of the box brings welcome relief.

Sitting up from his spot on the floor, Jason finally responds to her question. "Let's let it rest. I don't want anything more to do with this box today. I may never want to activate the damn box again."

With only a brief glance passing between them, Jason picks up the box from the bottom, carries it up the stairs, and carefully hides it away in a closet.

For now, neither of them wants to talk further

black box

about what had happened. Tomorrow starts of a new workweek. Clothes need to be washed, food needs to be bought, and the house needs cleaning. Sometimes, the mundane chores of living are a welcome respite from the mysteries of living.

Chapter 6. Frustration

Smithsonian laboratory, Washington, D.C., the next week.
Maryland suburbs, Thursday.

The week was long and difficult for Joseph and his people.

They assembled in Joseph's main lab, a large dimly lit open space with high ceilings and non-descript walls. The only thing that distinguished the space was what occurred therein, often occurring and brightly lit in the middle of the lab.

When Joseph and his staff gathered around the central work table on Thursday and reviewed the week, they had information but no good answers. On one hand, there is a consensus on what the objects are not. He and his staff now believe that the two objects are not what they initially seemed to be, that is, carved artifacts of some distant past.

Microscopic tests of the carvings at first gave some indication that the two objects were carved and polished. But the more they examined the objects, the less this seemed to be the case. They were just too smooth. What at first glance seemed to be the patterned chisel marks of a master craftsperson, turned out to be the

black box

precise and systematic marks of something more akin to modern machine processing. The individual variations of human craft were not there.

Further, the objects did not pass the age test. They were not very old at all. In fact, all the dating methods clearly showed that the two objects had come into being only recently. These two objects could have been made as recently as the past couple of weeks, possibly as recently as last week.

Joseph's thoughts wander back to the description of the two objects given them by the engineer. He was convinced that Ti was thorough and that she knew what she was doing. She definitely believed that the "carving" markings were not on the objects she sent to Washington.

Fortunately, Ti had taken a series of photographs of the objects. Arrangements had been made to have the digital photos emailed from South America to Washington. The photos had arrived yesterday evening.

As they examined blow-ups of the photos, Joseph sees that the engineer was absolutely right. The objects she found were perfect. By comparing her photos to the objects they had and the similar photos they made, he notices strong evidence that the objects were changed, switched or both. Given the very brief time over which the two objects were out of their hands, the evidence points to a switch.

Even if there was a switch, the critical question is what exactly are these objects and what is their purpose. The stone chamber, either the original or the fake, may have only been the container for the black box and nothing more. The fake stone chamber was destroyed early in Joseph's analyses and was fairly unremarkable.

On the other hand, the original stone chamber, which is missing, is a whole different story. Using the Ti's photographs, Joseph and his people were able to determine that it was probably as "perfect" as the original black object was. Still, they so far have been unable to find any further signs of its existence.

The fake black object in his custody is as unremarkable as the fake stone chamber. Initial x-rays of the black object showed it to be an empty box. After he was quite sure it was a fake, Joseph had his people become more aggressive in trying to find out what was inside. In one of the experiments, the black object almost exploded because of the stress applied to it. As with the stone chamber, modern manufacturing could explain most of how the box came into being.

Unlike his analyses, Maria's work on the couple in Maryland was getting some initial information on the function of the original black object. That seemed to be where they needed focus their attention now.

The more Joseph thinks about the whole affair, the more it seems as if someone has tried to convince them that these might be carved artifacts from the distant past. Since the parcel was marked for the Smithsonian, that someone had to assume the ruse would be discovered fairly quickly. If so, someone went through a lot of trouble to buy what might only be a week's worth of time. If Maria is right based on the couple and this weekend's activities, that was going to be the only time gained.

Though "investigations" are not exactly her forte, Maria tackles this one with the same tenacity that she does any problem. She had dug in hard for the past week. Now she waits for this morning's events to unfold as she waits in her car a few blocks from the couple's suburban Maryland home.

From what she learned so far this week, somehow, something happened between the hand-off

black box

from the engineer in South America and the pick-up in Washington.

Maria, as did Joseph, had a gut feeling at the beginning of the week that the objects they had did not match what the engineer found and sent to them. But now, Maria questions her investigation's propriety. She and her people were doing an awful lot of expensive and tricky investigative work based on something yet unproven.

Her investigation began in South America. Interviews of Ti, the engineer, and the airport crews were done quickly, but thoroughly. Everything that engineer said was verified. Ti agreed to a lie detector test. She passed easily. Whatever else is going on, she wasn't lying and she wasn't involved in the switch or the loss. It's also is clear from the interview transcripts that the objects she found were not the same as the objects they had.

Being concerned about her find, Ti held on to the parcel until it was placed in the baggage hold and the baggage hold was locked. Her eyes never left the plane until the plane left the ground on its way to the United States. While her actions were unusual, she stated that she saw this find as terribly significant and that she was determined that nothing be left to chance

Next Maria and her investigators focused on the plane's time during the Miami stop. The parcel would have gone through customs and been subjected to all the security checks that packages coming out of South American are subjected to. Normally, Customs officials would have checked the parcel as potentially being part of the illegal drug traffic trade. However, through arrangements Joseph and Maria made with the U.S. embassy in South America, the parcel was marked for special handling and instructions were given that it be hand-carried through the whole process. The attached note stated that the parcel contained archeological artifacts potentially of great antiquity and value. As such, the parcel was handled carefully and simply. In Miami, one customs officer with an unblemished fifteen-year record took responsibility for it from the baggage hold through customs inspection and back into the baggage hold as it was locked and the plane was sent on to Washington, D.C. No the problem wasn't there. It had to be Washington.

From then on, the parcel's path was not clear. Having cleared customs in Miami, it did not go through customs in Washington. Then when the plane landed at Dulles Airport, the baggage crew had been busy. Still, the parcel was given special treatment and a baggage handler was directed to take special care of it. But here was where the "chain of evidence" broke. A new and unknown baggage handler took care of the parcel. In picking up other luggage from a West Coast flight on his way to the baggage claim area, at most, the baggage handler had no more than three to five minutes to himself to do whatever it is he did.

All this "evidence" seemed to point to a pre-planned switch. But again there were nagging questions for Maria. Who knew about the parcel? Who knew enough to make the apparent duplicates? Who had the ability or the time to make the duplicates? Was it one person or were there more? It's hard to conceive how one person could have done it alone.

There had been a switch, but how did the original objects get out of the airport? Where were they now?

Her first theory was that the missing baggage handler walked out with the original objects and probably still had them. That was relatively easy to do. But so far, she found nothing but dead ends with respect to the baggage handler.

All the airport crews had gone through extensive interviews, all had had background checks, and all passed

black box

lie detector tests without a hitch. With respect to the baggage handler himself, only five sets of people had ever seen him. Among them were the baggage crew on the South American flight, the baggage crew from the West Coast flight, the crew at the carousel, the lost-luggage claims person, and the Maryland couple with whom the claims person had worked. Everyone except the couple was questioned. No one saw the man before and none of the airport personnel saw him after his interaction with the claims person. The man had vanished completely. Apparently, the man was there for one primary reason, to handle the parcel. The unanswered question was whether he left with the bag himself or passed it on to someone else.

The one other unknown is the Maryland couple who lost their luggage on another flight. Had it not been for their interaction with the baggage handler, it is unlikely they would have been noticed. For a while now, Maria's attention focused on their possible involvement. Initially, she thought that they might be accomplices and that they somehow took the parcel out of the airport. But here the testimony of the claims person was most persuasive. Ms. Link stated emphatically that the couple was as perplexed as anyone about the luggage mix-up and that they did not know the baggage handler prior to the airport encounter.

Maria ran background checks on the couple. The results did not fit the profile of people intentionally involved in a baggage switch. Checks of phone records showed no indication of interaction with people in Washington or South America during this period. They were out of town during the critical time period from when the objects were found until they were switched. Part of the reason for not subjecting them to questioning was that their careers and personalities did not fit the role. While the couple was still being investigated, they were receiving "special handling".

What Maria did learn about the couple was that the mystery baggage was to hand-deliver their missing luggage on Saturday. Here again, the luggage claims person was the key. She remembered the discussion and still had the partially filled-out claims report and the couple's phone number. At first, Maria wasn't sure that the luggage was ever delivered. She had the claims person make the call and without hesitation, the couple confirmed that the handler had returned their luggage on Saturday. They said nothing to indicate that there were any problems or that anything unusual happened.

Maria paused for a moment to think about the baggage handler. For someone who went through great difficulty to handle the missing objects, he had made a major mistake. If he just had gotten the luggage to the couple faster, the incident would not have involved the claims person or been linked to the second flight and the couple.

So far the couple was the only viable lead Maria had. Desperate for some answers, Maria decided to start watching the couple on Wednesday and to install surveillance equipment in the couple's house on Thursday.

Maria strongly suspected that out there somewhere were the objects found by the engineer. Though she did not know their significance, she nonetheless knows that these objects were important. Someone had done a sophisticated job of switching the objects in a short period of time. Something couldn't be buried for a long time, be dug up, and, within days, be substituted with almost exact duplicates. Either someone planned this long ago or someone had other methods at hand.

Now, early on Wednesday morning, Maria meets her two-person surveillance team in the neighborhood

black box

where the couple lives. She tells them that she wants to move quickly since the couple is the only remaining lead they had. The investigation into the baggage handler had virtually stopped for lack of any promising leads.

She asks her team to go over what they know about the couple and their behavior.

Her senior investigator, Ted James, gives her a quick report. "In most ways, Taj Curie and Jason Kalder are ordinary people. The couple has no children," he says, flipping through his notes. "During the week, Jason leaves the house around seven o'clock in the morning for work. He arrives at work a half hour later. Taj is out of the house by 7:30 and starts work at 8:00 in the morning. They spend their days at their jobs and tend not to arrive home until between six and seven o'clock in the evening. They do not have a housekeeper. A neighbor kid exercises their dog in the late afternoon. The kid comes in after school, sometime between four and five o'clock in the afternoon."

"Any indication of anything unusual this week?" Maria asks.

"Not that we can tell," Ted responds. "If they are involved, they really haven't shown any outward signs. Once in a while, one or both of them will either have later afternoon meetings or evening meetings that keep them away longer. We don't know if that is unusual without accessing their work schedules."

"You asked us to check the place out for possible installation of electronic surveillance," add the junior investigator. "We've done that and we don't see major problems. If you want it installed for the weekend, we will probably have to do it tomorrow. The two of them have a tendency to take off part or all of the day on Friday. If we wait until after tomorrow, we can't be sure how much uninterrupted time we'll have inside the house."

"What about the dog?" Maria interrupts. "Will we be able get inside the house with the dog being there?"

"We think so," Ted hesitates. "Dogs are always unpredictable, but this one does not seem to be aggressive. Based on what we see when the neighborhood kid walks the dog around the block, she's pretty friendly and bribable. We'll probably just need an expense voucher for dog treats."

"Maria, what's your pleasure on this one?" Ted asks.

"Let's proceed. We've already lost several days worth of information," Maria replies. "Before I came out, I received authorization to make this as legal as possible. Tomorrow morning after they leave, you go in and install the surveillance equipment. I can't afford to wait. I want to see what these people know about the missing objects and what they do this weekend. Maybe it will be for nothing, but we don't have anything else to go on."

She arranges to meet the surveillance team near the couple's house at five o'clock the next morning.

Arriving in neighborhood before dawn on Thursday, Maria sees the team's parked van. Parking her car behind a set of bush-like pine trees, she walks over, checks to make sure she is not seen, and climbs into the van.

They start to watch the house. Six-thirty comes and goes and no one leaves the house. Taj and Jason are either running a bit late or Maria and her people might have to forget it for that day. Then, just before seven, the door to the house opens and the couple walks together out to their cars. They kiss good-bye, get in and start their cars, and drive away. Maria breathes easier. She and her people wait a half hour to make sure the couple hasn't forgotten something and doesn't return early. Everything looks okay as they prepare to go into the house.

Their cover for this expedition is that the gas

black box

company is doing a special spot check on potential meter replacements and gas leaks. They have fake identification papers which should take care of any suspicious neighbors. Their plan is to work their way through the neighborhood. The three-person team wears the same uniform to keep track of each member of the team.

After working through the first few houses without any problems, they come to the couple's house and the houses on each side of it. This is the key time. They approach the three houses at the same time. As Maria and the junior investigator knock on the two adjacent houses, Ted moves quietly around to the back of the couple's house. In both adjacent houses, a person is home, listening to Maria and the junior investigator's explanations, and showing them where the gas meter is. Meanwhile, Ted approaches the back door of the couple's house.

Knowing that time is slipping away, Ted goes to work on the back door lock.

Inside the house, he hears Amber woof. "Easy, big dog," Ted says.

As the lock clicks and the door unlatches, Ted reaches into his pocket for treats. He throws a few through the crack in the door and waits a few seconds. He hears crunching. So far, the plan is working. The dog is buying into the bribe. Ted opens the door just large enough to slip through, then quickly closes it behind him. As he turns, he realizes that he's facing a very large Golden Retriever. The dog looks happy and surprised, glad that the stranger had the good manners to bring her plenty of treats. Amber wags her tail and nuzzles Ted's boot. Ted relaxes. The biggest danger posed by this dog appears to be licking someone to death.

Since they couldn't bring in a ton of surveillance equipment without raising serious suspicion, he's been selective. He has an abundance of microphones. He has only three cameras. The cameras and microphones are very small and have transmitters that link to the equipment in the van.

As Amber swallows the first few treats in one large bite, Ted slips her a few more.

Moving from the kitchen into the dining room, he notices movement at his side. He stops and looks to his left. In the window, a large black cat lies in the morning sun and flicks his tail. If menacing looks were an indicator, the black cat is a bigger threat than the dog. But the cat seems content to sit still as long as he doesn't violate its space. Ted moves on quickly. The dog follows.

Doing the upstairs first, Ted installs microphones in the master bedroom and in the hallway between the rooms to pick up most of what is said upstairs.

Moving downstairs, he installs listening devices in almost every room, including the basement workshop and out on the screen porch. While on the porch, he hears Maria talking to the next-door neighbor. Their plan seems to be working.

Next, he installs the surveillance cameras. For the sake of privacy, the team decided not to do the upstairs master bedroom. So instead, he places the cameras in three other places that the couple might use to discuss or look at the missing objects.

The first camera is placed in the basement workshop. The combination of a dust-covered, curtained window and some utility shelves provide cover. On the main floor, he puts the second camera in the den. He places it on a large, high bookcase where the books had obviously not been moved in years. He wants to put the last camera in the living room.

Time is running short as Ted scans the living room for a place for the camera. As he looks around, both the cat and the dog eye him. He throws a few more treats to the dog. He throws a few to the cat as well. No

black box

big surprise, the cat ignores them completely. The dog doesn't. Excited, she barks at him a few times.

Ted needs to get this done quickly. He looks up and sees a built-in bookshelf with several art pieces on the top shelf. It is fairly high up and out of the way. Standing on a chair, he looks at the top shelf and sees the comforting sign of untouched dust. He pulls the last tiny camera out from his pocket and installs it next to one of the art pieces.

Immediately, he pulls out his small walkie-talkie and signals to the other investigator who by now has returned to the van to activate the equipment. Each device must be checked. All the devices work fine, but the camera in the living room needs to be turned about twenty degrees to get the full view of the living room. Ted gets back on the chair, makes the adjustments, and receives the signal that everything is set.

As he slips out the back door and locks it again, he checks his watch. Fifteen minutes has elapsed, about what they had figured. He leaves a note on the back door from the gas company, checks outside for leaks, and checks the gas meter located at the back of the house. He moves on to another house. He sees Maria approaching another house further down the street.

About a half-hour later, they return to the van and move it about a block. Then they wait. There are still many hours to go before the couple returns home from work.

Shortly after six o'clock, Jason, and then Taj, returns home. They prepare and eat supper, and talk a bit.

Little useful information is picked up during that first day of surveillance, but a few things are clear. The couple has the black box, but not the stone chamber. It's clear that they do not know why the baggage handler gave it to them. The baggage handler is the key, thinks Maria as the surveillance winds down for the day And what is most intriguing is that they apparently did some experimentation last weekend and something amazing happened. Unfortunately for Maria and her people, this preceded surveillance.

Friday night is going to be key. The couple stopped experimenting with the box during the week for reasons that are not completely clear. It had something to do with their cat. Their next opportunity is this weekend. The couple had put aside Friday night to continue their experimentation with the black box.

The hours pass very slowly on Friday afternoon as Maria and her two investigators wait about a block away from the couple's house. Shortly, the couple will return home from work and the evening's activities will begin. More will be learned that night by everyone, if all goes as planned.

About five o'clock on Friday afternoon, the couple arrives home from work. Maria's surveillance team starts their recording equipment.

As Maria sits in the surveillance van waiting for the couple to finish supper, she feels that her team is making real progress. Finally, most of the pieces are falling into place None of her people believe the couple was involved before that night at the airport. It still isn't clear to Maria or, apparently, to the couple, why they were the recipients of the black box. All efforts to find the baggage handler went absolutely nowhere. Without him, the couple is now the focus. After all, they have the black box.

For a while, Maria and her people aren't sure the couple will ever use the box again. The couple's "success" on the previous weekend scared them badly and they show reluctance toward further experimentation. Maria's people could have recovered the black box today during the day. They chose not to. As of Thursday night, the couple stated that they planned more experimentation

black box

on Friday evening.

    Maria's people could also go in, grab the couple, and force them to tell what they know. But they are already learning a lot from the surveillance equipment. Besides, that aspect of "cloak and dagger" is in disfavor these days. Better to learn what they could, then take the black box back when the couple is gone or asleep.

Chapter 7. First Conversion

Maryland suburbs; the next Friday evening.

The week was hectic and work occupied both Taj and Jason. Little has been said between them about the black box or the experience of the previous weekend. They are unnerved and upset with themselves over how they handled the whole episode. Both agree that their courage and reason will probably return. Friday night is set aside for further, but careful, exploration.

With supper behind them, the time has come to re-engage with the black box. They finish the dishes quickly and prepare themselves for the new trials.

" First things first," Taj says. "We're still both a little shaky from the experience with G. I want both G and Amber as far away as possible from that black box and whatever it does. This is not a time for animal experimentation."

"Somehow, I suspect that we really lucked out

black box

when G survived the first encounter with the box. We might have hurt him. We might have lost him completely." Taj reaches down and picks G up, letting him curl up in her arms. "I still get upset whenever I think back to that night. We could have handled it better, much better."

Jason responds, voicing similar concern, "I know we could have and should have. When I saw him frozen and then saw the second identical cat, all I thought was that something very bad was going on there. Fortunately, G seems to have not suffered any ill effects. In fact, he seems to not been affected at all. It is like nothing happened."

"So far nothing bad has happened," Jason reassures Taj as he reaches over and strokes G's black forehead. "If we are careful, probably nothing will. Maybe there's some good in all this. We just have to be better at finding it. Maybe we'll find it tonight."

Following through on their precautions, Amber and G are safely locked away downstairs.

Jason and Taj go upstairs together, dig out the black box from the closet, and return to the living room. Curtains are drawn.

"What do you want to drink?" Jason asks.

"Bottled water with a twist of lime is probably about the most exciting thing I want to drink," Taj replies, standing in the entrance hallway. "This seems like a pretty good time to have a very clear mind. I'll go get them. I'm already halfway to the kitchen."

With drinks in hand and the black box sitting silently in front of them, Taj asks "What's the strategy?"

Clearly, last weekend's unplanned adventure was

unsettling. During the week, each of them considered calling someone up and handing the black box over. But they did not call. They did not hand it over. For one thing, they had no idea who to call that they trusted with this box. But somehow handing over the box doesn't seem like the right thing to do anyway. In some ways, keeping the box carries a level of comfort and relief from a different sort of anxiety.   In the back of their minds is this nagging thought that the black box was given to them for a purpose. After all, there is some reason to believe that their receiving of the box was not a complete accident. Somehow, the baggage handler seemed to be more than just that, but neither could quite determine what that more was.

"Both of us think that we might have been given the box for a reason, maybe a good reason," Jason notes as he takes a drink of his water. "But even if that is the case, why us? We just don't fit what I might guess would be the profile of who you would give something like this box. We may not be absolutely ordinary, but we're not that far away either. We can be pretty boring people at times."

"Who knows?" Taj interrupts, starting to grow impatient with too much talking and too little doing. "Maybe it was a mistake. Maybe the person or persons who put it in our suitcase didn't know what the box can do. Maybe someone just decided to give it to ordinary people like us and see what we would do with it."

"Little did they realize that we had the potential to be cat killers. Or cat cloners. Or whatever it is that we almost did," she says wryly.

"Enough talk," she pronounces, looking up at the clock. "Showtime. Let's get on with it. Again, what's our strategy to be?"

Sighing warmly at her impatience, Jason suggests a strategy. "Let's keep things simple. We'll take small

black box

steps to see what it can do and, most importantly, what it can do without killing anything or anybody.

They both decide that the first test will be with a simple object, in this case a kitchen bowl. Taj places the bowl in front of the box at about the same spot at which G had stood. As best they could recollect from last weekend, the box emitted some type of low powered light that embraced G.

"Okay, we've got the bowl in place," Taj says, her voice quivering. "Let it all begin."

"First, the two of us touch the black box on the four top corners at exactly the same time," Jason instructs.

"Good, the box is coming to life again. See the lights appearing on the top of the black box. Now, on with the rest of the experiment."

Just as before, Taj touches the "record" light that, in turn, is followed by the brightening of the "m to e" light. As they had vaguely remembered from their earlier experience, a faint white light comes from the black box and envelopes the bowl.

Also as before, Jason pressed the "m to e" light, triggering the "e to m" light that subsequently lights.

"Okay. This is it!" Taj takes a deep breath and touches the "e to m" light.

As had happened days earlier, a second object, the bowl, appears. Again as before with G, the second bowl appears to be a perfect duplicate of the first. The "verify" light is blinking. Not without some uneasiness, Jason readies himself to press the "verify" light.

He pauses.

"Listen, why don't you step back a bit?" Jason asks of Taj. "Just in case something happens to me, I'd like to know there is someone who is still alive and able to call the paramedics."

"No way!" Taj protests. "I'll stand one step back

and to the side of you. But I'm not about to miss out on this. If you're worried, let me do it and you move to the far side of the room."

Also not ready to be that far away from what might happen, Jason reluctantly agrees and proceeds. He reaches down and presses the "verify" light. They wait nervously. No change in the bowls. After a few moments, a new light appears and is flashing. This one is marked "delete." Both bowls are still there.

"Oh, wait a minute," Taj cries in indignation. " This I don't like. What's this 'delete' light supposed to mean. 'Delete' lights and keys always make me very uneasy."

Having been raised in the world of computers, a "delete" key always stirs up fear. Images of massive critical data files being lost forever cast about in their heads.

After about 30 seconds of inaction, the second bowl disappears.

Another step taken, but the result is apparently the same. A second object is created, but then disappears.

"Since our experience is that certain lights being pressed have the effect of triggering other lights, there is reason to believe that the 'delete' light is an action based on what else we have done," Jason suggests as he tries to think through what the function of the "delete" key might be." If I'm guessing right, pressing 'delete' will delete one or the other or both of the bowls. It would seem unlikely that it would come up at this time if it is there to delete something else. I don't think it's designed to delete the operator."

"You better hope that this is not a way to deal with the unauthorized use," Taj cautions, looking warily at the box. "You have to admit, having the box delete the unauthorized user is a pretty clean way of discouraging any riffraff from misusing it."

black box

"Just kidding," she teases. "I think you're probably right. I promise not to rush downstairs and huddle with the animals when you press it. And I forgot! It's my turn isn't it? Do you promise not to run off either?"

They both settle in and agree that the loss of an old bowl is of small consequence, assuming that it is all that gets deleted.

With little hesitation, they proceed again. Just as earlier, they move through the sequence of lights to the point where the "delete" light is flashing. As it's her turn, Taj presses the "delete" light. She steps back quickly.

This time, the second bowl does not disappear. However, the first one does.

"Do you realize what this means?" Jason exclaims in horror. "If we had proceeded as we did tonight, our G, the original, would be gone and we would be left with what is either G, or his clone, or something else that is apparently indistinguishable from G himself.

"Clearly, the 'delete' key is critical to completing whatever process this black box puts objects through." Jason peers at the now dark light panel. "Unless I am missing something, there are no remaining lights other than what we have pushed. 'Delete' seems to have the function of completing the process by deleting the original object."

Quiet for a moment, Taj suspects Jason is right and wonders what exactly happened here.
The black box, seemingly to have accomplished its function, is dormant again. All the lights are out. Once again, it is a featureless black solid doing nothing.

As they sit there in silence for several minutes, Taj and Jason slowly re-build their courage. As scared as they are by what might have happened to G, they are even more excited about the discovery.

"More??" Taj breaks the silence expectantly.

"Definitely more!" Jason replies.

Having survived the process with their excitement and curiosity intact, they move on to other tests with other objects.

"We need more complex objects to test the box's capabilities," says Jason as he glances around the living room. "We need objects with moving parts. Objects that are electrical. Let's start there."

Jason continues talking as Taj rifles through the living room junk drawer. "But let's stay away from live objects, at least for now. I shudder whenever I think of what might have happened if we had pressed the 'delete' key that night. I mean what would have the second cat been?" He shakes his head.

"Let's just say that, after our experience with G and what we just saw with the bowl, how about we stay away from animal testing? Way far away!"

"Good idea!" Taj responds with relief. "Look what I found for our test. An old wind-up clock that still works. Also, our battery-powered radio. These should help us determine what the black box can and cannot do.

"I want to try the clock first and see what happens." Taj says as she moves toward the black box.

Jason nods. Taj is on a roll now. This could be a long night as she will probably want to run everything in the house through the black box to see what happens. Sometimes, her curiosity seems to know no bounds.

"Hey, pay attention. Wake up and get with the program," she calls at him.

The clock is already placed in the area where the black box seems to "look" for an original object.

"Wait, I forgot to wind it." Taj reaches for the clock, winds it up, and makes sure that the second hand is moving. "I want to see if this little box can handle an object with moving parts."

"Here we go," Taj says out loud as she and Jason

black box

touch the box on the top four corners and activate the box. The "e" light comes on. With the process begun, she starts to press the lights on the black box. First, she presses the "record" light. The black box responds by enveloping the clock, the only object within close proximity of the box's front left, with a faint glow. At the same time, the "m to e" light comes on. Taj proceeds to press that light. The box responds by illuminating the "e to m" light. She continues by pressing the "e to m" light. On comes the blinking "verify" light and the second clock appears.

Jason and Taj cautiously lean over for a moment and look at the two clocks. The second clock looks identical to the first. Both clocks are frozen in place. Neither second hand is moving. Taj presses "verify" and watches as the somewhat ominous "delete" key appears and its light starts to flash. With a bit more confidence that nothing too terrible is going to happen, Taj presses the "delete" key. Both of them watch as the first clock disappears completely. Their eyes then expectantly turn to the second clock. It seems to be the same clock as the first clock. The time is the same.

Then they make the key observation. On the new clock, the second hand slowly works its way around the clock's face.

Within a few moments, the black box goes dark again.

"It works!" Taj proclaims. "This little black box can handle mechanical objects as they operate and make a second object, or whatever it's doing, that appears to be identical to the first. The second object is identical in what it looks like, but also in how it operates. If my time on the second hand is correct, it's keeping time just like nothing happened."

"It certainly does!" Jason agrees. "One thing I noticed though is that the box seems to freeze the objects while it is processing them. Both clocks stopped for those few moments between the 'm to e' light being pressed and the 'delete' key being pressed. I wonder... Let's try the radio."

It's now Jason's turn. He picks up the radio that Taj brought in earlier. As with the clock, the radio is placed at the upper left corner of the black box. Jason flicks the radio's "on" switch.

"Here we go," Jason says as he flicks the clock's switch. " Let's get a station with some body-charging rock and roll. There we are. Showtime!"

Jason proceeds through the process with the black box and the blaring radio. As soon as the "e to m" light is pressed the second radio appears, but the sound stops. Both radios are silent. Both are frozen as if time stopped. They are surprised by the sudden silence and Taj puts a hand on Jason's arm to urge him to continue.

Following through with all the other steps, he faces the flashing "delete" key and presses it.

Immediately, the second radio starts blaring as if unfrozen. Jason and Taj jump as the momentary silence is filled by music from the second radio. As before, the original radio has disappeared.

There sits the second radio. It is playing the same station as the original radio. It is playing at the same volume as the original. Once again, it appears the box had made an exact clone, in this case, a clone radio.

Slowly, Jason leans forward and turns off the clone radio.

"Well now what?" he asks Taj. "We've done a simple object. We've done an operating mechanical device. We've done an operating electrical device. I suspect the next test should probably be with something that is alive but inanimate."

"Like a plant," says Taj as she jumps up and starts from the room. "I say we go with a plant and I know just

black box

the one."

Returning quickly from the kitchen with a small rubber tree plant in a clay pot, she places the plant where the original radio had been. The "cloned" radio is set off to the side.

"Let's stop for a moment and say what we are both thinking. No animals. What we are both thinking is that we're not ready for animals," Taj continues. "We both want to know whether or not the box can pull it off, but somehow a live animal dredges up all the images of old science fiction films. The plant seems a logical, but safe, next step. Agree?"

While the two talk, the light catches a silvery web crafted between two of the lower branches.

"I agree." responds Jason. "At some point, not tonight, we will face the question of animal life. Maybe we can use something like an insect. No pets though. We keep the pets locked safe in the basement."

As has Jason before her with the radio, Taj takes the rubber tree plant through the process. The result is the same. During the process, there are two seemingly identical plants for a few moments. As the "delete" key is pressed, the original plant disappears and the second plant remains.

"Okay, let's look at this plant closely and see what we've got," says Jason as he examines the plant. "The leaves are still green. It's alive. The plant seems to be unaffected by the whole process, though we can't be sure on that point. For the next few days, we should keep a close watch on the plant to see if something negative might happen over time. From what I can tell, nothing has been lost in the process."

As Jason takes one last look at the plant, he lifts the leaves on the plant's lower back side. "I appear to be even more right than I thought," he quietly says to Taj. "Absolutely nothing has been lost in the process. Look here."

In her rush to run the plant through the process, Taj had not really taken a close look at it. Now they see that their experiment has accidentally gone beyond plant life. In a small web hidden deep among the leaves is a small spider. The spider, indifferent to all that happened, continues creating the web critical to its continued life.

"There's a spider in there, a real live spider," Taj exclaims. "You're right. Everything apparently did survive the black box. That spider is just as alive as it was in the original plant. It's just spinning its web as if nothing happened. I doubt that it even knows that something occurred."

Though too small to examine carefully, the spider seems to confirm what their G had confirmed days ago and more. The black box, without damage, either transported or converted both inanimate and animate objects into second "clone-like" objects.

.   They sip their water and sit there contemplating what happened tonight. Many thoughts are running through their minds. Is this just the final realization of the fictional "transporter" of "Star Trek" fame or is this black box something else?

In their minds, this black box is something beyond. For a few moments as the box processes the objects, there are two, apparently solid and complete, objects existing at the same time. Maybe the box just "moves" objects. Maybe the box creates a "clone" and the original destroyed or something. The Star Trek "transporter" just moves one or more objects from one place to another. Besides, the "transporter" is fiction, part of a distant future. The black box is part of their current reality.

Finally, the excitement takes its toll on them. They are concerned and weary. They hear noise from the basement. Amber and G are getting rambunctious.

black box

With some reluctance, they take the black box, place it back in the suitcase, and stash it away in the hall closet near the front door.

As they and the two pets head upstairs to bed on this warm summer night, they hear a small noise outside. Amber growls, but only briefly. Sleep is priority for everyone. With the warmth of the night, the window air conditioner is turned on in the bedroom and the door closed. The whole household, pets and all, settle in for the night.

"Tonight has been fruitful," Maria says to her team. "Over the past few hours, we learned a lot as we listened to and observed the couple. Several things are clear. Taj and Jason are innocent bystanders who are intelligent and curious. They have been successful with the black box and, fortunately for us, talkative."

"Once we take the black box, as we will shortly, Taj and Jason will be even more confused and angry over its disappearance. They will try to find out who took it. But who will they be able to turn to? Who will believe their story? Hopefully, no one will. There will be no proof. We will make sure of that."

"The only wild card is the missing baggage handler. Without him, they are stuck. With him, they could get help. However, his appearance would also give us an opportunity. Given the opportunity, I will snatch him in a second," she says as the team sets up its plan to retrieve the box.

In a stroke of good fortune, the black box is in a

downstairs closet. The whole household is asleep in the master bedroom, with the air-conditioning drowning out most of the sounds from the rest of the house.

About two o'clock on Saturday morning, Maria and her team make entry. Amber's faint growl is heard, then nothing. No other stirring occurs in the bedroom upstairs. Surveillance cameras are retrieved. The upstairs microphones are left behind, a hopefully acceptable risk.

The black box is taken.

Jason, Taj and the pets wake early. More excitement is expected today.

As Jason shaves upstairs, he hears a shout from Taj. It is something about the box. He calls down to her.

"It's gone!" Taj shouts. "The black box is gone."

Chapter 8. Experimentation

Smithsonian lab, Washington, D.C.; early that same morning, Saturday.

Joseph is uneasy this morning. The black box is in their hands, but he knows it wasn't volunteered. Though kept in the dark by Maria during her surveillance, he now knows about the box's "retrieval." He now knows about Jason and Taj's experimentation. The surveillance tapes show him how to access the black box and, to some extent, its use. This is getting out of hand. Even before now, steps were taken that he could not accept ethically. Still, he is torn. There is the intriguing mystery of the black box. For now, he has to set aside what was done and the ethics ignored and the laws broken. Maria is going to have to search her conscience on this one, though he knows he will have to live with his own soul searching. For these next days, he will put on his lab coat and see what the black box can do, where it came from, and what is its purpose. He will try to make this all worthwhile.

Joseph assembles his team by a wall of the large, warehouse-like lab room in preparation for the upcoming experiments with the black box and speaks to them. "All of you know a bit of why you are here, that it has something to do with a find made in the South American jungle. Let me show you what it is. Let me introduce you to the 'black box."

His team follows him over to the center of the laboratory where stands a large heavy white table. On it stands only one object. He turns on a set of bright lights above the table, fully illuminating the object.

"What you see here is a black featureless object," Joseph continues. "If you look at it more closely and handle it, you will find nothing to indicate that it is anything other than a black solid of somewhat light mass. Trust me. It is more than that by far."

"Based on experiments conducted in another location, but under less rigorous research conditions, we know some of what the box can do. What it can do is nothing short of amazing, though we do not yet know exactly what it is doing. We only see the results."

"If this sounds cryptic and unconvincing, that's probably how it should sound. Over these next days and weeks, we will learn much more and this may all be much clearer to you and, to me."

"Joseph, if I may break in for a moment...." Maria interrupts him, in a tone implying authority, to address the entire team. "This research team, while a primarily a Smithsonian research team, is involved in a joint effort with the federal government. Both of our organizations have been involved in this project from the beginning. Both have a lot of interest in solving the puzzles surrounding this black object. We may have slightly different reasons for our interest, but we share the common goal of knowledge."

black box

"I and my people are not here to interfere in any way with what you are about to do. Our role is to serve as observers and to keep our superiors informed on the progress made by all of you. We wish you luck. Given what we know so far, I think you will find this to be an exciting research effort." She nods at Joseph, signaling the end of her speech.

Joseph clears his throat and resumes his explanation. "Let me first tell you what this unassuming black box seems to be capable of doing. Let's assume that I've placed a physical object to the front and left of the black box. If I do certain things to the box, it becomes active, revealing a series of lights and keys. When those keys are pressed, certain things happen. The black box envelops the object in a low light, seems to "recognize" the physical object, and enters something in some way into the box's memory. When certain other keys are pushed, a second, seemingly identical, object appears to the front and right of the box. Both objects are there at the same time. Both are real physical objects, not holograms or anything similar. As the keying sequence is completed, the original object disappears, leaving only the new second object, apparently identical to the original."

As Joseph scans his research team, he sees the skepticism in their faces, but he thinks he's piqued their interest. He looks over at Maria., "Show them," she words.

"Now I suspect that you are all skeptical about all this," Joseph paces calmly in front of the group as he speaks. "I would not want you any other way. Today, I want you to be scientists at your best. I want you to ask the tough questions, subject our experiments to further testing, and suggest alternative explanations. Be vigilant against tricks. We do seek truth here, no matter what that truth may be.

"Let's begin with a test," he says as he prepares to duplicate the first experiment of the Taj and Jason. "I am going to place this multicolored kitchen bowl to the front of the black box. This will be our original object. Maria, please come over here and help me activate the box."

"When you observe what Maria and I do, you will see that the box apparently needs two people to activate it initially. We place our fingers on the four top corners of the black box, thus activating the box."

Nothing happens. The black box remains inactive. Murmurs come from the research team and Maria's observers. Joseph and Maria pause for a few moments.

"Now you might ask, which side of a featureless black solid is the top?" With Maria's help, Joseph flips the box onto its other side. "Unless we are all wet on this whole thing, it's probably not this side."

The observers snicker good-naturedly.

"We've now turned the box over and will try it again with the other side."

As Maria and Joseph repeat the touching of the box, the box comes to life, and the initial set of lights comes on.

Much louder murmurs permeate the room. Maria steps back as Joseph presses on.

With the bowl in front of the black box, he moves through the whole process, resulting initially in two bowls and then, when the process is done, resulting in only one bowl, the apparent duplicate.

"What happened?" asks a research team member. His question releases floods of other questions from other team members. One asks, "Joseph, do you honestly believe that this is no illusion and there are two real physical objects?"

"Let me answer the last question first," Joseph replies. "I can't be absolutely certain. However,

black box

everything I know about the box and what it can do leads me to conclude that what you see is real and no illusion. The box does something to physical objects. The real unknowns are what and how. In the back of my mind is the nagging third question, why?"

Joseph gestures to the group of researchers. "That's why you are all here, to help answer these and many more questions. Enough of the preliminaries, let's find out what this box can do."

"First, we'll duplicate the experiments conducted and the results achieved by earlier 'researchers'."

With that, Joseph and his team begin duplicating the experiments conducted by Taj and Jason, but without the accidental experiment with the cat G. From one bowl, there comes a second bowl. From one radio, there comes a second radio. Finally, from a living green plant, there comes a second green plant. The team adheres to all the details of Taj and Jason's experiments: the green plant comes with a live spider. To clear up one of the uncertainties of Taj and Jason's experiment, Joseph documents that the living spider is on both first the original plant and then on the second plant.

Just as the surveillance tape demonstrated to Joseph and Maria, the experiments demonstrate for the research team that the black box apparently creates a second object, a seeming duplicate of the first. But then again, the original item always disappears when the processing is completed. They wonder if the original item necessarily has to disappear for the process to be complete. If so, why?

Once the basic premise of the box is established, Joseph and his team try to decode the system of letters and their corresponding lights on the top of the black box.

Given what seems to be happening with the black box and what would, to some extent seem obvious from the letters, they tentatively decide that the lights and letters probably mean the following. "Record" is the light and key that starts the whole process and seems to start the function, whereby the black box ascertains what the original item is that it is to duplicate or move. Though they don't know how it does it, the "record" key seems to cause the black box to search for an object to the front and left of wherever the box is. The object or objects within that approximate distance are enveloped in a faint glow. This may mean that something is happening to them or it may be the box's way of signaling that it is "recording" and will process later.

With respect to the letters "e" and "m" letters, Joseph and his people now assume that these probably signify "energy" and "mass" respectively. That is what one might expect from a device that seems to convert an object's mass either for the purpose of transportation or duplication. They are still unclear over what the initial "e" light was, though it might have something to do with energy levels in the black box or in the conversion process or both. It is the only letter and light combination that is in the reverse order and does not operate as a pressable key.

Continuing from there, "m to e" then signifies the changing of mass to energy. This implies that somehow the box is taking the mass of the original object and in some way dealing with it as energy. Since the original object still is there at this point in the process, the original mass may not yet have been converted into energy. As for the next set of letters, "e to m," their best guess is that this signifies the changing of energy to mass. This made a bit more sense since this is when the second object appears, as if mass is coming into being. Whatever else the box is doing, it seems to take the original item and put it through that conversion process.

The "verify" letter and light combination

black box

functions to see whether or not the first and second item are really the same. The final light, "delete," completes the process by eliminating or moving the original item. Without pressing it, the process always terminates within 30 seconds and the second item disappears.

But what exactly does the "verify" light do? Their best guess is that it somehow checks to make sure the second item is the same as the first. Some testing is needed.

"Since we made a guess at what the 'verify' key does, let's try a series of test just to see if that's what it does and, if we're correct, how sensitive it is to changes," Joseph instructs his team.

"For the first set of tests on the 'verify' key, we'll focus on the original object and use plastic building blocks. We'll connect the building blocks together into the shape of a toy human robot with two separately powered, motorized arms."

"For our first tests, we move or change the first item, the toy robot." A researcher brings Joseph the building block robot. He puts it to the front and left of the box. "Ok, activate the box," Joseph tells him. "Proceed with the keys and stop before we press 'verify.' We'll split the original robot in two pieces. Leave the second robot whole and see what happens. Press verify and ...."

"It's disappeared," exclaims a researcher. "The second robot disappeared. The original robot is in two pieces as we left it."

"Exactly," notes Joseph. "Physically changing the original object itself seems to terminate the process. The 'verify' function recognizes that they are no longer the same objects. Let's try a variation on this theme."

"This time we'll start with half of the robot." The researchers move quickly to get a better view of Joseph's experiment "We put it through the process. There's the identical one-half robot on the other side of the box.

Now, before we press 'verify' let's put the original robot back together into a whole robot. Then we'll press 'verify.'

"See. Something different happened. The duplicate one-half robot created by the box does not disappear. But look at the original robot. The original one-half robot, the same as our duplicate one-half robot, is gone. But the other half, which we tried to attach, is just lying there. The box seems to ignore additions to the original object or objects once it has gone beyond the 'record' stage."

They perform other tests to confirm that physically changing the original object in the middle of the process terminates it. Adding items to the original makes no difference; the additions are ignored no matter how much the added items are physically linked to the original. However, if the researchers make even a small scratch in the original object when they add items, the process terminates. Even the smallest scratch precipitates termination.

"Let's take a different approach," suggests Joseph. "We'll focus on the location of the original object."

Moving the original has little effect. Just before hitting 'verify,' they try putting the original object inside other objects. They put it behind walls. The box keeps track of the original as long as it is not changed itself. But there seems to be a distance limit. From further than one hundred yards, the verification does not take place and the process terminates.

"Okay, we've worked with the original, it's time for testing the duplicate," Joseph says after a few hours of testing have passed.

When they test "verify" with respect to the seeming copy, the black box is much more sensitive to changes in the item, but not at all to changes in location. The black box seems to keep track of the second item no

black box

matter where it is or how far it travels. Time seems to be the only limit. After 30 seconds without pressing "verify," the process terminates and the second item disappears.

Changing the second item in any way terminates the process. Other things can be placed on it or next to it, as long as the second item itself is not altered. Just as with the original, a scratch made on the second item terminates the process. Unless it is an exact copy of the original, the black box will not "verify" and will not process.

They then proceed with testing the black box in other ways. In a series of tests to see how the box handles objects of different weight, they find that whether the object weighs one ounce, one pound, or one hundred pounds makes no difference. The black box succeeds each time in making an identical copy.

Their testing then moves on to handling more than one object at a time. Here, the black box has no difficulty dealing with any number of original objects or of objects within objects. During one experiment when the research team is tired and a little loose, the box is given the challenge of dealing with a live plant inside a 300 pound safe with a glass of water on top of the safe. There, on the right side of the black box, stands a 300 pound safe with a glass of water on top of it. When they open the safe, there is the live plant.

They debate whether or not to try small animals. This was the point at which Taj and Jason experienced their great trauma. Taj and Jason's concern reflected the whole ethics of animal experimentation, but this was not a major ethical dilemma for Joseph and his team and even if it had been, Maria and her team would have pressured them to move forward.

So they proceed with animal experiments. Without hesitation or miscue, the black box individually handles a white rat, a bird and an ant when sedated. They try again with unsedated and animate animals. No problem. When they perform the same tests with the animals as a group, once again the black box performs as expected. There, to the right side of the box, stands the white rat, the bird and the ant looking as healthy as can be.

Though it does not matter whether the animal is alive or not, or animate or not, the black box has its own way of dealing with the issue of movement. Once the process begins, the black box freezes the original object and the duplicate, though only for a maximum of about one and one-half minutes. It's the box's own variation on suspended animation.

"Might there be some way for the suspension process to be made to last longer?" One of the researchers asks Joseph as they watch the original ant and duplicate ant be momentarily frozen in motion.

"What must it be like for the animals during this period of suspension? Does it hurt them?" Joseph asks back. Still, he has the team move on.

They bring in animals of all kinds from nearby research facilities. They are going to test the capacity of the black box.

"Is there any limit to how much mass the box can handle?" He adds this question to the long list of questions they've already sketched out. "We know it can handle say 400 pounds. But can it handle really big objects?"

One female researcher, who had become quite an enthusiastic participant during the day and has been responsible for many of the more creative objects converted, pauses for a few seconds before saying, "Let's find out. I'll be right back."

All of a sudden, Joseph hears a loud rumbling sound moving in their direction. Through the doorway

black box

comes the researcher with her prize. From another part of the lab, a large portable safe, weighing over a thousand pounds, is wheeled into position.

Joseph smiles. "You brought the safe," he tells her. "Why don't you do the honors and see what this little box can do?"

With zeal, the woman researcher proceeds through the process, but to an early termination. This time when the process is carried out, the black box goes no further than the "m to e" light. The researcher tries it again. At the same point, it terminates the process. There is a limit for the mass of the object. Yet they have had success in the past with objects that had more volume than this safe, though these other objects had substantially less mass.

Utilizing a laboratory scale and different objects with different weights, they estimate that 500 pounds is the limit of what the black box can handle. Getting back in touch with the animal research facility, they arrange for a young heifer, about 450 pounds, and an older cow, considerably more than 500 pounds, to be brought in. They put them through the process. As expected, the black box can handle only the 450-pound young heifer.

By that time, it is nearly midnight on Saturday. Most of the research team still functions, but not at full capacity., "What do you say that we call it a night?" Joseph suggests to Maria. "The next tests get much more complicated. A few hours sleep would help all of us a lot."

Maria looks over her own people, many of whom look weary, and agrees. "Close it up for the night. We've learned a lot about our little South American find. Lock it up in the vault. I'll make sure that the night guards are posted outside the vault and keep this place secure."

With that, they secure the black box inside the vault and everyone except the guards leaves for the night, with the experiments to resume at one o'clock tomorrow afternoon.

At noon, Joseph arrives at the laboratory. As he walks in and greets the guards, he thinks, "From yesterday's work and the work of Taj and Jason, we learned so much about this box's functions. But there is so much we don't yet know. To some extent, the phrase 'black box' is a very appropriate term here. If ever there was one, this is the proverbial 'black box,' a device that does something, but no one knows how or what is inside making it happen."

Over the next week or so, Joseph plans to return to basic questions about the box itself, testing the material of which it is made and checking it for energy before, during and after it processes objects. More x-rays and other imaging techniques will be used. Preliminary x-rays done first thing yesterday indicated that the box is a solid object with no internal parts, or at least no internal parts that the x-ray device can measure. But more of that kind of testing is for next week; today needs to focus on the box's functions.

By one o'clock, the research team and Maria's observers arrive.

"Today, we begin with the more complex questions and complex experiments with the black box," Joseph announces as he opens the session. "We have two lines of questions that we'll tackle over these next hours. The first line of questioning is the following. Is the 'copy' really the same as the 'original' object? Here we will try a whole range of measures to see if we can discern any differences."

"The second line of questioning has to do with what exactly the box is doing. Is the black box moving

black box

the original item or copying it or both? We see and feel two distinct objects at one point in the process. But what is the case when the process is complete and there is only one object left?"

With that introduction, they begin the day's work.

The first set of tests is to determine whether or not the black box is moving the original item or copying it. Here, Joseph suspects, no test will be conclusive. Much of their time is spent debating how they can possibly design the test so as to accurately and definitively answer the question.

"Listen," Joseph interrupts. "What I hear all of us saying is that we don't know of any other tests than those we did already that will answer the question. Everyone agrees it's a critical question, but no good tests are available to get the answer.

"Let's go over what we think we know already. The box appears to be a copying process rather than a transportation process since the original and the "copy" co-exist in time for up to one and one-half minutes. Thus, the device may be destroying the originals that we have used in the tests. I, for one, am in no big hurry to be 'converted' by this black box until this little question is resolved."

"Maybe the box doesn't 'destroy' the original but puts it into some state of suspension," the female researcher says. "Sort of like what it does to animate objects during the processing."

Joseph nods. "But if so," he points out, "the key question is where are these originals. If so, we put an awful lot of objects, including a 300-pound safe and a 450-pound heifer, in this suspended state yesterday. It must be getting terribly crowded."

"On the other hand, there seems to be no practical reason why the black box might not be able to do both. Possibly the box temporarily creates the second object to make sure that transporting can be done without harm. Only after everything checks out and the operator presses 'verify' and 'delete' does the transporting take place. Possibly the 'delete' key is deleting the temporary object to make way for the actual transporting of the original. But there are a lot of capabilities that are 'unknowns' for us right now."

This line of inquiry proves to be shorter than Joseph expected. Maybe the next line of questioning will bear more fruit.

"Is the 'copy' really the same as the original object?" Joseph asks. "So far, we probably are inclined to say that it is. All of our earlier tests seem to indicate that it is. This again may be one of those questions that we cannot answer with complete certainty.

"So how should we proceed? Let me suggest that the first step is to check the status of the two items during the time period when both the 'copy' and the 'original' apparently exist."

Here, tests are conducted by the research team between the pressing of the "e to m" key and the "verify" key as well as between the pressing of the "verify" key and the "delete" key. In conducting these tests, there are a couple of significant problems. For one, they have an extremely limited amount of time. If the "verify" key is not pressed within one minute, the "copy" disappears. Subsequently, if the "delete" key is not pushed within 30 seconds, the "copy" disappears.

A second testing problem results from the two objects being "frozen" during the conversion process. The object no longer functions. The internal workings of the objects, like blood flow or electrical activity, are suspended. There are limits to what the research team can measure since both objects are temporarily frozen in place during the process.

By every measurement they can make, the two

black box

items, the original and the apparent copy, exist in their entirety at one point in the process. They both have the same mass and dimensions. They are both solid or liquid depending upon the item used. They both operate the same either mechanically or electronically. Because the two objects are frozen during the process, these latter tests are conducted on the original object before processing and on the "copy" after processing. For all the team's tests and sophisticated measurements, there is no distinguishing the before and after objects. The black box apparently adds nothing, subtracts nothing, and makes no modification.

"As I see it, the results of the tests are fairly conclusive," says the female researcher. "Nothing we can measure indicates that there is any difference between the two objects. But there still may be a difference we don't know how to measure."

"You're right," responds Joseph cautiously as he taps his chin thoughtfully. "Are we failing to measure something?"

Joseph considers whether or not he should make this a troubling point. He looks at the two teams. He knows he can't avoid the question most likely on all their minds.

"I suspect most, if not all, of you are harboring thoughts of what the black box will do to human beings.

The teams glance uneasily at each other, then nod yes.

"Clearly, virtual certainty will be essential before anyone should even think about human beings going through the 'black box' process. We'll put that question aside for later deliberation."

Joseph clears his throat. "But we're not done yet."

A quiet observer for some time now, Maria speaks up from behind him. "I've seen you all measure all kinds of standard physical properties of objects. You have found no discernable differences. But one thing you have not measured is the impact on mental processes. The animals you have tested so far did appear to suffer any harm, but you did not formally test for change. That's where I believe we should focus next."

"Agreed," says Joseph. "The intriguing question is what is the black box doing or not doing to the mental process. Is that also duplicated? Is there harm? Is there benefit?"

For this test, they turn to two monkeys, a male and a female, as test subjects. Certain cognitive tests are given with respect to the mental capabilities of the monkeys. The black box is engaged and produces "duplicate" monkeys. The same tests are done on the "duplicate" monkeys.

A research team member specializing in cognitive abilities reads off the results to the other team members. "We see some indication that the 'duplicate' monkey retains the learning from the cognitive tests performed on the 'original,'" he tells them. "But that's more likely just a problem with the impact of testing itself. If the box is creating a duplicate, that's what should happen since the original monkey will have learned from the tests as well."

"Yet other than that, we find no discernable difference between the original and the duplicate monkey. They 'think' the same. They have the same knowledge. They behave the same. It is as if nothing happened or the monkey had just transported a small distance."

"I suspect that we are all in agreement to this point," suggests Joseph. "There is now every reason to believe that the black box can either create an exact copy or can move the original from place to place without any alteration. But again, there is no certainty!"

"As I see it, now the main remaining question is

black box

about humans," Joseph notes uneasily. "But let me be clear on this point for the research team and the observers in the room. We still have much to learn before anyone should even think about proposing a test of the 'human' aspect of the black box. This is far too early a time to even begin to deal with that issue."

Looking up at the lab's large clock, Joseph realizes that it's close to midnight and time for the team and observers to call it quits.

"After all, this is only our second day of testing," he tells them all. "Much more will hopefully be learned about the black box over these next weeks and months. We'll talk about this more tomorrow."

As Joseph steps back, he looks over at Maria. He senses the absence of patience in her and, to even a greater extent, her observers. He hadn't asked who they were and she hadn't offered to explain their presence. How much time does he really have to deal with the "human" aspect of the black box in a careful, scientific manner? Maybe a month, but no longer. Maybe less. Maria walks by him, heading for the door. Maybe less.

Maria turns briefly as she nears the door. She glances at her observers first and then at Joseph. Deep worry is what her look communicates.

Chapter 9. Personal Conversion

Smithsonian laboratory, Washington, D.C.; one week later.

Almost simultaneously, both Maria and Joseph check the clock in the lab. It reads six p.m., but both know that it's much later in terms of perceived time.

Over the past week, they have conducted more experiments on the black box's function. They repeated previous tests. They tried different objects. They tried to fool the box in subtle ways. They made changes in the objects themselves or in their location. Two unmistakable conclusions emerged. First, the "original" object and the "duplicate" are the same by any measure available to the research team. Second, the black box does one thing and, apparently, only one thing. Using an original object weighing 500 pounds or less to the front and left of the box, the black box, either by duplication or transportation, brings about an object to the front and right of the box that is indistinguishable from the original

black box

and may even be the original. To the best of their knowledge, it does nothing else.

With respect to the box itself, they tried every scanning device to learn more about what is inside the box. Consistently, the scans show the box as a solid object. Testing the box material is made with every known method of analysis came up with nothing other than what they felt with their own hands and saw with their own eyes. The box is made of a black, impervious, glasslike material.

They tried to see what happened when the box is activated. In general, they picked up some type of energy readings, but it was too large to make any sense. The energy readings change during the box's processing, but the team has been unable to figure out in what way. The energy levels seem to be lowest when both objects exist. This might suggest that the box has energy of its own that it uses to temporarily have the "original" and the "copy" co-exist.

The research team's attempts to impact on the box's surface have been to no avail. They found nothing that would suggest a way to get into the box. There are no openings. The material of the box remains impervious. Nothing, not strong chemicals, mechanical tools, or powerful lasers, made even a hint of a blemish.

As each day passed, Joseph felt the level of tension and impatience build. While the research team continues to learn new things, it isn't enough for Maria's "observers." Increasingly, her observers are asking questions, very tough questions. Each question has one of two underlying themes. The most forthright has to do with the unanswered question about what the black box would do to a human being going through its process. The less forthright theme has to do with the black box's potential for doing other things than they had discovered so far. Underlying the last question appears to be the box's potential as a weapon.

The last thought makes Joseph shudder.

As Sandy Hart[5] sits in the laboratory that day watching the research team's work, her thoughts go back to how she came to be here. "Volunteer" seems to her to be a strange term for what she is. While she technically volunteered for this project, she feels she had little choice.

When this project was placed before her, admittedly in sketchy terms, she knew that it was her duty to volunteer. She did so without hesitancy.

She knows this is far from a risk-free mission. More so than usual in a non-combat situation, all five of the volunteers were told to get all their lives in order and have been told to behave as if they were going into a combat situation from which they might not return. Each of the volunteers proceeded accordingly. Sandy visited her mother in Chicago, but wishes she could have talked to her Dad as well.

For the past week, Sandy has sat in this laboratory watching the research effort. There were no doubts in the observers' or her mind as to why she was

---

[5] She made the choice to enter the military after finishing her bachelor's degree. The military helped pay for her college education, but this is not what brought her together with the military. She always had a strong sense of public duty. The military isn't the only way to fulfill that sense of public duty, but for her, it fits.

Her father had passed away a couple of years earlier. Still, her mother and her grandparents, all four of them, were glad to see her. Sandy isn't married, although, for many reasons she kind of wishes she was. She's seriously considered it, but has yet to meet the right person. Today, being unmarried makes one less complication for her to worry about.

black box

here. There is the black box. There is the research team trying the conversion process on virtually everything, except human beings. Here sit five human volunteers.

Some people in the room, especially Joseph, seem anxious whenever the question of human testing comes up. Others in the room talk of little else and seem to have little discomfort with the prospect. But then, the ones who were talking are not the ones who would be doing the testing. Sandy is less sanguine on the feelings of one of the key "observers," a Dr. M.L. Tarry. It's not that she is comfortable with what he is saying: it's more that she is not as uncomfortable.

As the late afternoon is about to turn into evening, Sandy watches the testing carefully, especially the tests with the monkeys. Joseph and his team do a pretty thorough job of testing. Unfortunately, there are certain questions they cannot answer with complete certainty. The "human" question is one of them.

From the discussion going on around the room, Sandy sees that things are coming to a head even now. She clasps her hands around her head and leans forward in deep thought. For Sandy, little time remains for soul searching. Little time remains for answers. So much is at stake, and she has to be sure of herself.

Among Maria's observers that late afternoon is Dr. Tarry[6], a military scientist known for his work on the

---

[6] At fifty-five, his life is now devoted to his research. He and his wife divorced. They do not see much of each other any more. His two grown children have independent lives of their own. He sees them infrequently. He is comfortable with that being the case.

human aspect of warfare. Much of his work focuses on human performance, or as how the military sees it, strengthening the human being as soldier. Certain people believe that his work holds much greater promise than does work on missile defenses and high performance bombers.

As he sits along the wall, his thoughts turn to his work.

Others worry about high-tech, non-human weapons. So does Dr. Tarry, but from a different perspective. His is a more complex challenge. He tries to develop a hi-tech human being better able to deal with and survive those weapons. Still, that's not what brought him into the military and not what keeps him here.

In an era when civilian research funding is getting tighter, he can see military research funding is growing. By sliding over to the military side, he is relatively assured of having funding for his research for many years to come. Besides, the civilian side of research is limited and much less interested in his line of research. Only in athletics and, to a lesser extent, business, is there much interest in the concept of human performance.

Yet he's still betting that, like a lot of other military research, his research work would end up having it greatest impact, positive impact, in the non-military world.

So far he's not had any major ethical conflicts. But now there is this black box. If it can do more than transport or duplicate, then there might really be something.

"Sure, it can either move objects modest distances and maybe duplicate them," he thinks. "Maybe. But what real value is that? So far, its value is not much more than that of a magic show. Entertainment value is not enough. There has to be more. I have to find that more."

black box

"Joseph and his research team have had their chance," Dr. Tarry decides as he stretches his legs and rises. "They're good researchers trying their best. Caution is not bad, but they are far, far too cautious. It is time for them to step aside. If not, they will be moved aside."

Both Maria and Joseph see control over the situation shift away from them. Joseph is under increasing pressure from his superiors. The pressure on his superiors is coming from very high up. The terms "progress" and "funding" are more and more closely linked. For the Smithsonian, this is a much hotter item than they are used to handling. Even his superiors know there is an obligation to science that is not yet fulfilled. The word circulating the lab is that the Smithsonian might lose control over the box at any time.

Maria is nervous about today. She's come to like Joseph and deeply respect his work and ethics. She wishes circumstances were otherwise for them and wants him to know more about her and her more about him.

As the week passes, the number of heated arguments outside the lab increases. Maria is worried. She argues for time and a carefully reasoned scientific process. Her observers argue for a major shift now. She's losing the argument and is only a telephone call away from losing direct control over the project. Given that one of her observers, Dr. Tarry, left the room about an hour ago to make a progress report and given the report she made at lunchtime, the next phone call will be it.

As the phone rings, Maria is waved over to take the call. The tone of voice on the other end is unmistakable. Her superiors' patience is gone. They want answers to the larger questions now, not later. Dr. Tarry, her lead "observer," is being given control. They apologize, but the apology is more perfunctory than real. She is to stay on and oversee the project, but is not to interfere. As she looks across the room, she sees that Joseph is being given the same orders. She waves across to Dr. Tarry, motioning him to come over. With a knowing look, he does. When they look at each other, there is no sign of animosity by either. They are both just doing what they have to do. They both have to work together. It will not be easy.

    She passes the phone to him.

    While the phone conversation continues, Maria assesses Dr. Tarry. "Dr. Tarry is a highly intense man who does not tolerate fools or those he perceives are fools," she reminds herself. She's not sure what he thinks of Joseph and her. His patience is surely not in large supply either. As the work was not progressing quickly, it was obvious that his mind and body were pacing. While noticeable, it wasn't much of an issue. He was just an observer, just one of the players. Now things have changed. Now he is in control.

    When the phone call ends, Dr. Tarry moves to the center of the room and conferences briefly with both Maria and Joseph. Though they already know, he states that the project is now his and so is the responsibility for what happens next. The pressure is now on him. He can and will tolerate no interference. But he would very much appreciate their counsel if and when solicited.

    Joseph and Maria both agree to stay with the project for the duration.

    With these formalities taken care of, Dr. Tarry addresses the people in the laboratory. "You need to know that I was just been directed to take over the project," he tells them. "For security reasons, all except the two senior researchers and my senior people are to leave the room. I know. I know. I hear those sounds of unhappiness and disappointment. I understand your disappointment and thank you for your valuable contribution. We are cutting back the research team substantially and you are no longer needed."

There is no confusion. The look on Dr. Tarry's face says it all. They are to leave and leave quickly.

Most people do so. A few hesitate until they see the guards posted at the door. The five people to the one side begin to get up from their chairs. Dr. Tarry motions for them to stay seated. They sit back down.

"There's one exception to that rule," Dr. Tarry announces. The five volunteers should stay sitting where they are."

Clearly the "human" issues of the black box are about to come front and center.

As was the case since the beginning of the project, an electronic record is being kept of all the experiments and their results. Dr. Tarry walks over toward the recording booth in which the woman who oversees the recording sits and controls the equipment and the recordings.

"Is everything ready?" Dr. Tarry asks in more of a demand than a question.

She assures him that all the equipment is working and that they have three working cameras prepared to record the results of the next experiments. Dr. Tarry wonders a little about her tone of voice; she's clearly not happy about all that's going on here and she's not alone on that point. On the other hand, she should be a bit happier since she at least is getting to stay and watch.

Returning to the center of the lab and the spot where the black box sits, Dr. Tarry turns to the main camera and announces the next phase of the experiments.

"I and my superiors carefully reviewed the

experiments to date, especially those with monkeys and chimpanzees," Dr. Tarry states as he lays out the justification for what is to come next. "In our view, every important test that could be conducted has been conducted. There is absolutely no indication that the black box is harmful to the objects it processes. There is every indication that it is capable of handling a human being. That is the next phase of these experiments."

With that, he states, "A group of young military men and women have volunteered to be part of the next experiment. As you must have noticed by now, they are sitting along the wall."

The volunteers' chairs creak loudly as they look straight ahead, trying to hide their apprehension.

Off to one side, Maria whispers to Joseph. "It would be interesting to ask them about just how much 'volunteering' they really did when approached for this project. I doubt this would stand up to any 'human subjects protection" review."

Joseph nods.

"This is not going to be easy for them," Dr. Tarry continues. "But they are here and they are trying to prepare themselves for facing an experience that, to the best of their and our knowledge, no other human being has ever gone through. They need us to help get them through this experiment safely."

Dr. Tarry then begins to set up the next experiment. He turns to the corner of the room and asks for a volunteer to be first. They are hesitant. To be first and survive would be a great honor. To be first and die or be maimed without anyone else ever knowing would be no honor. After a brief moment, there is movement among the volunteers.

A young woman with "Sandy" on her ID tag steps forward and walks over to where the black box is. She glances at it. She finds the spot used so often in earlier

black box

phases of these experiments and stands there silently.

For everyone involved, with the possible exception of Dr. Tarry, seeing a human being in that spot takes their collective breath away. They knew it would happen, but the shock is no less. Joseph and Maria feel that this is all wrong, that more time is needed, and that too much is still not known.

It doesn't matter what they think now. The experiment is going forward as planned by Dr. Tarry. His authority and his direction are not subject to question.

A few minutes pass and Sandy still stands, waiting. Dr. Tarry's team moves around her in a flurry of activity in preparation for the first "human" experiment with the black box. On the lighted table, the black box also sits, waiting. The juxtaposition of the human, Sandy, and the black box sets the stage for this historic experiment.

"Sandy, are you ready?" Dr. Tarry asks.

She does not look at him. She does not speak. She just nods her head affirmatively.

"All right," he says. "Then I think we proceed." His voice softens from its normal authoritative tone for just a moment. "Sandy, let me assure you. Everything we know tells us that you will not feel anything and that you will not be harmed. I'm going to count down from five and then press the first key. I will proceed through the lights fairly quickly, just giving our people enough time to observe the results of each step. Do you understand?"

She nods.

With that, Dr. Tarry and his lead researcher activate the black box. The other researcher steps back out of the way. Dr. Tarry counts down from five to zero. He presses "record."

On comes the "m to e" light. Somehow, Joseph hoped that the black box would refuse.

After about ten seconds, Dr. Tarry proceeds to press that light. The "e to m" light is illuminated. No change in Sandy. She is still standing there, as before, quietly.

Another ten seconds pass and Dr. Tarry, less quick this time, presses the "e to m" light. Almost instantly, the second Sandy appears.

No one dares to make a move. No one wants to move, fearing that somehow they might inadvertently mess up the process with Sandy suffering the consequences. Even Dr. Tarry is caught up in the moment. He looks back and forth at the two "Sandys," and forgets to push "verify." After a minute, the second Sandy disappears.

Everyone gasps. Dr. Tarry is annoyed by the fact that he failed to hit the "verify" key.

"Sandy. I'm sorry," says Dr. Tarry, the only one to speak through the silence. "I was just so amazed. There were two of you. For those few moments, there were two 'Sandys' co-existing in time."

Most are surprised to hear Dr. Tarry apologize for anything.

With that, Sandy almost comes apart. But she doesn't. She hasn't spent days building up her courage and putting her affairs in order to miss out on this piece of history. So far, she's survived. The completion of the process would be a whole other leap into the unknown.

For Sandy, she believes that she will be leaping across a small amount of space as she, in her current form, will either cease to exist or be moved. Either a new Sandy will take her place or the old Sandy will be in a new place. Will she still be the same Sandy? If not, how will she change?

Knowing that even great courage does not

black box

necessarily last forever, Dr. Tarry asks Sandy if she is ready to proceed again. She tells him yes.

Even he seems a bit awe-struck by the courage of this young woman and wonders, "How would I behave if I were in her place. I think I might not behave as well."

"Fine, then. Let's get on with it," Dr. Tarry announces sharply. "Same procedures as before but we'll go all the way through."

This time he moves through the lights faster. After pressing "e to m", the second Sandy appears and both Sandys are frozen in place. After only a few seconds, he presses "verify."

In seconds, on comes the "delete" light. Both Sandys are standing there, frozen.

Dr. Tarry feels a pinch of fear as he glances back and forth between the "delete" key and the two "Sandys." He realizes that he might be about to send this young woman to death or worse.

He decides to push through his fear. He's programmed himself to complete the move. He presses "delete."

The original Sandy disappears. The second Sandy does not.

There is no movement, until Sandy begins to move and check herself over. She is trying to ascertain if anything about her is altered. She is unsure, looking for help among faces she hardly knows. She looks pleadingly for a friendly, understanding face.

Turning to Joseph and Maria, she asks them, in as calm a voice as she can muster, "Am I all right?"

Quickly, they both move to her. They try to assure her that everything appears to have gone perfectly. As it turns out, neither finds it that difficult to say. In the back of their minds, they do believe the black box works. They believed she would be safe.

Once before, when Joseph and Maria lunched

together, they talked about the "human" question. Somehow, the box is intended for human beings and not just for rats and cows. None of the people they knew in this world would go through all this effort to create something as sophisticated and powerful as the black box just to move or duplicate plants and animals. Why would anyone do this, if not for human use? But then again, what *is* its use for humans?

Joseph and Maria are eased out of the way as a physician and nurse are called to examine Sandy. Dr. Tarry wants to know if anything varies from the baseline information they have on Sandy from testing on the previous weekend. The doctor and nurse examine every conceivable part of her body for change. They check out all her body functions. They quiz her on all kinds of information from technical to personal. They test her reasoning.

All this takes time. By the time the doctor and nurse finish their first phase of testing, it is very late, eleven o'clock at night. The medical team cautions everyone that they can't be absolutely sure until they complete a couple more days of tests and observe Sandy closely. But, in their combined and considered judgment, the Sandy who stands before them now is exactly the same as the Sandy who volunteered to go through the conversion process only hours earlier.

The experiment has not failed. The entire team has a big success on their hands. Her fellow volunteers hug Sandy partly to comfort and congratulate her and partly to relieve their own pent-up anxiety.

Dr. Tarry motions sharply to Maria and they both walk quickly over to the telephone. As she walks, Maria sees that Joseph is also reaching for a phone.

In minutes, phone calls are made to the higher-ups who have been waiting for further results. While they had been somewhat relieved by the preliminary reports

black box

hours earlier, they are still on edge. Maria's career, as well as others', might be on the line.

When Dr. Tarry returns from his phone calls, he announces that further tests are postponed until at least the next morning when high-level government officials will be attending.

As Maria starts to walk over toward Joseph, Dr. Tarry stops her for a moment. "After we go over the tapes with our superiors tomorrow morning, maybe I can convince them to slow this whole thing back down again," he says quietly. "They got their 'human' experiment. Maybe they will allow us to hold off future human tests for a week or so until we all see how Sandy does."

Maria is shocked. She strongly encourages his plan, wanting to support any sign of human concern in this man. She assures him it's the right thing to do before she says goodnight.

"I think Dr. Tarry learned a small bit of humility tonight," she tells Joseph as they leave together. "Going at a slightly slower pace is sounding much more comfortable to him."

Maria and Joseph shake hands. They look at each other and smile, then reach out and hold each other tightly before separating to congratulate each other.

They look over at Dr. Tarry as he leaves the lab. They look over at the volunteers saying good night to Sandy. They think about the higher-ups and the military flavor of the last few days. All of sudden, they both have a gnawing feeling that failure might have been a better outcome.

For both of them, so many questions remain unanswered. Is this all the black box can do or are there still secrets which it holds? Is the black box a transporter, a copier or a transformer? Does it move objects, clone them, or convert them? Is it capable of doing all of these?

They are saddled with big questions and no clear answers.

Even more so, there is still the nagging question of why. If only they can find the bearded man. They both feel he can provide the answers. But will he share the knowledge? Why should he?

In the recording room outside the main laboratory, Kathryn Graves, the woman handling the recording, is terribly distraught over what she saw today. She asks herself under her breath, "What black magic was carried out this day? What's going on here? Is this sacrilege?"

Quickly and quietly, she duplicates the recordings. Having done that, she locks up the original recording and leaves. She knows she isn't coming back. She has to get this recording into the right hands. She feels that this all has to be stopped. To the very depth of her soul, she believes that "conversion" is immoral and the black box is the tool of some devil.

black box

Chapter 10. Anticonversionists

Washington, D.C.; the next Friday afternoon.
Network television broadcast, later that Friday afternoon.
Suburban Maryland; later that Friday evening.
Streets outside White House, Washington, D.C.; weeks later.

As deadline approaches, the Washington editor of the evening news is not happy. Her people were slipped three videos that are either a grand hoax or a major piece of science fiction turned reality.

According to Kathryn Graves, the woman who gave them the videos, the Smithsonian Institutions is involved. Phone conversations with two lower level Smithsonian research types indicate words are coming out from some less-than-happy researchers about being thrown off a hushed up joint project between the Smithsonian and the Pentagon. So far, Smithsonian officials are saying nothing. They neither deny nor confirm the story. The only clue is an off-the-record remark to the effect that if the story were true, the Pentagon would be in control and the press might want to talk to them.

Calls to the White House and the Pentagon are being ignored even more than usual. Still, no denial came from either. There is too little denial. There is too much silence. This is looking less like a hoax. And the government and the Smithsonian are strangely nervous.

As one of her reporters runs into the editor's office, she blurts out, "My Pentagon source is showing a bad case of nerves and trying to dance around on the authenticity of the video. The story he is trying to sell me is that it is just a hoax. He says no such experiments took place; no so-called black box exists. You want to know what I think? It just doesn't feel like a hoax. My Pentagon source would have been more successful at convincing me if it were a hoax."

The editor calls in the reporter whose territory includes the Smithsonian. Motioning him towards her desk, she fills him on the details. "You need to squeeze your sources again. Remind them that we have the video. Remind them that our experts believe it is real and unaltered. This time indicate that the network believes the video to be genuine and the black box to be real. If the Smithsonian doesn't come clean on the story now, we will imply that the Smithsonian and the Pentagon together may be participating together in a cover-up. Trust me. That will not be a particularly positive image for the Smithsonian."

The reporters depart quickly and start hitting the phones.

As the editor paces in front of her desk, she thinks about the people in the video. Dr. Tarry has already been deep-pocketed by the Pentagon. He is nowhere to be found and it's clear that they won't find him before the evening news airs. The same goes for Sandy Hart, the person she really wants to find. But the real race is on for who gets to the two original project leaders first, the network or the Pentagon. Both project leaders, Maria Mendez and Dr. Joseph Form, were not at work today and are apparently together. The editor isn't confident that if they do find Maria and Joseph the two

black box

researchers will be willing to say anything.

The phone rings.

As the editor grabs the phone on the first ring, the word is good from her field reporter. The reporter found both former project leaders, Mendez and Form. Mendez and Form were shown the video. Mendez started to deny the video's authenticity and then tried to walk away. She is someone fairly high up in the federal government. The other project leader, from the Smithsonian, stood there shaking his head. After pressing him for the upwards of an hour, the reporter got him to confirm the story. Mendez later confirmed the video's authenticity in deep background, but refused to appear on camera. The Smithsonian researcher, Dr. Joseph Form, reluctantly agreed to talk on camera. Form is doing this on his own and without Smithsonian sign-off.

The editor sends her Pentagon and Smithsonian reporters back out to their sources for comments. This time the secrecy dam cracks. The Smithsonian confirms the story, but says it was never intended to be a "military" sponsored experiment. Even the Pentagon gives ground. They confirm the basic story. Their version is that the black box was found in South America and they are just trying to help the Smithsonian discover what it is and what it can do. One of their soldiers, Sandy Hart, volunteered her assistance to the Smithsonian and participated in that phase of the test recorded on video.

With the Smithsonian and the Pentagon confirming key aspects of the story, the editor has no reason to hold back. She leans back in her chair and smiles broadly. She knows that the evening news just got one hell of a lead story.

At six o'clock, one-half hour before airtime, the

White House and the Pentagon make a last-minute attempt to have the story pulled for national security reasons. The network executives refuse to accept the "national security" argument and decide to broadcast the story as planned. In informal, off-the-record conversations, White House and Pentagon officials reluctantly concede that they were caught unprepared by the leak of the video and are not in a position to make the "national security" argument work.

On the evening news, the lead story is that science fiction has become reality. The network news anchor tells the stor a new piece of "black box" technology. We interviewed the Smithsonian researcher, who is one of two former project leaders, and we believe his story to be credible. Both the Pentagon and the Smithsonian, after initial denials, now confirm the historic event. Let me warn you that the video you are about to see may be disturbing, especially once you realize that it is not science fiction."

The network shows the most critical five minutes of the video, now authenticated by the Pentagon and the Smithsonian. The video itself is devastating, especially the indelible image of the two "Sandys."

The video and the story transfix millions of people across the world. The video clip plays time and time again across broadcast and cable networks and plays in every country around the world. The clip is picked by websites and fuels blogs worldwide.

Sandy is an instant celebrity. But no one can find her. Everyone wants to know if she is okay and they want to know what it is like to be "converted," the term used by some of the scientists. Part of the interest is concern for another human being. Part of the interest is in what may be the significance of "conversion".

The black box, the truly silent figure in all this, becomes a somewhat ominous sign, meaning different things to different people. Questions start to arise as to

black box

what exactly the black box does and where it comes from. Some people see it as a sign of something good; other people see it as a sign of something evil.

Hour after hour, day after day, the video is replayed. Two images dominate – Sandy and the black box.

Arriving home from the church on that same Friday evening, a minister sets down her briefcase and starts to go toward the kitchen for a cold soda. As she passes by the living room, her husband calls out, "L.O., come quick. They've got some crazy story coming about a human experiment and a black box."

"I'm coming," she responds as she walks into the living room where he is sitting. She stands behind the couch, sets aside her crutches, puts her hands on her husband's shoulders, and watches the story unfold on the evening news. She does not like what she sees.

L.O. focuses on the image of the black box, silently and mysteriously doing what it does. She focuses on the image of Sandy Hart.

"What did they do to her?" she says to her husband, indignation in her voice. "Am I right that this black box is supposed to have taken this woman, created a duplicate of her, and then 'deleted' the original woman?"

"They're not sure on that yet," her husband replies, gesturing towards the newscasters on TV. "It seems like there is agreement that there is a duplicate woman, seemingly identical to the first. On what happened to either of them, there are different views. One view is what you said. Another view is that the original woman is transported from one spot to the other. Apparently, there were a lot of tests done on animals and other things before they tested it with her."

"It's not right," Reverend L.O. Moses murmurs to herself as she goes out to the kitchen for the soda she started to get earlier.

" I can kind of see what happens to the body when this black box does what it does," her husband calls back to her as she makes her way to the fridge. "But my question is 'what happens to the soul?"

"A good, moral question!" Reverend Moses responds as she turns away and heads out to their den.

Leaving her husband to watch his programs in the living room, L.O. turns on the television in the den and begins watching the ever-expanding news coverage on the black box and Sandy. As the hours go by, she continues flicking back and forth among the channels trying to pick up whatever is being shown and said about the human experiment.

As the television images move in front of her, she keeps playing the morality question and implications over and over in her mind. She keeps returning to her husband's question about what happens to the soul. While many of medical science's near miracles with the brain raise difficult questions about the soul, no medical advance raises as troubling a question as does this little black box. L.O. isn't anti-science. She hasn't ever been anti-science, and as far as she's concerned, when religious faith and medical science combine forces for good, she's always amazed at what 'miracles' occur. But this is something else entirely.

She continues watching the television. Whenever the black box appears on the television screen, she feels confronted by what it does and what it signifies.

Neither view of what the black box does allows her to walk past the question of soul. Most religions, including hers, do not allow for a soul that can be moved from one physical body to another physical body or that

black box

can be duplicated so as to occupy two bodies simultaneously.

Her husband comes to the door "L.O. Time for bed," he says softly. "It's almost one o'clock in the morning."

"Not for a little while," she responds, waving him away. "The more I think about this, the more I am troubled. I worry about what this black box does. I worry about where it might have come from. I worry about what it means to people who believe in a God and in a human soul as we do. Where does this leave us?"

"I don't know either," her husband responds. "But you can't resolve it tonight."

"You're right," Reverend Moses says reluctantly. "Go to sleep. I'll be there before too long."

Her husband heads up to bed, switching off the lights in the other rooms as he goes.

Leaning back, she thinks back about how she got here and what it means for where she goes from here.[7]

---

[7] Fortunately, at the age of twenty, she acquired an ally and a mentor within her religion's hierarchy. Her mentor was a man seen by many as the symbol of tradition. But he saw what was happening to their religion. It had lost strength in numbers and commitment. In an era when women were finding their own way, his religion, which was his life, was failing to adequately address the vital and full role for women. In L.O. Moses, he recognized the potential for re-directing his religion. In his view, helping her was helping the religion in which he believed fervently.

Though it might well have happened without his help, everything moved faster with it. By the age of twenty-five, L.O. completed her training and became the Reverend L.O. Moses, the first woman to hold that title in her religion. With her in the pulpit, more women came. More men and children came as well. People, even outside her own followers, tell her she touches them deeply and strengthens their faith. She tells them that they do the same for her.

This past year when she turned 47, she began a Sunday

Religion has been integral to her life since childhood. There was little doubt as she grew up that religion would be her life. There is the slight complication about her being a woman in a religion where virtually all of the "reverends" were men. Her talent for oratory, the intensity of her beliefs, the strong following she generates makes it difficult for the authority structure to ignore her. There are times when they tried to re-direct her energy into more traditional roles for women. She rejected that re-direction.

Her preaching is strong because her beliefs are strong. She is there to save the souls of the people who come to her. She is there to help the lives of the people who come to her. Her followers are important to her for how they live now and where their souls will go after this life.

She blinks as again the image of the black box appears on the cable news program and is juxtaposed with the image of Sandy.

"It is morally wrong," she says, gripping the

---

morning televised church service. She has a small audience. Her mentor, still a source of support, encourages her, but cautions her to use the power of television wisely. He says that others have not. She understands the temptation all too well. But she assures him that she will work hard not to fall into the trap of money or power. She also requested that he keep a watch on her and confront her if she goes wrong.

But there is another great influence on her life. She is a survivor. Having survived polio as a child, she now has to live with post-polio syndrome. The disabling condition means that she must live with crutches. She learned to live with that reality. She moves pretty smoothly through life, just not as fast as others when it comes to mobility. Up on the pulpit, her limitations disappear. In many ways, it is as if the strength that she has lost in her legs moved into her mind and her voice.

black box

remote. "What that black box supposedly does runs head-on into the basic belief structure of my religion and any other religion built upon the existence and sacredness of the human soul."

"What right do these people have to play with people's souls? What right do they have to play God? Is the young woman different after the process? If you believe in a human soul, you almost have to believe she will be different after this process, this sort of conversion."

"Here I stand as one who could greatly benefit from 'conversion.' How my life would change if conversion could make me walk again without crutches. But no way am I going down that path!" L.O. shuts off the television and turns off the lights in the den, preparing to make her way upstairs.

"From all that I'm hearing, there is no reason for me to believe that this black box exists for the purpose of doing good. There is the great risk that it exists for the purpose of doing evil. After all, I see it playing with the issue of people's souls if not the souls themselves."

As L.O. adjusts her crutches she realizes that what she fears is that the black box is the devil's hand on earth and that this process, this 'conversion,' is not just science gone astray, but the devil's own work.

Taj and Jason are in the midst of the usual Friday night fare -- supper and the evening news -- that same evening. They flip through the channels to see the evening news' lead stories. They hear the word "black box" and stop switching channels. They instantly recognize the black box. But for them the shock is greater as they see the two Sandys. For them, it drives home what happened that night with their cat G. The black box is real and it really did what they saw it do.

They now realize what happened to the black box. The federal government broke into their home and took it that night while they slept. They feel violated, cheated, and scared. Being quiet had probably protected them until now. What will happen now that the whole world knows about the black box? What should they do given what they know? Should they try to reach the project person in the report, Dr. Form? He seems to feel as they do, with both deep fear and curiosity.

Weeks pass, but not so the controversy.

Outside the White House, a new religious group, who calls itself "anticonversionists" and is led by Washington, D.C. minister Reverend L.O. Moses and other religious leaders demonstrates with increasing anger. In an outpouring that is only weeks old, they sound a new battle cry for a significant portion of the aligned and non-aligned religious communities. Ever since the videotape aired, the charge of "humans playing God" has put the scientific community on the defensive, to say nothing of the federal government, especially the Pentagon and the White House.

Above the crowd comes a strong woman's voice. "For several weeks now, all of us have engaged in a pitched battle with government and science over the black box," Reverend Moses shouts over the noise of the demonstrators. "They say it may do good and its secrets need to be known. In the time they have had it, they have yet to find one 'good' thing it can do for anyone. We say it is evil and its place is not on this earth."

She leads the crowd in chants of "Ban the Box," "Save the Soul," and "Destroy the Devil's Hand." After a few minutes, she yields the microphone to another

black box

religious leader and steps away from the podium.

As she leaves the rally later that night, she questions whether or not she's right. Is there any possibility this black box was created to do good? There is always the chance that God sent it here for that purpose. Maybe, just maybe, we do not comprehend God's purpose.

"But no," she tells herself. "This is the devil's hand at work. Through all the many meetings we and the other religious leaders have with government officials and leading scientists, the message is the same. Science and government think it might do good. But so far they can get the black box to do only one thing, moving or duplicating objects."

The scientists tell her they still don't know where it came from but they have no reason to believe that it was made on earth. The technology is far beyond anything known by science on this planet. All the scientists and government people say is that they believe it may have been left here some time ago, possibly by an alien race. They admit they don't "know" that. It's just that no other explanation is any better. This further fuels the anticonversionist fire.

Having the religious movements label the black box's process as "conversion" was her call. She wasn't the first to use the term. She heard the term used in the news footage of the experiment and later, by some of the scientists. In her view, the term "conversion" is useful because it brings together the scientific and religious aspects of the black box. What it means isn't easily answered. For the scientists, "conversion" refers to the change of matter into energy into matter, a basic process used by the black box in its duplication/transportation of objects.

For the anticonversionists, it is a bit different. The original call by all of them was to stop "artificial conversion," in effect to get humans to stop playing God. When she says that they are against artificial conversion, some television and radio talk-show types refer to them as the "anti-artificial conversionists." After a while the term stuck, except it is shortened to "anticonversionists." Her movement has come to be comfortable with the label.

In part, this label makes more sense as a new movement emerged against L.O.'s call for the black box's destruction. This other movement wants to use it on themselves. They call themselves "conversionists." Fortunately for the anticonversionists, the conversionist movement is still small in numbers and disorganized.

As anticonversionists, they've staked out a very clear position. They demand a stop to research in this area. Engaged in what they term a "holy war," they view themselves as protectors of the human soul. Their battle against artificial "conversion" is no less than a battle against evil. The lack of knowledge or consensus about the black box's origins leaves open the possibility of a nonhuman creator. For some anticonversionists, that nonhuman creator is no one other than the Biblical devil. Others of their people are not sure what kind of nonhuman or human 'devil' may be involved.

Out of this emergence of devil imagery has come another image. Conversion is seen as the "devil's work." The black box is the new tool of the devil, the so-called "devil's hand," Biblical devil's hand at work on modern day Earth.

As for herself, Reverend Moses is not quite sure what kind of "devil" is at work here. Though her mind keeps debating that point, her outside work moves ever forward. For now, she believes that some kind of "devil" is involved. It matters less which kind, human or otherwise. Someday, people may find out who this devil was or is.

black box

Off to the side and far enough away to be out of sight, Joseph and Maria watch the anticonversionists' rally in fascination. Wherever this movement is going, the two of them are at least partly responsible.

Each of them has an arm wrapped around the other. "We are part of all this," Joseph says to Maria. "With the coming of the black box, all kinds of questions are being raised. Some are legitimate and some aren't. Regardless, this society is wrestling with a very large force that it doesn't understand and doesn't know how to handle."

"The box itself is an exciting piece of technology," Maria says back. "But it's the larger question it raises that is most intriguing."

"Take the anticonversionists. They understand that a human being is processed through by this mysterious black box. The 'in' term today is "conversion." But their question is very simple. What about the soul? As scientists, we tend to focus on the physical aspects. As religious followers, they tend to focus on the religious aspect. From their belief structure, they are asking a very legitimate question, one which I sincerely doubt any of us has the ability to answer."

Joseph nods. "These kinds of questions always bring me back to Sandy," he says. "She has become a religious symbol. To some, she is a symbol of good. To others, a symbol of evil. But for me, Sandy is such a good human being and the black box did not change that."

"Yesterday we got another request from Reverend Moses and her followers for the government to produce Sandy immediately," Maria tells him, filling him in on that day's work. "We will refuse just as we have in the past. Producing Sandy will not change anything. It will just feed the hysteria that's already rampant. There's nothing anyone can prove by Sandy going public. Besides, we have to protect her. We all got her into this situation. "

"I honestly doubt that we'll go any further than the network interview we had her do a week ago. Nothing was settled by it other than the fact that she is still alive. The anticonversionists got more intense. Beyond that, a new group of people is developing, the conversionists. When they see Sandy and her angelic face and smile, they believe that conversion does good. From everything I've seen about Sandy before the conversion occurred, she is the same person before that she is today. There's no evidence that the black box did anything, positive or negative."

"We can count on the right Reverend L.O. Moses to keep this whole thing going," says Joseph as they start to move away from the rally. "The black box is now the cornerstone of her television ministry, a ministry that now reaches hundreds of thousands of people each week."

"She keeps it simple," he explains jokingly. "Open each week with a one-minute videotape of the so-called "conversion" of Sandy. Cry out for the lost soul of Sandy. Challenge the devil's hand to release her soul and leave this earth. Challenge the earthly authorities to produce the devil's black box and destroy it for all to see."

"Amen, brother," Maria interjects. "Nothing less will satisfy the right Reverend Moses and her many followers. It's been an awfully long time since this nation was torn over the issue of the devil incarnate and the battle for souls. Maybe not since the days of the Salem witchcraft trials.

"Ooh, that thought drives the cold deep inside

black box

me." Joseph shudders. "Let's go home."

Chapter 11. Weapon

Pentagon research lab, Washington, D.C.; several weeks later.
Large, abandoned building, Andrews Air Force Base, Washington, D.C. area, that afternoon.

In the days that follow the leak of the video and the interview with Joseph and Maria, the black box project is pulled out of the Smithsonian lab and moved to a secure Pentagon research lab. At the Pentagon, there is much anger about the video. There are recriminations against Joseph and Maria for the interviews. For a while, the two of them are denied access to the project. The Smithsonian considers withdrawing Joseph from the project completely. For several weeks, Dr. Tarry and his people, all military research people, work on the black box project by themselves.

A few weeks ago, things began to shift. Many scientists and researchers are extremely distrustful of the Pentagon having total control. They call for more involvement by the scientific community and for the Smithsonian to become involved again. Likewise, within the government, some of the officials responsible for science policy argue against the military's total control of the experiments without oversight by science agencies.

black box

Ultimately, the White House intervenes. The Smithsonian is asked whether or not it is willing to be involved once again. With some reluctance, the Smithsonian agrees, though the institution remains uncomfortable with the relationship with the military. The scientific community convinces the Smithsonian of the dangers of letting the Pentagon run this project without the scientific community. As for the other federal agencies, they are permitted to join the project as well. They assemble a small research team to join the Pentagon and Smithsonian teams.

The question comes up as to who will coordinate the respective teams. The White House directs that the Pentagon will be the lead. Many disagree, but are overruled. The White House designates Dr. Tarry as the overall project leader. Joseph and Maria are offered the chance to once again be team leaders for the Smithsonian and the other government science team. Initially, the Pentagon balks at this because the two are identified with the network broadcast. But, it is countered, they had nothing to do with the leak of the video. The person who leaked the video was a civilian military employee who just joined the project a few days before the incident. She was fired and, in order to keep her silent, is being threatened with prison time if she speaks out further about the experiments. She agrees, but only because she already said about everything she knows to the media and to the anticonversionists' leader, Reverend Moses. When the Pentagon realizes they are at risk of losing the whole project, they back off and accept Joseph and Maria.

Dr. Tarry weighed in on the side of allowing Joseph and Maria. Though he saw them as having little value when he first took control of the project, he now has a greater appreciation for both of them. Yes, they are more cautious then he and his superiors, but that is exactly what he wants for right now. Contrary to his superiors and contrary to his initial feelings, he is not concerned about moving too slowly, but about moving too fast. Besides, he argues, it is only fair that they stay involved. If not for them, the government would not have the black box and would not know most of what is known about the black box.

Maria and Joseph re-join the project.

While the scientific community is involved again, there is no doubt as to who has control. The Pentagon, with direct orders from the White House, has it, at least for now. Also, what was implicit before is explicit now. One primary goal of the research project is the black box's potential as a weapon.

In some ways, Dr. Tarry is as concerned, as are Maria and Joseph, over what could happen if the black box is used for military purposes. When Dr. Tarry finished his doctoral degree and decided to join the military's research program many years earlier, somehow he had always assumed he would never face any "doomsday" type device, or as least nothing more powerful than the doomsday devices already in existence. He came in as a soldier and a scientist with his allegiances to his country and to scientific pursuit strong. Today, he still sees his role as a combination soldier and scientist, but this not an easy combination.

In no way did this come home to him more than when he was ordered to take over the black box experiments and proceed with human experimentation. He didn't need to be ordered. He wanted the responsibility and the opportunity. He knew human testing was the necessary thing to do and he knew that they had exhausted all the preparatory testing. He felt that the black box was intended for human beings, though

black box

there was nothing specific and concrete to support this "feeling." While ready to proceed, he also knew that the risk of what they were doing was great.

That day he stood only inches from her and could see every emotion-generated movement in her body. There, that day and forever after, he and Sandy became trapped in their roles as soldiers that neither will ever completely escape.

For the immediate future, the pressure for human subject experimentation is off, but only until the next breakthrough. All the needed research can be done with complex animals and complex inanimate objects.

In the first days following the experiment with Sandy, he was able to convince his superiors that they needed at least a week to conduct follow-up tests on Sandy and to observe her for any possible changes in her physical or mental being. Before that week ended, the story broke with the leak of the video.

Many in the scientific community and on Capitol Hill sharply criticized the Pentagon for moving too fast with human experimentation. After that, even Dr. Tarry's superiors were increasingly reluctant to proceed with human experimentation. Eventually, everything will settle down. Then they will re-start human experimentation.

Several weeks after the experiment with Sandy, Dr. Tarry sits in his office thinking about what an amazing, though unnerving, time this is. The black box is a huge leap beyond today's science. It can do things that no other human device can do and does it with technology they do not understand. Still, unless they can unlock more capabilities, it is little more than a curiosity with no any other practical significance.

There is a knock on the door. The door opens and in walks a familiar figure. As she walks across the room, he is taken aback by how she seems to have changed since when he first interviewed her before the experiment. Nothing in her medical records indicates that these changes have resulted from the effects of the black box. More likely, Sandy always had many of these radiant qualities, qualities that might or might not have emerged in a military environment. She is bright and quite pretty, all qualities that pre-date her encounter with the black box. Sandy also suddenly has become a "cool" person. Her confidence in herself is strikingly greater than before the experiment. But again, anyone who stepped to the brink of death, looked at it squarely, and survived is likely to acquire a very large dose of self-confidence.

"Good morning, Dr. Tarry," Sandy says with a soft smile as she takes a seat across the desk from him. "I want to thank you again for these off-the-cuff and off-the-record discussions we have been having lately. It's a relief to be away from the research team. I know they mean no harm, but it's just that everything I do is recorded on video and or on the computer. At least here, I find a few moments of respite."

"I know that feeling of being in a fish-bowl," Dr. Tarry replies. "Only by comparing myself with you do I feel less observed. You need some time away from observation. I've instructed the observation team to discontinue 'every-moment' observation. But for now, I'm still looking for some way to get you off the grounds so that you can regain some contact with the outside world. This is proving difficult. There are people high up who are not at all comfortable with you leaving the research compound, even with an armed escort and even to another secure area. They're not worried about you doing something. They're worried about what somebody might

black box

do to you." Dr. Tarry gives Sandy an admittedly fatherly look. "Honestly, so am I."

He always feels good about their conversations. For both of them, it is a chance to be themselves. It wasn't that way in the beginning, but has developed this way as mutual trust grew. To a large extent, their relationship is one that combined aspects of being father and daughter and of being colleagues. They are good and trusting friends, but each of them could use other people. Neither really has anyone else to turn to. Maybe when Joseph and Maria return, they will both have additional people they can trust.

"Can we talk some more about the black box?" she asks, knowing the answer will be yes. "After a month of your team's probing and my own 'soul-searching,' I still don't know what the black box did to me, if anything at all. I don't know if I just moved around a bit or if I am another person, identical to the person I was."

"Yes, that struggle for answers goes on for both of us," Dr. Tarry replies as he sighs. "No one, except possibly the missing baggage handler, knows if the black box is 'good,' is 'evil,' or just 'is.'"

"Then we're all stuck," Sandy says. She throws up her hands. "It seems to be our nature as human beings to want to know everything about this mysterious black box. We hope that what we learn will be that it exists for a good purpose and that what it does is 'good.' If the contrary is the case, we can only hope that some of the precautions you've told me about are sufficient. As we both know, the Pentagon has one primary purpose for this project, to discover whether or not this box has 'weapon' potential." Sandy looks out into the main office behind her where soldiers and researchers fill out paperwork and plan the next day's tests. She leans in towards Dr. Tarry and lowers her voice. "This prospect concerns us both"

A few days later, Joseph and Maria re-join the project at the Pentagon site and re-unite with Dr. Tarry and Sandy. In a meeting with Sandy, Joseph and Maria, there is the excitement similar to old friends meeting after having survived a disaster. There is the coming together of colleagues who realize that on their shoulders rests the heavy responsibility of uncovering secrets and making sure that, ultimately, the revealing of these secrets is for the greater "good."

Joseph and Maria are in awe of the Sandy who is now their colleague. She is now, and maybe always has been, a fun and confident young woman. Out of uniform and in civilian clothes, she is a stylish dresser. She is "cool" in her attitude and behavior. And, she is "cool" in how she talks and interacts with everyone. Is this the Sandy of before conversion or just the Sandy of after conversion? Or, are the two Sandys one and the same? Is the black box a factor in the Sandy of today? These are questions that remain difficult to answer.

With the expanded project team assembled, Dr. Tarry goes over the work that's occurred in the weeks since the experiment with Sandy. In trying to discover the function of the black box, the team has not resolved some basic questions that will be critical to their future work.

Both Joseph and Maria are amazed to look at the man, Dr. Tarry, who stands in front of them. A major transformation has occurred. The intensity is still there, but humanity now dominates his attitude and behavior. What they seen now is a colleague struggling to find the right answer to a complex endeavor upon which they have all embarked.

"Though we assume that the box is virtually, if not totally, impervious to outside forces, we wanted to

black box

make sure," Dr. Tarry explains. "Making every reasonable effort to ensure that no permanent damage is done to the box, we tested a range of methods for getting through the surface of the box. Nothing had even the slightest impact. We did not try anything like a weapons-grade laser because we believe it will not have any impact. There's also another reason. If that powerful of a laser does have impact, we suspect it will destroy the box. Obviously, that would be totally and absolutely counter-productive and stupid."

"Next we tried to learn about the box's insides using various non-invasive techniques. Testing electrical forces told us that something is going on inside, but we have yet to figure out what the tests mean. We'll come back to this later.

"Testing magnetic forces in the box got us nowhere. We went through the full range of materials-analysis technologies and got absolutely nothing for our efforts. We know no more from that than what is obvious from human sight and touch. Imaging techniques using x-rays or sound gave no indication about the interior. Either there is nothing there beyond a solid object or imaging technology cannot penetrate the box's surface."

"Let me clarify that point," Dr. Tarry says, pausing for a moment as he sees the dismay on the faces of his team. "Not that there isn't anything there, it's just that we can discern nothing other than that something goes on inside the box during 'conversion.' We've come to use that term as well because it fits with the black box's apparent conversion of matter to energy and then back to matter."

"Back to my earlier point about energy levels," Dr. Tarry continues. "When conversion occurs, energy levels within the black box are virtually immeasurable. When the box is dormant, there is also a tremendous amount of energy in the box. If our measurements are correct, this box contains a massive accumulation of power. But we're not sure our measurements are correct. The levels, both during dormancy and conversion, are so high as to be immeasurable. We are talking about numbers in the magnitude of the energy generated in the core of a large nuclear reactor. It is difficult to conceive of this little black box producing, using, storing, or containing that kind of power. If nothing else, that kind of power should destroy the box."

"As unbelievable as your figures about the energy levels are, it does address a dilemma we face," Joseph interrupts. "If the box actually creates a second object exactly the same as the original, then that would require a tremendous amount of energy. Since the box does not seem to draw energy from any outside source, all that energy must be stored inside the box. To some extent, your measurements on energy levels suggest that is exactly what the box is doing. If so, the 'delete' key may be the trigger to the box's recovering needed energy from the original object."

"Could be." Dr. Tarry nods in agreement. "We will keep analyzing the energy issue, but we have pretty much concluded that the box is not going to yield much more information on its make-up. Any creative ideas on tackling the question of the box's make-up will be greatly appreciated. In the meantime, we return to work on the box's function, on what the conversion process can do."

"Let's break now," he instructs them as he finishes his update. "For those of you working with me these past weeks, the lab looks different today, relatively empty. There is good reason for it. We're moving the next phase of experimentation to a larger facility, a hanger and maintenance complex at Andrews Air Force Base. We'll meet here in a half-hour, get on a bus, and drive out there. We'll eat lunch there and then I'll resume the briefing and return to the issue of function."

black box

Just after one in the afternoon, Dr. Tarry resumes the briefing session at the abandoned hangar. "Now, I am presuming that all of you who were not part of the early experiments read the reports, including the experiment with Sandy. By the way, Sandy, who all of you met earlier, will be here observing these experiments. Obviously, her interest is more than just passing."

"Our work on the black box's function is focusing on four possible capabilities. The first is transportation, that the box can move objects from one place to another. The second is duplication, the capability to make a second object exactly the same in every way as the original object. The third function is transformation, whereby the box can take one object and make into another object that is entirely different. Finally, the fourth capability is creation, the most troubling and intriguing of the four. If the box can "create," then the box can produce virtually any object either from nothing or from nothing more than energy."

As Dr. Tarry has presented the agenda for the day ahead and the necessary background for the coming experiments, they are ready to begin the next phase.

For this phase, Dr. Tarry's choice of an abandoned hanger and military facility provides large and small spaces with partitions of different materials. It also puts his research team at some physical distance from his superiors at the Pentagon. Dr. Tarry feels that distance and less pressure is prudent for these next experiments.

The early tests will focus on the black box's ability to deal with distance and its resistance to various materials. Throughout these tests, Dr. Tarry will utilize two objects, both complex. One is animate -- a monkey; one is inanimate -- a fully functioning prototype of a computerized laser weapon.

    For the first test, they place a monkey in front of the black box and proceed through the full process. At the end of the process, there is the "duplicate" monkey, about one foot to the right of where the original sits. Next, they move the second monkey between pressing the "e to m" and "verify" keys. They do the same again, but this time between the pressing the "verify" and "delete" keys. Moving the duplicate monkey has no impact by itself. The duplicate can be moved anywhere as long as it doesn't take more time to get there than the black box allows between steps in the process. If it takes longer and the keys are not pressed in time, the process is terminated and the duplicate monkey disappears.

    With respect to the "original," there is a distance limitation. As long as the original monkey is still in the box's range, about one hundred yards, there is no effect on the process. Once an object is "recorded," which places the object somehow in the black box's equivalent of "memory," the box tracks the original's location as long as it stays within the box's range. When the original object goes outside that range, the box can no longer "find" the original and terminates the process, leaving the original as it was. The duplicate disappears as expected.

    On the next round of tests, they try placing barriers between the original object and where the second object is to appear. The process is unaffected. They place the original monkey in an open, then closed, two-ton safe. The black box ignores the safe, which is too big for it to handle, and moves the monkey, which it can handle. When the metal safe is placed in the receiving area, the black box immediately finds an open area for the second object. Trying different size safes and other cabinets, they find that if the space is sufficient, the box places the second object in it. If it is not, it finds the closest open area for the object. The same results hold true when the

black box

sophisticated inanimate object, the laser weapon, is used. When a large solid object is placed in the receiving area, the black box finds an open receiving area, as long as there is some safe space within about a hundred yards. If there is not one, the process terminates.

On the one hand, the box is apparently designed to go through great effort in order to complete the conversion process, scanning a large amount of territory and analyzing the characteristics of objects within that territory. On the other hand, it is apparently designed with an inviolable override protection to ensure that the original object is not harmed and with a termination procedure if there is no "open" place.

To some extent, these experiments confirm the black box's capability to transport the original object as well, assuming that the second object is the original object transported. Dr. Tarry, Joseph and Maria are bothered even now by their inability to discern whether the second object is an exact duplicate or the original relocated. If the second object is the original, then the black box is capable of transportation. But they have yet to find a way to directly control the box's placement of the second object, the duplicate. Indirectly, they by adjusting the surrounding environment, they can cause the box not to place the duplicate in certain places. But there is no way for them to exercise anywhere near complete control since the box can scan such large areas of territory.

Little further is discovered about transportation during this phase of the experiments.

Proceeding to the next round of experiments, they focus on whether or not the black box can produce duplicates, or clones, of the original. If this works, clones of people and duplicates of weapons can both be made. If possible, they need to find some way to retain both the original and the second object. In all past experiments, either the original or the second ceases to exist depending on how far the process goes. But there is always that brief time period in which both apparently exist. This is where they will concentrate their attention. Once again, they proceed through a whole series of tests on the two objects during this critical time. Every test they perform produces the same result. The first and the second object have no discernable differences. Their chemical make-up is the same. Their dimensions are the same. All their component parts are the same.

The interim stages of the process are sensitive to certain types of change. In the one-minute period before the "verify" light is pressed, either object can be changed as long as they are restored before time runs out or before the light is pressed. In the case of the laser, a component can be taken out and put back in during the one minute period and not affect the process. If the component is not replaced, or is placed in a different position, or is replaced by what appears to be an identical component, the process terminates and the second object disappears. The same proves true for the 30-second period between pressing the "verify" light and the "delete" light. Apparently, the verification process continues to operate until the original object is "deleted" or the total process terminates.

Unfortunately, not every test can be performed since both objects are "frozen," meaning that they do not function during the interim period. There is no way to test whether or not the original and the copy function identically. As confirmed by earlier experiments, the original and the copy are exactly the same, including their functions, once the process is fully complete. The fact that the two seemingly identical objects co-exist for a brief time period argues for the second being the duplicate of the original. But this seems almost unthinkable. For that to be true, the original monkey has

black box

to be gone. Even more unthinkable, the original Sandy has to be gone. If the originals are really gone, has something been lost in the process? If so, what?

In the backs of all their minds, they keep hearing the arguments that passed between the anticonversionists and the conversionists over the issue of the black box and the human soul. These are questions and arguments that trouble them, though in particular, these questions trouble Sandy the most.

On the other hand, they contemplate what it will be like if they can make the major breakthrough and retain the original <u>and</u> the duplicate. Not only could they create clones of humans and machines, but they could potentially create cloned black boxes. If all these possibilities could be unleashed, the world would become a very different place. For now, this is not happening, and everything else is wild speculation.

As he watches the research team work and sees the small pieces of progress they have made, Dr. Tarry realizes that the ethical issues surrounding the black box dominate more and more of his thinking. Should they even be looking for the box's 'weapon' potential? Or should they turn all their resources toward what it might do to mend bodies and cure diseases? Should they stay away from human experimentation completely? Why? Is it the 'soul' question that stays with him or the 'man playing God' question? He's not completely sure this internal ethical debate is a good or bad sign, though he suspects it's a good sign for his own ethics. He wishes his superiors were more bothered by the ethical consequences, but maybe they have considered these issues and have just not discussed them with him.

He leans back in his chair and thinks back to how

this all began. His thoughts again come back to the original and fake stone chambers and the fake black box. According to his hypothesis, the fake stone chamber and the fake black box were probably made by the original black box. As improbable as this seems, no other explanation serves any better.

If his theory is correct, this black box can do a lot more than they've already seen. This theory may open up a whole new area of exploration -- transformation. Maybe the black box could do more than just make clones or move objects. Maybe it can transform matter from being one thing to being another thing and be controlled in some way so that it could make the original stone chamber, seemingly perfect and strong, into a second chamber, less perfect but more closely resembling something a human stone carver might make. He sighs as he realizes that his ideas are largely a whole lot of maybes.

But sometimes, he lets his imagination drift further. There were times, when he thought of the transformation possibility, that another term crept in: creation. This concept stirs deep fears and great exhilaration. Suppose the box could create a stone chamber from nothing or from pure energy. Can't it not create something else, maybe a human being? Maybe more than one human being?

He thinks back to the letters displayed on the box. He thinks he understands them better now. Apparently, the box's basic process takes the matter of the original object and records it into some type of code. Then, it converts that code, if not the matter itself, into an energy equivalent. Using that code, it somehow converts the energy stored in the box before the process began into the matter of the duplicate. To do that, it probably uses the code of the 'original' object. When the 'delete' key is pressed, the black box recovers the energy it expels in

black box

making the duplicate by 'deleting' the original object and absorbing its energy."

"Just what all can this black box do?" Dr. Tarry mutters to himself, thinking over the implications of "transformation." "If 'transformation' can really happen, this will throw an enormous amount of fuel onto the already heated debate between the anticonversionists and the newly emerging conversionists," he says out loud. He's not sure that more fuel is what is needed right now.

As the weeks pass, transformation remains elusive. If the black box has the capability, they are not able to access it. In the end, nothing is proven one way or the other.

At the end of what seems one of the longest days on this project and with the entire research team gone, Dr. Tarry sits and stares at the box. The black box seems to acquire an air of indifference sitting by itself. Dr. Tarry is frustrated and his frustration goes on growing. Like always with this project, he's feeling pressure from above.

"If we can just get inside the box, maybe that leads to something further," he thinks. "On the other hand, maybe it will just destroy the box and leave us with nothing. I have resisted pressure to again try to open the box. My gut tells me that the key lays somewhere on the box's surface."

"Somewhere on that dark surface is a way to reach other capabilities. Jason and Taj accidentally discovered that the key is touching the four top corners simultaneously. Maybe therein lay other keys. Maybe other combinations of touching other places will activate other capabilities. That is where I will focus our resources next." Dr. Tarry strokes his head with his hands. "That is, if I have any time at all."

Chapter 12. Conversionists

Downtown Washington, D.C., several weeks later.
Downtown Washington Hotel, a few months later.
U.S. Capitol grounds, Washington, D.C., one month later.

For several weeks now, the anticonversionists, led by Reverend L.O. Moses, reign over the issue of the black box. Their vocal condemnation of the black box and the "conversion" process has put the federal government and the scientific community on the defensive. Government officials and scientists ask for reason and patience as they try to learn more about the black box. The anticonversionists' call for the box's destruction continues to grow. As the anticonversionist movement expands and the black box research yields no new breakthroughs, some government officials and political advisors are more open to destroying the box and ridding themselves of an increasingly messy political problem.

Reverend Moses becomes a global personality as other people in other countries are exposed to her television ministry and see the video of Sandy Hart's "conversion." While the televised images of Sandy and the black box are critical to the growth of the anticonversionist movement, these same images reach many other people who are affected very differently.

On the balcony of his downtown Washington apartment, Christopher Carey[8] appreciates the warm afternoon sun and considers his life.

As the sun starts to drop below the skyline, he thinks about his life and where it is going.

"Whenever I think about my future, the image of the black box interferes." These images reach out to him and offer something he finds nowhere else.

Christopher, like many of his friends, taped his own copy of the conversion of Sandy. Just as is Reverend Moses, he's captivated by the image of the black box and Sandy. But, while Reverend Moses is fascinated in a negative direction, he's fascinated in a positive direction. He plays the video over and over again. Every time, he's left with the same impression: here is something that is strange and wonderful.

Christopher does not belong to any organized religion. Over the years, he has had contact with various

---

[8] As a single man aged 40, he continues to search for many of the important things in life. He had a couple of good relationships with women, but none has yet led to marriage. In some ways, he regrets that. In other ways, this has given him the freedom to pursue his career and travel. Someday soon, he suspects that he will find the right woman, develop the right relationship, and marry.

His career is on track. Within the past six months, he's been promoted to Vice-President of a moderately-sized television and radio holding company at which he began his career ten years ago. People say he has strong management and leadership skills. Others suggest that he consider going on the air. It's not my direction, but he hasn't ruled it out completely as he enjoys those few days when he goes on the air to cover for someone."

black box

organized religions but never found what he needed. He is not against organized religion, though he is troubled by some of the things some of the religions do.

But Christopher is not completely happy with a life without some of the things that religion provides. Re-watching a tape of a recent anticonversionist rally, he notes that just like them, he seeks that higher purpose to human life. He seeks answers to how the universe came to be as it is and ways to grow personally. Something is missing that is needed. This is a nagging problem for which he might never find a solution.

"But then there is this black box," he tells himself. "There is this video of the conversion of Sandy. What is all this? Can this have any meaning for me?"

He understands that "conversion" was initially a term the scientists used for the physical process through which the black box put physical objects. He also understands that people, like Reverend Moses and her followers, grabbed onto this idea and labeled it "artificial" conversion. To them, the scientists soiled the only right use of the term, that of the conversion of a person to faith in God and religion.

"Maybe there is something else there," he thinks as he contemplates the issue further. "Suppose conversion is neither neutral, as the scientists believe, or negative, as the anticonversionists believe. Suppose conversion is positive. Suppose conversion is somehow a cleansing process. Or maybe an enriching process. If so, the black box may be a way for people to reach the higher levels of existence to which many aspire. Some have found this higher existence in organized religion. Black box conversion may be another way. Maybe it is the way. Maybe it is the way for me." As he surveys the city from his balcony, Christopher feels inspired for the first time in a long time.

     Conversionists begin to communicate via the web and meet as small groups on college campuses around the United States. The video of Sandy Hart's conversion by the black box is now the equivalent of a cult film, though it's only a few minutes in length. The conversionists are not necessarily of one mind about the value of the conversion process or even what it is. Instead, they are of one mind in seeing this process as positive. Some attach religious significance to it. Others see it in more individualistic terms. Some adopt the name "conversionists." Some use other labels. Other resist labels of any kind.

     For some conversionists, Sandy's disappearance after the experiment raises her to the level of sainthood. Some see her in the same way Christians see Jesus Christ. There are also conversionists who do not see her as a saint, but generally see her conversion and growth as something to which they aspire. Her network interview does little to change this. Her bright and positive personality dominates the interview and adds additional credence to the view that conversion either made her, or helped her, grow.

     Besides, many conversionists want to believe the black box plays a role. After all, they are searching for something just as people who join organized religion are searching for something. Some believe the box does everything and the person is but a passive player. Others believe it is the full and active partnership between the box and the person that results in conversion and, subsequently, personal growth. For many conversionists, it is the essence of the person that the black box sustains when it generates the "duplicate" person.

     Many conversionists believe that the black box cleanses the person's body or the soul or both. After all,

black box

the scientific experiments documented that the box rejected the inclusion of any foreign matter. All that is left after conversion is the pure duplicate of the original. While "soul cleansing" may or may not be a too large leap from the box's rejection of matter being added after the process began, the conversionists believe it supports, if not confirms, their view.

For many of the conversionists, the black box's potential lies in a cleansing process. They see the stern, somewhat fearful look on Sandy at the beginning of the process. They then see the serene and joyful she had look as the process ended. Many conversionists concede this may be nothing more than a person feeling relief after surviving a potentially risky experiment. But still. There is something about Sandy that captures them.

Even though they are reminded about what the experiments really show, the conversionists ignore the scientist's observations that the black box does nothing to the original, other than duplicate or move it. Why should they believe the scientists? But, the scientists are unable to completely rule out that a "physical" cleansing occurs and they agree that they just may not be able to measure the effects of the cleansing.

Beyond the issue of cleansing the physical body, is the issue of cleansing the soul. Here the issue is irresolvable. Scientists do not know how to measure aspects of the human soul. Therefore, they can neither support nor refute the contention that the black box cleanses the soul. The belief that the black box cleanses the soul is, and may always be, a matter of faith, much like the underpinnings of most religions..

On the other side of the argument, the anticonversionists feel the essence is lost, or is at risk of being lost, in conversion. For them, the risk is that only the body, not the soul, survives conversion.. If it is truly lost, the most extreme among them believe that it is lost to the devil. As with any large movement, the full range of views is reflected among the anticonversionists.

While the anticonversionists become an international movement quickly, the conversionists' numbers are relatively small, but they are growing more quickly in numbers in recent weeks.

In a world where reality is far from everything most people hope for, and this hope is a precious and sought after commodity, the black box offers the hope of something better. For many conversionists, this hope is much of what they hang onto in order to survive. If they could only put themselves and the Earth through the conversion process, all the bad things would go away. The earth would be cleansed. The earth and the people on it would become as serene and bright as Sandy. Likewise, the conversionists' souls may be cleansed and they will be that much nearer to human perfection.

Some conversionists are less sanguine about souls, but no less enamored by the potential for human growth. As people seeking a higher plane of consciousness and being, they feel the black box offers hope for escaping the limitations of the past and present. With it, people may be able to break these bonds and be left with only their pure individual beings, much more in control of the future.

As is the case with the anticonversionists, the conversionists have very little "reality" upon which to base most of their beliefs, but that matters little. For the conversionists and the anticonversionists, they see the black box and they see Sandy. This is far better than trying to believe that some religious figure of significance is appearing on someone's refrigerator or even a church's wall. And this is far better than depending upon the passing down of writings and observations from ancient times, the foundations for most organized religion today.

black box

People can interpret this black box as they wish. No one appears to be in a position to prove them wrong, or, prove them right.

With the meeting over, Christopher watches as about 200 conversionist leaders from around country leave the room and head back to their home communities. The group came a long way in the last 48 hours in uniting what will never be a totally united movement. "That's all right," he thinks. "That is one of the hallmarks of conversionists. They are never ready to fully yield their own personal freedom and beliefs to anyone else."

"Life among the anticonversionists is so much simpler," Christopher senses. "Sometimes, I wish it were so for the conversionists as well. The anticonversionists organize against one single image, the black box. Being against a single, simple image is so much easier than being for multiple, complex images. The latter is the lot of the conversionists and they are richer for this. But it makes it much more difficult for conversionists to organize into a coherent whole when the situation calls for it. And right now the situation definitely calls for a coherent movement prepared to take concerted action."

Before he heads off to a side room where the two most prominent persons from the two main factions of the conversionist movement wait, he decides to take a brief walk through the hotel's indoor garden. The hotel is between conventions so the garden is virtually empty.

"The conversionist leadership showed their followers a united front for past two days, but only because they face a common enemy," Christopher thinks to himself. "If and when that is no longer a threat, they will all likely go their own ways again. For now, it is clear there is only one person who can lead them in the days and weeks to come. Unfortunately, I am that person."

Only a couple of months ago, Christopher saw notices that groups of conversionists from the D.C. area were going meet. He had no agenda in going. It was just an opportunity to get to know people and share views. But almost from the beginning, he noticed a strain among them, primarily along the two factions. The whole meeting started to fall apart.

On the one side, there was the "religious" faction. This faction wants to develop an organized religion similar to the anticonversionists. Groups representing this faction have popped up around the U.S. In organizing their meetings and, in a few cases, setting up actual churches, they use various names incorporating the term conversion.

For most of these people, the soldier Sandy is the key. Her conversion is what they personalize and, at times, almost deify. Many of these people elevate Sandy to the level of saint. Some do not go quite that far. Theirs is a belief based upon the existence of human soul, similar to the basic belief of the anticonversionists. Their belief in the human soul is coupled with a belief that the black box is here for good.

Wherever the black box came from and whoever brought it, this group is convinced it is brought for the purpose of cleansing human souls, not unlike a baptism. For those who believe in a heaven, the black box helps them to reach it.

The second faction, the "non-religious" faction, is made up of very different people with a very different foundation for their beliefs. This part of the conversion movement is a collection of individuals simply labeling themselves as conversionists. They emphasize that this is conversion with a lower-case, not a capital, "c."

black box

For them, the black box process is the cleansing of the physical being. Through conversion, the essence of the physical being is kept and the unwanted residual, that which detracted away from the essence, is discarded. As they see it, through conversion, the physical spirit is released to soar to new heights.

For them as well, the image of Sandy is the underpinning of their beliefs. Sandy is not deified, but is seen as a physical human being who, in partnership with the black box, achieved a much higher level of existence. While not true for all these people, most of them wanted to follow Sandy and experience for themselves "conversion."

When the arguing started, Christopher looked around the room. He listened to the debate and saw the two factions. He realized that he wasn't strongly tied to either faction. He understood what drives both of them and their common ground. As the meeting wore on, he moved around the room, trying to cool down the heated discussion. At one point after several people from both factions spoke, someone asked him to speak. He's not sure why, but he said yes.

For those few minutes, he went back to what had brought them all together, the black box and the possibilities it represented. He told them that it did not matter that the box meant different things to each of them. That is what the black box is, something which has the possibility of helping each of them get to where they want and need to go, even if this is to different places.

When he finished speaking, he was asked if he would lead the next meeting's discussion and continue his role as peacemaker and as their leader. He agreed.

They are all "conversionists" and, as of today, they unite behind him. When Christopher considers that prospect, he bursts out in laughter. "How lucky are they to have me as their leader?" He shakes his head. "If God really exists, I sincerely hope that he or she will have mercy on both the conversionists and me. We are both going to need it."

Christopher looks at his watch, realizes he needs to get on with his meeting, and heads back to the hotel meeting room.

As he enters the room, both conversionist leaders stop what obviously was a heated debate to rush toward him.

"Listen, Christopher," shouts Margaret Tyler, the leader of the non-religious faction. "We have a real problem with this whole organized religion and soul business of Matthew and his people. There are times when they sound as sanctimonious and intolerant as the Reverend Moses."

"Christopher, we're different people in many ways from Margaret's conversionists," Matthew Stone counters, jumping in. "We're not just a loose collection of people with beliefs ranging all over the philosophical map. No way are we going to lighten up or stop our own kind of evangelism."

Christopher places his hands on their shoulders. "I wish I could say that this is the first time I've heard this particular debate or the first time that I've heard you two debate this," he says softly. "Stop beating up on each other. You've got much in common. Let's focus on that."

"If we don't follow through on the commitments we all made in the last two days, we're all going to lose something none of us wants to lose. Even as we meet, Reverend Moses turns up the pressure to have the black box destroyed. All three of us saw her interview on the Sunday talk show. So far there is no counterforce to her. By joining and activating your two factions, we can be

black box

that counterforce. That is your commitment to me. Let me assure you that I will not let you back away from this commitment."

"Our press conference this morning has started things moving," Christopher assures them. "The television networks, wire services, and major newspapers were here. They're hot after a story. We'll just have to see how the networks play the story as tonight's lead."

Though their difference are unresolved and probably irresolvable, they set these differences aside, at least for now. Much depends on their willingness and ability to pull together. Their adversaries are united. They cannot afford to be otherwise.

Under Christopher's leadership and the facing threat of the anticonversionists, the conversionists begin to pull together and organize. As they see the increased strength of the anticonversionists, their own fervor grows and so do their numbers. The time has come for them to counter the anticonversionist movement and prevent the destruction of the black box.

A month passes.

On the U.S. Capitol grounds, the conversionist rally begins. Already, tens of thousand of conversionists have entered the grounds. More are entering by the minute.

Christopher climbs up to the podium and surveys the largest gathering of conversionists yet. "On both ends of Pennsylvania Avenue today, politicians sit watching our every move," he tells the crowd. "Just one month ago, they were ready to cave in to the anticonversionists and cast off what many of them saw only as an unpleasant campaign issue. They were ready to destroy the black box, the symbol of conversionism. Our symbol. Today, with thousands of you telling them 'No,' I can assure you they are having serious second thoughts."

"To any of you politicians, including the President, who may even now entertain the destruction of the black box, we say emphatically, 'not if you want your jobs!' If the black box is destroyed, we will hold you responsible. We will make sure that your next election campaign is your last."

"Each and every one of us here today has our own reason for joining this fight. Each of us has our own beliefs about the black box and its power. Where we stand united is in the common belief in equal access to the good it can do." Christopher rests his voice for a moment before he continues, his voice falling loud and clear over the crowd.

"We do not just stand against the box's destruction, though we stand solidly on that issue. We stand for the people's right to access the black box. We stand for the people's right to conversion."

"No government, no matter how powerful, has the authority to deny its people access to the symbol of its revered religion and personal beliefs. <u>Our</u> government is doing exactly that. <u>Our</u> government has no right to do so. We demand that <u>our</u> government relinquish control over the black box and return it to the people."

The crowd cheers fierily.

As he leaves the podium, Christopher surveys the crowd. He hopes that he is doing enough and that the strength of the movement is enough. While many politicians are now neutral and some now support the conversionists' position, he knows that is not enough. In the back of his mind, he knows the easiest solution is still for the black box to disappear or be accidentally

black box

destroyed. But he remains unsure as to whether they will ever have enough clout to stop that from happening. If their people can just find it themselves, they might be able to protect it.

As time passes, both movements grow quickly and internationally. Both now have strong leaders effectively articulating their cause. For each movement, the black box symbolizes their differences.

Where is the box now? In general, most believe that the Pentagon has it. The Pentagon does not deny this.

Politics continue to play a big part in the black box's fate. As the conversionists and anticonversionists both grow in number and power, politicians feel increasingly trapped in this "lose, lose" situation.

Now, many anticonversionists embrace the view that the box has probably been on Earth for some time. Along with that, they believe that the black box was used in that distant past. They see the black box as the devil's hand reaching into Eden. Without the black box, many believe that God's original plan would be in place and "Eden" would exist. For them, the black box is the source of original sin or the result of it.

To the conversionists, the black box is the equivalent of the "holy grail" and sought with the same fervor. The government's hiding of the box is no less an outrage than a wall around Jerusalem. Conversionists demand access to the black box. They demand the right to conversion. Court suits are filed. Laws guaranteeing access to the box are introduced. The pressure to bring the black box out into the open grows quickly.

Already, politicians on each side of the issue have won and lost elections on this issue. For most of them, they wish the box never existed. There was a time when the destruction of the box was an easy solution. No longer. Now the ramifications of its destruction are potentially as great as its being accessible to the public.

black box

Chapter 13. Probe

Pentagon research lab, Washington, D.C.; days later.

As Dr. Tarry turns on the desk lamp in his office, morning light is some time away. Today is the critical day.

He hears a light rap on the door. "Come on in," he calls out, moving to greet his visitors.

Maria and Joseph walk in, their faces as somber as Dr. Tarry's.

"Dr. Tarry, morning," says Maria as she takes a seat. Joseph sits in the other chair nods hello.

"As you both know well, we've got a very big problem here," Dr. Tarry begins. "There's so much more to learn about the black box, but it will take time and patience. We don't have either. My superiors and yours are no longer tolerating delays. One way or another, the mystery of the black box has to be settled and settled quickly."

"Sadly, we agree," Joseph interjects, collapsing into his chair. "The whole environment around this project becomes less stable as each day passes. Even within the project, things are getting increasingly difficult." Dr. Tarry motions for him to go on.

"Both on the research team and among the higher ups, there is the growing presence of conversionists and anticonversionists. Some have lost their objectivity. The two anticonversionists on the research team are torn between their responsibility as project researchers and their belief as anticonversionists. Increasingly, they feel pressure to use their access to carry out the demand for the box's destruction," Joseph points out.

"And as for the two conversionists on the research team, you see them watching the others to make sure the black box is not harmed. When they look at the box, it is always with reverence. I have no doubt that they are under pressure to grab the box and get it away from the lab and into the protective hands of the conversionist leadership."

"But there are also other forces," Maria interrupts. "Dr. Tarry, as you know well, the project is at a dead end according to the military. They are more and more convinced that the only way we will solve the riddle of the black box is by going inside. They are ready to risk the destruction of the box if that is what it takes."

"So far, only the scientific community holds the military in abeyance. For how long, I don't know. Just as we are meeting this morning, there have been meetings going on all around this town over the past couple of days. The decision-making situation is fluid and active."

"My guess is that the final call will come out of the White House," she says. "They see this project as the 'kiss of death' or the proverbial political 'third rail'. The arm's length relationship has changed. There are new forces moving there and I think they may be nearing a decision to intervene."

"That's confirms my thinking," Dr. Tarry says as he also sits back in his chair. "These past several months have taken a toll on my physical and mental reserves. I

black box

am losing my will and my ability to hold off those who are willing to risk it all in order to find answers."

The meeting ends with a growing sense of pessimism in each of them. Time is just about to run out.

With an hour before the research team is to assemble, Dr. Tarry turns in his chair, looks out the window to see the sun starting to rise in the morning sky, and thinks, "Though only months passed since this all began, it seems much longer. I am worn down. I know it. If the higher-ups think they are frustrated, they should feel what it's like to be in my spot. The external pressure from them. The tensions among the research team members. The internal pressure I put on myself."

He picks up the remote control and activates the video camera in the lab. The box sits silently, unyielding of its secrets.

"For all these months, Joseph, Maria, my research teams and I tried everything short of going into the box itself. The arguments I made against doing that have less sway as the days pass. Only one argument, that the box could potentially be destroyed, held off my superiors in the last few days. There is no obvious way to enter the box and the box resists all attempts to enter it forcibly. Entering it will probably require means so powerful as to result in the total destruction of the black box and possibly more. We don't know what powers the black box may have to protect itself."

Outside the scientific community and the military, there is a less-defined, but no less influential message coming from key decision-makers. The message is that the loss of the black box may present fewer problems than its continued existence.

As breakfast is brought in, the President and a special advisor take their seats.

The man sitting across from the President was initially recommended by a close friend of the President's from his university days. His friend told him about a man, very well grounded in many of the scientific aspects of the infamous black box, who has been meeting with him off and on for a couple of months. This man impressed his friend, not only with his knowledge of the science of the black box, but also with the politics of the black box. Knowing the difficult situation facing the President, his friend suggested that the President meet this man.

From their customary background checks on the man, nothing unusual emerged. According to the paper trail, George William has a Ph.D. from a prestigious university and is already working as a part of the "black box" research team. Because the first meeting between the President and Dr. William was also with the President's friend, little additional checking was done.

As soon as they met, the President hit it off well with this personable, bearded man. Though young, Dr. William is intelligent and politically savvy. While he is able to answer all the President's questions about the scientific aspects of the black box, it is answers to the political aspects that make him especially valuable. To date, he counseled the President to not involve himself directly, to leave it as a science and military matter, though this course will change shortly.

"Mr. President," Dr. William begins, "let me respectfully suggest that it is now time for you to move to a different phase with respect to handling the black box issue. Until now, the prudent path was one of keeping a certain distance. But circumstances are changing."

black box

"As I indicated to you two weeks ago, I recommend a change in policy concerning the black box.

Knowing that this is coming, the President asks Dr. William to describe his rationale for the change.

"Mr. President, until now, your position was to let the science community and the military make key decisions collaboratively," Dr. William responds. "To date, that served you reasonably well. More was learned about the black box. Human conversions were stopped, which slightly diminished pressure from the anticonversionists. The conversionists' pressure was not overwhelming because their numbers were relatively few."

" The military has lost its patience. The scientific community is running out of further avenues of research. The anticonversionists are increasingly fearful that human experimentation might start again. The conversionists are now very strong and in a much better position to force the issue of human access to the black box out into the political process."

" From what you told me last week, politicians from all sides of the issue are quietly, very quietly, passing the word that the black box is a major political liability. This view is bi-partisan. If there is some way to make this whole thing go away, to disappear, many influential politicians will be very grateful to you."

"But George, isn't that risky for me?" the President asks, concerned.

"Mr. President, less so than if no action is taken. Less so if the box's destruction or disappearance is, shall we say, accidental," responds Dr. William. "The military believes the only way to get more answers is to go into the box itself. The anticonversionists want the box destroyed and believe this might accomplish that goal. Only the conversionists will be a problem. Our only bet is that their outrage over the box's destruction will be less than their growing outrage over not having access to the box."

"Your decision should not be to have the black box destroyed. your decision is to unlock its final secrets by probing the interior of the box. You will say that it is your sincerest wish that nothing adverse results from the probe."

"If and when the box is destroyed, your role will be to comfort the conversionists, those who mourn the 'accidental' loss. Everyone else will be relieved and not need your comforting."

The President and Dr. William talk on for another half-hour. Ultimately, the President agrees with the strategy. He picks up the phone, calls Dr. Tarry's superiors, and issues the necessary instructions.

At noon that day, one of the researchers informs Dr. Tarry that he has a call. He excuses himself and goes into his office. He has little doubt what the call is about and what will be its outcome. He starts to argue the decision until he is reminded for the second time that this decision was made by the President himself. Agreeing to proceed as instructed, Dr. Tarry hangs up the phone. He looks out the window as if looking for some inspiration, some divine direction. He finds none. He heads back to the lab.

Maria and Joseph meet him just outside the lab.

" Do we have no alternative but to open the box?" Joseph asks.

"I'm afraid so," Dr. Tarry responds, tired. "We have no alternative. Apparently, this decision comes all the way from the President. There is no recourse."

Maria nods understandingly. "Joseph, it was bound to happen," she says, giving him a sympathetic

black box

glance. "We're just not making any significant progress. It's not that there isn't more to analyze; it's just that there are powerful forces out there with different agendas. I'm sorry for all of us, but none of us are surprised."

"All we can hope is that we won't destroy the box," Dr. Tarry says.

To them, the black box almost seems like it wants itself to be destroyed rather than yield its secrets. Who knows? Maybe, in its own way, the black box is demonstrating the greater wisdom.

Thus, the attempt to open the black box begins. Going back to earlier experiences with the stone chamber, the initial experiments are performed on the "fake" black box since it is similar to the real black box, at least on the surface. While no conventional cutting tools made substantial inroads, the fake does not appear to be impervious. The laser weapon used in earlier experiments is the likely candidate for breaching the fake box.

When bringing out the laser weapon, Dr. Tarry orders the area cleared. The original black box is locked away. The fake black box is set in place on the lab table in the center of the room.

The laser weapon is armed and set for cutting. With the fake black box in its sights, the cutting begins. Though the cutting is slow, it proceeds until it cuts all the way around the top.

As the team shuts the laser down, Dr. Tarry walks over to the box. "Let's see if we have been successful to this point," he says.

He lifts the newly cut top off. To their disappointment, on the inside, it is only a hollow box.

Joseph picks up the fake box to examine it. "The

fake black box seems to be made of the same material, a sort of glass, throughout. The walls of the box are very thin as might be expected given its light weight. Nothing else is remarkable." He shrugs and hands the fake box off to Dr. Tarry.

As Dr. Tarry takes the fake box from Joseph he notes that what *is* remarkable about the fake is its the interior seems to confirm one theory. "This box is made of a material unlike any other material we know," he tells Joseph. "It is not made by any process known to any of us involved in this research project."

"More so than even before, I am convinced that my transformation theory is the most viable," he goes on. "Some yet unknown process made this fake box from some unknown material. I continue to believe that the original black box is the best possibility. Transformation, maybe even creation, might just be possible."

As they clear the fake box off the research table, they retrieve the original black box.

As the research team prepares to cut the original black box, Dr. Tarry tells them that he suspects that the 'real' black box will be much more difficult to deal with than the fake, but he wants to set up the experiment in the same way to start and to set up the laser in the same way.

The laser is armed and set for cutting. Dr. Tarry fires it. Nothing happens to the black box. He tries again and again, slowly moving up through the laser's power range. Even though they try the full power range of the laser, no cutting occurs. The black box is unaffected.

"Possibly if we try bursts at full power, this might have an effect," one of Dr. Tarry's researchers suggests.

Dr. Tarry hesitates. "Why? Should I?" He thinks. "I want to stop the whole process. But I know that I

black box

don't have that option yet. I have to proceed, at least through this last laser experiment. If this last one fails, there are no other more powerful tools immediately available. Then, and only then, I can call it a failure and gain more time to explore the outer face of the box."

Again, the laser is set up and armed. This time it is for more powerful, but briefer bursts of energy. One of the researchers, the bearded one who suggested the last strategy, makes another suggestion about changing the orientation of the box with reference to the laser. Distracted by another researcher's question, Dr. Tarry nods in agreement.

The researcher picks up the box and re-orients it. As he places it back down, Dr. Tarry happens to look back. He notices that the researcher's handling of the box demonstrates a certain familiarity. He watches how the researcher's fingers, all ten of them, touch the bottom of the box in a particular way. He even thinks he sees some brief activity on the surface of the box, a faint glow at its bottom.

Dr. Tarry's researchers are asking more questions about what will happen next. He's got no time to focus and he needs to proceed.

As he fires bursts at the black box, he moves up through the laser's power range. Nothing happens as they near the peak power of the laser.

In the final test, they set the laser's power at maximum. While Dr. Tarry makes the final adjustments on the laser, George, his bearded researcher, touches the box and makes one last adjustment in the box's position. Everyone steps back behind the protective shielding.

The final firing of the laser occurs. At first, nothing happens. Dr. Tarry feels relieved. The black box has survived.

Then, within seconds, the box is gone. Everyone runs to the table where the box stood only seconds before. Nothing remains. The black box disintegrated.

Dr. Tarry, Sandy, Maria and Joseph, and the rest of the researchers stand silently around a now empty lab table. They had thought the black box survived. They had thought, somehow, that they had been granted a reprieve. But the box is gone.

Quickly, Dr. Tarry, Sandy, Maria and Joseph go over to the video monitor. They re-run the video of the final experiment. Again, in the video replay, the box just disappears.

"Did it disintegrate?" Maria asks. "Or did it just disappear?"

"Can't tell." Joseph shakes his head. "The video is inconclusive."

While the four pore through the video, researchers examine the tabletop. No one can find any remnants of the box, not even dust.

They run the entire video of the laser experiments. They run the last phase time and time again. Nothing happens that they can see until they go to maximum power bursts.

As the despondent research team closes the lab down for the day, Dr. Tarry keeps replaying the last few minutes of the video. When he sees hands touch the box, it reminds him of something he saw. He focuses in on George, the bearded researcher, in the video. He notices the placement of George's fingers in reorienting the box. He thinks he sees a faint glow at the box's bottom. He watches carefully as George touches the box's bottom just before the final laser burst.

As the laboratory begins to clear of people, Dr. Tarry looks around for George, but doesn't see him. He asked if anyone had seen George William, the researcher

black box

with a beard like his own. No one remembers seeing him after the final laser burst and the disappearance of the box.

Over the next few days, Dr. Tarry makes a series of informal inquiries about the research team members in order to find out more about George. Try as he does, he is unable to find any clues as to what happened to the researcher. Personnel cannot find records of George ever being on the project.. In talking to some of the people overseeing security clearances for the research team, they are sure that there were papers on George at one point and that they were returned to personnel. Somehow, the records were lost or someone took them.

Dr. Tarry knows George was there. George seemed knowledgeable and helpful, at least before the box disappeared. Now he is gone. So is the black box.

Chapter 14. Loss

Washington, D.C.; the next day.
Washington, D.C.; the next Sunday.
Washington, D.C.; a few weeks later.

In the evening news studio, the crew and cast wait nervously. They are about to air video of the black box's destruction. This is an historic newscast with wide implications. All the networks have the video and each network knows that what they say about it will greatly affect what subsequently happens in the streets.

As the evening news broadcasts open, the words said across the country are similar. "Earlier today, while researchers attempted to open the mysterious black box, the black box was accidentally lost. A powerful laser destroyed the box."

"According to government spokespersons, the research team made little progress recently. After much consultation, the President decided the only way to learn more was to open the box."

"During an attempt to cut open the box using a high-powered laser, the box apparently disintegrated. There were no remnants."

The networks then proceed to show clips the

black box

government-provided video of the experiments and the box's disappearance.

"Earlier attempts to learn more about the box already concluded that the black box was capable of either transporting or duplicating objects. Researchers remain unsure as to whether it did transportation, duplication or both."

"While anticonversionists are rejoicing tonight, there is great sadness and some anger among conversionists."

Dr. Tarry is interviewed. He is tired and disheveled. He states that he's afraid the black box will always remain a large mystery. "There is no doubt in our minds that the black box was capable of either transportation or duplication. You see the videos of the experiments demonstrating this capability. Unfortunately, we were never able to get beyond this point."

"So then, did the box have any real value or significance?" The interviewer asks.

"In the black box, we had a wondrous device that did things that no other device known to mankind can do," Dr. Tarry responds, his voice low with disappointment. "But the box was also much like a good magic trick. It was fascinating, but what good was it beyond being entertaining?"

"What we did, if duplication was what it did, was to take an object and make a duplicate of it. We could not get it to make multiple copies of anything, machine or animal. Essentially, it transported an object the grand distance of about two feet, maybe more if you played around with the box's environment. So in the end, what good could it do? The answer, from what we know, is absolutely none. But it sure was fascinating to watch it do what it did. "

"So what happens next?" the network interviewer asks.

"We will continue to review the results of earlier experiments, but we really don't expect to learn much," Dr. Tarry responds in a less-than-convincing manner. "With the black box lost or destroyed, our work is limited. Our work will pursue certain advances in technology that might be possible.

As Dr. Tarry fades out, a Presidential spokesperson comes on. She states that the black box is now a part of our history, but unfortunately, that is all it will ever be.

When questioned about the fate of the only human being to have gone through the conversion process, the spokesperson assures the audience that Sandy Hart is well and suffers no ill effects from the black box experience. "The scientists concluded that the black box had absolutely no effect on her. Earlier today, most people saw her looking healthy and happy in what will be her final public interview."

The reporter asks if this means that Sandy will not be returning to public life. "The government is assisting Sandy by giving her another identity," the spokesperson responds. "This is to protect her from 'crazies' who are a threat to her personal welfare. Regrettably, these are necessary precautions to protect her."

"Let me make an important point," she says. "As the President said in his press statement earlier today, the loss of the black box is a mixed blessing for the nation. No doubt, some people are very happy over the box's loss. However, for those who have adopted conversionism, the President extends his deepest sympathies and sincerely hopes they can find other ways to channel their energies and find the fulfillment they are seeking."

Few people are convinced by her words. The network anchors play the story neutrally, not wanting to

black box

do anything to incite the anger of the conversionists or to provide fuel to the suspicions of the anticonversionists.

As most people expected, the conversionists are angry. Some feel they were robbed of an opportunity for a cleansing of the soul or that they lost the opportunity to achieve a higher plane of personal development. But they are all angry. And someone is going to pay for this loss.

Christopher turns away from the television set, in shock from the black box's loss. He knows it is true because he, as did the anticonversionists, had access to the research team. Leaks came regularly from the two researchers sympathetic to conversionism. The same is true for the two sympathetic to anticonversionism.

"How could they do this?" asks one of his fellow conversionists who has gathered at Christopher's home to watch the broadcast. "How could they be so careless as to destroy the symbol of our beliefs?"

"I wish I could just say it was their being careless," Christopher responds, trying to calm his friend while at the same time, be honest.. "They knew that opening the box was a high risk maneuver. Many politicians, including, I suspect, the President, hoped that the maneuver would have exactly the result it did."

"The pressure was immense to 'lose' the black box. The combination of anticonversionists and nervous politicians was too much for us to stop. Maybe in a few months, we might have been able to prevent this type of action. But we ran out of time."

There is a price to be paid for this treachery," he says, now addressing the other conversionist leaders in the room. "Many of our people will make their way down to Lafayette Square across from the White House over the next few hours. I want all of you on the telephones now making sure that the White House and Capitol Hill never forget tonight. The message to our people is simple. Tonight's protest must be peaceful, but must exude power."

Within hours after the network broadcasts, conversionists converge on Lafayette Square across from the White House. By midnight, the angry crowd numbers in the tens of thousands. No one visibly called for a demonstration. That would come later. No one needed to.

Standing across from the White House with his followers, Christopher realizes that phone calls were unnecessary. The conversionists will come anyway. They will be peaceful. Conversionists are sincere, caring people, and are not destructive.

Individual speaker after individual speaker shouts loudly to the large, unhappy crowd. The conversionists express years of pent-up frustration and jointly grieve the personal loss of their own future. At times, they comfort each other. At times, they feed each other's anger. As Christopher directed, no destruction takes place that night.

Christopher listens to the speakers spontaneously raising their voices. Especially one has a pronounced, positive affect on the massive outpouring. He speak convincingly that whatever they do next, violence is not the answer. Violence is the antithesis of what higher spirituality should be or what achieving a higher personal plane should be. His voice speaks to their grief and challenges them to reach a higher plane. He speaks of the black box as merely one means of achieving this plane. Within those powerful words is the message that much of it is up to the individual and the collective group.

As the bearded man leaves the podium, Christopher reaches out his hand to thank the man for his uplifting words. Christopher watches him merge back into the crowd before his own name is called and he has

black box

to proceed to the podium.

"Think about what you just heard," Christopher calls out to the crowd. "There is a wise, caring man. There is a true conversionist. People like him are the essence of what is good about conversionism. His words and mine are not intended to stop conversionists from acting against a government that we feel has robbed us. Our words are to set a positive and peaceful tone for how we do it. Our actions will be strong and unyielding, but they will also be peaceful and non-violent."

"Due to stupidity, carelessness and malicious intent, all conversionists have suffered a great and terrible loss. No half-hearted words from the President or other politicians will change that."

"To our government, listen very carefully. Our message is clear. We will be avenged for our loss. Those of you politicians, and I include you, Mr. President, who think that elections will not be in jeopardy once the black box is gone, are wrong. You will pay with your political life. We conversionists are many in number and fervent in our commitment. Starting now, we will organize to unseat every incumbent who unwisely chose not to take the pledge to protect the black box. Your inaction permitted this government to risk the box's destruction. Make other plans for the rest of your public lives. Public office is no longer an option."

"If we should ever be so fortunate as to again have the black box, we want to ensure that no politician will lack commitment to its protection and that we will never again suffer a loss like this."

"Let me end, not by speaking to politicians, but by speaking to all of you here and across the world. Many of you are conversionists for very different reasons. What we have in common is our belief that we are capable of rising to a higher level of existence. We rise to that higher level, in large part, by our own concerted action. We rise to that higher level aided by what the black box represents."

"The black box has taught us much. Humankind can break the bonds of its environment. We can break from the constraints of the past. With the black box as our guide, we can cleanse ourselves, maybe even our souls, of what holds us back."

"But the primary lesson of the black box is not of a technological processing of human growth. The box will not do all the work for us. It will only help clear the way. In the end, we are the agents of our own better future. We are the ones who must lift up our own selves and assist the rest of humankind to reach that higher plane of existence."

"Contrary to the wishes of the anticonversionists and many politicians, conversionism does not end tonight. Tonight, we begin the next stage of our evolution. Whether or not the black box exists, its image will always be with us. Fellow conversionists: tonight, we mourn. Tomorrow, we will go on with greater commitment."

As Reverend L.O. Moses watches the network news and the live coverage of the conversionist demonstration and the speakers, especially the bearded man and Christopher, she feels joy as well as deep-rooted suspicion.

People on the research team who were sympathetic reported that black box is apparently destroyed. If so, the "devils hand," is gone. But, she has serious doubts. After all, her people reported that no pieces of the black box were found. That might be explained by its being disintegrated. However, some part of the box, even as small as dust, should have survived.

black box

After all, the box was supposed to be virtually indestructible.

At first, L.O. thought there was a government cover-up perpetrated. Now she doubts this idea. Her government sources, placed well throughout various levels, give a consistent message. The government believes the box was destroyed accidentally. If it somehow exists, they don't have it either.

As Sunday morning comes, L.O. moves slowly into the pulpit as the television crews prepare for the broadcast. She sets aside her crutches. The countdown to broadcast is complete and she goes on the air live.

"Today, we come together to rejoice in the comfort that a major piece of evil has been removed from the world. The black box is destroyed. It is gone. The devil's hand has been cast away from humankind. We are free from its tyranny."

"No longer will the devil's hand work its evil deeds. Since the days of Eden, the black box has been with us. It was there at the time of original sin. It was there when humankind was cast out of Eden to roam the earth in misery. But no longer. We are free at last." L.O. sways in the pulpit, beginning to reach the rhythm of her sermon.

"Eden is once again within our grasp. But there is no miracle that will take us there. Much work remains to get us there. But, my fellow anticonversionists, the path is easier with the force of evil beaten back."

"We are different than some of the conversionists. We know that much of our destiny depends on what each of does individually. Some of the black box followers believe that the black box would miraculously and immediately transport them to heaven.

They were wrong. Some thought it would cleanse their souls, raising them above all earthly existence. They are wrong. The black box is not to raise up souls, but to destroy them."

"Even for those of you who do not believe in the Biblical devil, you know that a technological devil can be almost as destructive. So it was with the black box. Technology cannot transport or duplicate souls. The black box did what it did: it 'deleted' the original person, taking away the soul's body. It did nothing less than <u>kill</u> the original person and nothing more, as such a technological devil cannot touch the human soul."

"But if you believe in the Biblical devil, then the black box, the 'devil's hand,' was a threat to the soul. No one knows if the devil's hand was here to destroy souls or carry them away. Maybe its method was more devious. Maybe it just provided conversionists the vehicle to self-destruct their body -- in effect, to commit suicide and, as a result, damn the soul."

"For us, the soul is sacred, not to be risked at the hands of technological marvels or the devil himself. We fought for the black box's destruction. It is done. Now we must go on, together. Our movement will not end because Eden has not been reached. For months, our energies focused against the force of evil. Now, we must turn those energies, individually and collectively, to the forces of good. It is Eden, and all that Eden represents, that we seek. It is the final fulfillment of the human soul, here today on earth and hereafter away from earth, which we must achieve."

In the weeks after the box's loss, there is much joy among the anticonversionists. There is also ever-present suspicion.

black box

L.O. sits in her den and replays the video of the so-called "final moments" of the black box. She leans back in her chair and wonders if evil is so easily defeated. Is the devil's hand so easily cast out? And if it is, where is the evidence of its destruction?

"The video is one thing: anyone can manipulate a video," she mutters. "The government observers, including some who are anticonversionists, are pretty convincing. But then the government has a whole lot of reasons for wanting this episode to go away. There was good reason to stage a fake destruction or to destroy another fake black box." It's the latter possibility that bothers her a lot. What if the actual black box were not used in those final hours before its supposed destruction?

"Suppose it hadn't been destroyed, but just disappeared. There is no debris. If it disintegrated, where are the pieces or even dust? There had to at least be some dust." She remembers that the interviews with the observers of the final experiment suggest that the disintegration was so complete that the resulting fine dust particles were drawn through the lab's ventilating system.

"Maybe instead of being destroyed or switched, the box was transported somehow intact. Did the box have that capability?"

Unless the box re-appears, the issue will never be completely settled one way or the other. Some anticonversionists will always believe that the destruction was a lie and the devil's hand exists. L.O. suspects that she will always be counted among this group.

As time goes by, more and more anticonversionists are convinced that the black box exists as they see their efforts to restore Eden fail. Something is to blame and the black box is a natural target. The anticonversionists charge the government with conspiracy.

A knock comes at his front door. Putting down the papers he's been reading all day, Dr. Tarry gets out of his chair, moves around the desk, and opens the door. Facing him are two people he had initially seen as adversaries but who now knows as good friends.

"Hey, Dr. Tarry, how are you doing these days?" says Maria as she glides through the door and gives him a semi-professional, semi-personal hug.

"I'm fine," he replies. "How are the two of you? How's life for two people who are now significant others? Are you two ever going to actually marry or are you going to just keep hanging out together." He smiles.

"Beats me," Joseph replies good-naturedly. "So far, it seems to be working. Maybe we'll just leave it that way." He playfully touches Maria's arm. She smiles back at him.

"I was just thinking, as I saw the two of you in the doorway, how much things changed over the months since we last were together," says Dr. Tarry. "I kept waiting for you two to launch a counterattack. I think you kept waiting for Mr. Hyde to appear. Fortunately, he didn't."

"Joseph and I have been thinking back to the whole experience as well," allows Maria. "In some ways, it was like being able to almost touch a star. We seemed so close to what would have been a true technological miracle. And, then it was gone."

"When the team was disbanded, Joseph went back to the Smithsonian and I went on my merry governmental way. Lucky for me, the federal government never seems short of unpleasant problems to solve. "

"How's your work going, Dr. Tarry?"

black box

"My work is about as stuck as you might guess," Dr. Tarry shrugs. "I'm happy that they let me retain the lab and other resources to continue to play around with some of the possibilities suggested by our work with the black box. I even thought about trying to get you two assigned to work with me. But my work is strictly for the Pentagon for now and you know how they feel about non-military. I also know how you feel about the Pentagon. Maybe later under better circumstances?"

"Let us know," Joseph says. "Just like you, we invested a lot of ourselves in trying to solve the riddle of the box. We both want another shot."

"As both of you know, I developed quite a few theories about the black box and the missing baggage handler," says Dr. Tarry. "Nothing proven. Just theories and speculation. Would you care to hear them?" Maria and Joseph tell him yes. He ushers them into his small, but comfortable personal office.

"For one, I don't think we destroyed the black box. There's the missing researcher who was directly in contact with the box just before we did the final attempt with the laser. I thought back to how I hesitated at the time and how he encouraged proceeding. He even suggested how to place the box."

"In reviewing the video, I noted at least two occasions when he physically handled the box in the final moments. After his first contact, there are inconclusive indications that the box was active again, but not as it was when we were doing earlier experiments. There was a glow coming from the box's bottom, not top."

"Don't downplay your observations and suspicions, because we both share your 'theory' about the continued existence of the box," Maria scowls at him. "We would have said something, but we felt that it may have all been for the best. We never found the bearded man, but we assume he probably still exists."

"Let me tell you about a little coincidence I ran across," she continues. "Over the past few weeks, I did a little computer checking on all the people who were involved in some way with the black box directly or with decisions affecting the black box. Once I had that list, I looked for anyone whose involvement with an agency or otherwise was only during the time that the black box was known to exist. That list is fairly short, about ten people. I checked with some people to see what they could tell me about these ten people. Most checked out as nothing unusual. Several did not.

"Guess what the common element is for a set of these 'short-term' people? They are all males and they all have beards. One is the bearded baggage handler. A second is the very researcher, Dr. George William, you mentioned a few moments ago. A third is the man, using the credentials of Dr. William, who served as an informal advisor to the President. Since I had some video from the lab, I showed it to a friend in the White House. They are all the same person."

"Here is the video from the lab." She holds up the tape and walks over to Dr. Tarry's video player. "Here is Dr. William. But there is also one last place he appears, the conversionist rally outside the White House on the night the box is lost. Look at this speaker. See. There he is."

"Unbelievable. There he is," Dr. Tarry says as he falls back in his chair. "Everything makes sense now. This man had his hand in the whole series of events surrounding the box. He didn't just pass on the box and walk away. He was here the whole time. Who knows when else he might have whispered a word or turned a switch that affected the course of events?"

"He could have walked away with the box at any time. He had ample opportunity. Why didn't he?" Dr. Tarry's questions start spill out of him; they're so many

black box

that Maria and Joseph can barely keep track.

"Is he done? Is that speech his last act? It sounded like it could be?"

"But what has this all been about? Is the real mystery the technology of the black box or is it something else?"

"The unknown is the still unsolved mystery of the black box's purpose. Over the past several months, history records how humankind dealt with an apparent miracle that had no known purpose. Yes, the box did things that were magical and entertaining. But did it have any more lasting and significant value. Did it do evil, as some believed? Did it do good, as others believed? If it didn't do any of these things directly, did it somehow do them indirectly? Or, did it have no value, other than being an entertaining magic trick?

"I'm not sure we'll ever know," Joseph states, looking at them both. "But I heard his speech when it was first given. I've seen it on tape several times since then. If that really is him and he believes what he said, then the technology of the black box is not the answer. It is more about us as human beings. The answer has something to do with how we as human beings interact with something like the black box, what we are evolving into, and how we can achieve a higher plane of existence."

"For a brief moment in history, the world encountered an unknown and a small taste of the hope of an easy path to a higher human existence. The black box was given. The black box was then taken away," Joseph says slowly, folding his hands in his lap as he speaks. "During its time in human hands, the black box brought a mixture of hope and despair. There is some reason to believe that it helped bring human growth. Very different people with very different beliefs developed positively as they wrestled with the box's existence and its purpose. But, the black box has yet to help people fully reach their highest existence and fullest knowledge. It brought conflict. It has yet to bring peace."

Epilogue

Pentagon research lab; several months later.
Maryland suburbs; several days later.

    While everyone else has lost interest in the experiments, Dr. Tarry continues. Finally having convinced the Pentagon that they are not a risk, he hooks up with Maria and Joseph for further exploration. The three of them know that there is still a mystery here that deserves and, at times, demands their continued attempts to solve. As has been the case for several months, Dr. Tarry has the lab and a free hand to pursue this issue in any way he wishes. He is virtually forgotten by the government.

    As the three of them continue the research and their review of the earlier experiment records, they are increasingly convinced that the black box had the capabilities that they suspected. Joseph and Dr. Tarry think they discovered more about the basic principles of the mass to energy and energy to mass conversion. They begin the first experiments in this direction.

    Dr. Tarry, in reviewing the videos of the bearded researcher, Dr. George William, and the final moments with the black box, thinks he sees how additional capabilities of the black box are accessed. All he needs is the black box.

Off to the side, a bearded janitor observes as he has for the past several days. As they finish the first experiment, he seems concerned. Then his shift ends and he leaves for the day.

As he leaves, Dr. Tarry taps Maria on the shoulder and points to the door. She sees the bearded man leaving and nods back at Dr. Tarry. Joseph nods as well, picks up the phone and makes the call. At the same time, Maria grabs her coat and heads out a side door.

She sees the man turn the corner and start walking down the street. Another man, one of Maria's people, stands about a block away. Maria and her surveillance partner keep their distance, but stay close enough not to lose him. Each night, they have been able to stay with him longer before they lose him in a crowd somewhere. So far, he does not appear to realize he is under surveillance.

But then again, Maria is not so sure. He has always outmaneuvered them in the past, even as far back as the original switch at Dulles. Maybe he knows they are on to him. Maybe that is even his plan. Regardless, she will keep pursuing him.

They could confront him in the lab, but that is risky. While they want him badly, they want the box even more. They take the gamble to see if they can get both.

Damn! As she slides around the corner, she doesn't see him anymore. looks for her surveillance partner and sees him about a half a block away. He sees her. They've both lost the stranger. Frustrated, but undaunted, she waves him off and starts the trek back to the lab. Maybe tomorrow.

----

black box

Out in the Washington suburbs, Taj and Jason sit thinking.

The world seems quiet and normal in comparison after everything that's happened. Every once in a while, they notice someone doing surveillance on their house, but always at a substantial distance. They hired a private security firm to clear out all remaining listening devices. About a month later, they did it a second time to see if any devices had been re-installed. No listening devices were found. The firm told them what to look for in the future.

Apparently, the government doesn't have much interest in them anymore. No reason why they should. The government already knew everything they knew.

The more they think and talk about the whole experience, the more they doubt that the black box was destroyed. Their personal experience alone was not one that builds trust in the federal government. But they wouldn't be surprised if the government didn't have the black box either. They are struck by their experience with the baggage handler and the black box. There was special warmth that passed among the three of them on the day he delivered the luggage with the box inside. Over time, they came to believe that the baggage handler is the box's keeper and that he intentionally gave them the box. They no longer consider the incident an accidental occurrence.

But if that is true, why did he involve them at all? What should they have done with the box? Is their involvement now over or is there something yet to come? Something is missing. Something has yet to happen before this is done. They have not yet gone full circle with the black box and its keeper.

At times, they think they are just suffering from some kind of "save the world complex" and should get over it. Not an easy thing to do given who they are and where they want to go.

There is a knock at the door.

They open the door and immediately recognize the face. As much as he looks troubled, they look relieved.

The bearded man slips quietly into the house. Without a word between them, Jason and Taj close the curtains and direct him to the most secure spot in the house.

Once they feel safe, the three of them look at each other and embrace warmly.

They try to make him comfortable. He finds some security and starts to relax.. Jason and Taj look at the strong, but slightly weary, face. They realize that he's strong and still in full control of all that's happening.

First, he tells them of his own trust and confidence in them. Then he lays out the journey that awaits the three of them. Taj and Jason listen. They find some of the answers that they sought and feel once again the excitement of being in the center of making history.

black box

BLACK BOX -- INSTRUCTIONS
Level One

ACTIVATION

Using four hands, touch the box's top four corners simultaneously.
> (**Response:** Illuminates (1) the "e" light, (2) the "record" key/light. If no activity for 10 minutes, box shuts down.)

OPERATION

Place original object to the left and front of the box and press the "record" key.
> (**Response:** Illuminates original object by scanner beam. Illuminates the "m to e" key/light. If no activity for 1 minute, process terminates.)

Press the "m to e" key.
> (**Response:** Illuminates the "e to m" key/light. If no activity for 1 minute, process terminates)
> press the "m to e" light. Within a few moments, the "e" light flickers. Seconds later, the "e to m" light brightens.

Press the "e to m" key.
> (**Response:** Illuminates the blinking "verify" key/light. Box's object appears to right and front of box. Original and box's object inert. If no activity for 1 minute, process terminates.)

If box's object is acceptable, press the "verify" key.
> (**Response:** Illuminates the flashing "delete" key/light. If no activity for 30 seconds, process terminates.)

If black box process and outcome are acceptable, press the "delete" key.
> (**Response:** Original object is gone. Box's object remains. Box shuts down)

black box

Book Two: Save The World, Complex

Prologue

South American jungle, about a year later.

For a long time, this part of the jungle was quiet. No outside strangers came to visit. But all this is changing. Since the jungle remains inhospitable to humans, human visitors appear periodically but not often. Always the humans search for something. Always they stop at the dirt mound in the clearing. Apparently, they don't find what they look for because they leave with no more than what they bring. But about a month ago, a new group of humans came through the area. Like those before them, after a long, intense search, they found the mound of dirt. Once more, the mound is empty. More of these human visitors are likely to come: the jungle will never be the same.

The jungle animals have no memory of a year ago when a woman entered the jungle and left with the strange object she dug from the dirt mound. The animals do have a memory of when some time later, a group of people searched long and hard through this area, disrupting jungle life. These people found the clearing and the mound where the woman found the strange object. But at the mound, the humans found nothing of interest. No human came back for a while.

Today, something has happened. The change is subtle. Long ago, the mound collapsed somewhat as what was inside of it had been removed. Now the mound is fuller. Something has been re-inserted into the dirt mound.

One year after the black box disappeared from the Pentagon research laboratory, the black box reappears in the jungle and inside the dirt mound.

In one sense, only seconds had passed; in another sense, a year. A year ago, the black box was in the Pentagon research laboratory. Researchers fired a laser weapon at it, first trying to cut the box, then trying to blow it open. As a last laser firing was prepared, the bearded man touched the black box and activated it. With just moments to go, the box was made to disappear from the laboratory and to reappear here, in the earthen mound. Now, one year later, the box is back in the jungle.

In the future people will look back on what happened with the black box and how it happened. They will speculate on at least two theories. Initially, the primary theory will be the black box, as instructed, converted itself into a type of energy. At the same time, the box was programmed to reappear one year later in the jungle's earthen mound where Ti Ching, the engineer, originally found it. Under this theory, the box was capable of moving itself through space and time to place

black box

itself at a pre-programmed location.

Over time, this theory will lose some favor to another one: the black box was actually moved by a second box that used the fixed coordinates of the jungle's earthen mound. Under this second theory, the original black box is converted back into matter one year later by the second box pulling in the bound energy using the box's personal code, that is, the set of instructions for converting energy into a particular object.

Under either of these theories, people will raise questions as to whether the black box was in an energy state for the year or was transported someplace else and then came here, to this place at this point in time, by itself or through means of a second black box. And some people will think these issues of little relative importance compared to other questions about the black box.

Chapter 1. Search

Capitol mall
Washington, D.C.
South American jungle

During one of their rare free times on a Friday afternoon, Dr. Joseph Form and Maria Mendez take a leisurely lunch outdoors.

"This search for the black box and the bearded stranger is a bit much at times. Dr. Tarry is consumed by it. It is as if he races against death or a great evil force," Maria sighs as she unwraps the turkey sandwich she has brought with her from the office.

She shakes her head. "We know little more now than a year ago. Without the box, most of our work keeps dead-ending."

"I wouldn't have had it any other way, but I'm tired of all this 'black box' stuff." Maria shakes her head before taking a bite of her sandwich. She chews slowly as she looks out over the mall and the Smithsonian buildings. "We know nothing of what goes on inside. We may never know."

Sitting next to Maria on the bench, Joseph reaches over and takes one of the sandwich halves from

black box

her lap. "Remember back when we thought it might have been taken back to the jungle in which it was found? Or that maybe, we would find other clues there? Dr. Tarry, his search crew and you and I spent a week in that jungle, traipsing through the jungle day after day." Joseph smiles wryly. "The environment was almost primeval in nature. I felt what Ti felt when she first found the box."

"Though Ti didn't remember exactly where she found it, fortunately, she only traveled a day's journey from camp. We were lucky to have such a limited area to cover." He says between bites of sandwich.

Maria nods in agreement. "Even then, it took two days before we found the earthen mound," she points out.

"And the mound was empty, just as it was empty since Ti first took the box," Joseph sighs as he opens up his drink, still frustrated by the memory of that search. "Throughout that whole area, twenty searchers found not a single sign of anything unusual."

"Tarry was really frustrated," Maria says. "I don't know which drives him more. His anger over losing the black box or his fear someone else had it or would get it. And then when we returned, there were his military bosses. Even one month was more patience than they had."

"No rest for us though," she says, crumpling up her sandwich wrapper. "Here we go back into the lab. Government expert and Smithsonian scientist side by side trying to crack the riddle of the black box and its keeper."

"The keeper!" Joseph, as usual musing to himself and not completely paying attention, jumps back into the conversation. "Now there is your target! You spent months tracing any evidence of his existence before the black box was discovered. But you found nothing." Joseph speaks more quickly now, as he always does when he starts to get into a subject.

"You found no evidence that he existed after his last visit to the Maryland couple. Your surveillance crews know he was there. They saw him go in the front door and take in a package. By the time your people got clearance to go inside, the keeper was leaving out the back, again with package in hand."

"But Taj and Jason may still be the key," Maria says as Joseph catches his breath. "They're the only people who interacted extensively with the box's keeper. He sought them for some purpose. Not only did he apparently seek them in the first place, but he risked everything to see them a second time."

"Almost immediately after the keeper's visit, the couple lightened their 'personal baggage.'" Maria tells him. "They sold their house and rented it back from the new owners. They set aside a fair amount of money, much of it portable and distributed. They seem ready to move at a moment's notice. Then again, over six months has passed and they've made no major moves."

"Yeah. Right. No major moves other than threatening to sue you and the whole federal government for invasion of privacy," Joseph laughs.

"Our public relations image wasn't helped when my people broke down their front and back door, charged through their house, and demanded they produce the box's keeper." She shrugs. "By the time I walked through the door and saw how sloppily this little activity was carried out, all that remained was to do damage control. We pulled out quickly."

Joseph looks at his watch. He has some time left before he has to be back at the Smithsonian. "You never did tell me how that worked out."

Maria laughs lightly. "Well, if Taj and Jason had brought any press in, we would have been hung out to dry. Still, we maintain low level watch over their activities, including travel and credit cards."

black box

"Actually, I'm glad that part's essentially over. This work is more rewarding," Maria remarks, thinking back on the months of surveillance.

As they finish lunch and walk back to work, Maria has one last thought. "Tarry is more relaxed now that he is back to being a scientist and you're in your element and happier, even if all your questions remain unanswered. Like what's inside the black box."

As she moves away from the pulpit, Reverend L.O. Moses thinks about the deteriorating anticonversionist movement. The same movement that was so motivated when the devil's hand was here. With it gone, she finds it harder and harder to hold the group together. Some people see the threat as gone or suspect that it never existed. At best, she might be able to hold the whole movement together for another six months. Then it will be over.

As the television cameras sweep towards the choir, she sits down, humbled by the potential threat to the very core of a religion built on the concept of "creation" and a "soul." The black box strikes at these religions in the same way that the theory of evolution struck at an earlier time. Religion survived evolution and it will survive the black box.

Many people are cynical as to her motivation. But if anyone were to look at Moses' financial books, he or she would that this is not about money. All of the money contributed by movement followers and TV congregants was carefully used. Power isn't her motivation, either, though no one will probably ever believe that. No, rather, her motivation is that she believes in God. She believes in creation. And she believes in the devil."

Her's is a mission to fight evil, to fight for the

very souls the black box can take away. Unless God's hand is somehow reaching through the black box, its physical conversion process can't transfer the soul into the second body. If it is not God's hand, the soul is lost or there is no "soul" in the first place. Both possibilities are unacceptable to her.

Quite some time ago, Moses succeeded in getting 'black box' conversions effectively banned. With the black box gone, no one had reason to raise the issue again. But what would happen if the black box reappeared? The conversionists are now much stronger than the anticonversionists. If the black box reappears, Revered Moses fears she will lose the next round.

As the choir nears the end of the hymn, she moves back to the pulpit, readying herself for the resurrection of the black box and of conversion.

Christopher Carey, always uncomfortable with the mantle of leadership, leaves out the side door of the conversionist meeting. Nearly a thousand people attend this weekly meeting, but the "congregation" is much larger. The Washington congregation is still the largest, but is challenged by growth in all other areas of the country. The more people are frustrated by life in general and by organized religions in particular, the more people seem eager to move to embrace conversionism.

At this time, conversionism has several different types of adherents. One group, believing there is a "soul," sees the black box as cleansing that soul. The cleansed soul is what moves from the original person to the converted person. The other main group of adherents rejects the concept of the soul and sees conversion as a physical process of cleansing the physical person.

As different as each conversionist is, the one

black box

uniting factor is the black box. Somehow, everyone holds onto it. They see it and its conversion process as confirmation of their own personal beliefs. As opposed to organized religions with all their pronouncements, rules, commandments, and trappings, conversionism has none. Why? Simply, it is because the black box has never said a thing. Moreover, no one can verify that the box's keeper ever said anything. As such, all are free to make their own interpretation. It is the ultimate personal religion.

As he walks, Carey realizes that he could try to make it otherwise. He could try to make conversionism "organized." But conversionism is a movement of individuals, inspired by the black box's mystery and promise and organized only by their own personal value and belief systems.

When the black box was lost, Carey thought the following of conversionism might end for the other conversionists. For him, it didn't matter. As it turned out, it didn't matter for most others either. Christianity is a useful analogy here. Christ did not need to be present for Christianity to continue and even grow. The same is true for the black box. Now what would happen in a second coming of the black box or in a second coming of Christ is a whole other question. Second comings for any 'religion' definitely stir things up.

He knows he must keep himself prepared for a second appearance of the black box and its keeper. If it comes, many will fear losing the box again before their own conversion. Hundreds of thousands of people will want to be converted. In fact, too many people will want to be converted. There will be chaos.

This is partly why he spends this time emphasizing that conversion itself is not as important as the message of conversion. To Carey, the message is clear. People can control much of their own destinies and their own cleansing. Whether or not they have a soul is less the critical question than what they do with their lives. Whether their time is as short as one physical lifetime or as long as a soul's eternal life, people's mission should be to help make this world as good as they can. This means ridding the world of the bad just as the black box rids the person of the bad.

Even now, his people search for the black box throughout the world. It is their holy grail, after all. Maybe, they will find the original box; maybe they will find the keeper. Maybe, there are other boxes in other places. Maybe, there are answers as to its origin.

The conversionists have only two real leads. One lead is the story about a couple who interacted extensively with the box and its keeper. The conversionists were never able to crack through the government secrecy to find them. Yet, Carey knows they are near D.C.

Their other lead is where it all began, the South American jungle where the black box was found. After months of investigation, the conversionists found out the approximate location. Though his people searched the jungle for tens of miles in all directions, but nothing was found. Over the next several weeks, another group of conversionists will explore that area of the jungle. Maybe this time, they will find answers.

As he strolls into the post office, the keeper knows that the next stage of Earth's journey is about to begin.

The next phase could have been sooner. It was his call to make. But he waited. He wanted to watch people respond to the black box's first coming. One year is a reasonable time for observation. Nothing happened

black box

to negate the final implementation of his overall plan. Now, the time is right to proceed. Now is the time for the black box's full introduction into this world.

The black box's keeper is anxious to re-engage with Taj and Jason. He walks over to the window and purchases a stamp. As he moves toward the mail slot, he places the stamp on the letter he wrote and sealed earlier and drops the letter into the mail slot.

In the South American jungle, another round of human activity begins. It has been a month since the first group of conversionists found the area where the black box was first found. Today, another group of conversionists arrives and prepares to go out and find the location. Maybe the first expedition missed something. Maybe this group just wants to satisfy themselves. Or maybe something has changed.

In his secure office in a private research laboratory, Dr. Tarry reads over the report one of his staff has prepared for him. He had requested a full description of events with the black box and its known history up until then. Dr. Tarry rubs his temples and puts his glasses back on. It's going to be another long day.

First known contact was by Ti Ching in South America. The black box's first known use was by the keeper. That was when the keeper formed the original stone chamber for the box that was hidden in the earthen mound. Second use was again by the keeper. Intercepting the shipment of the box and the original chamber at Dulles Airport, he apparently re-formed the original stone chamber into a cruder version; he made a fake black box, again cruder than the original. It's not clear how the fake black box was made. The best explanation was that it was formed by the original box and may have used souvenirs from the Maryland couple's luggage as "building material."

The keeper then gave the black box to the Maryland couple, Jason Kalder and Taj Curie. Next, they used the box. Activation was accidental and their experimentation relatively crude. At one point, they almost converted their cat. After the government has installed electronic surveillance, it was also known that Taj and Jason did simple one-to-one conversions of both inanimate and animate objects.

After the black box was retrieved from Taj and Jason's residence, the next round of experiments began under the initial supervision of Dr. Joseph Jones and Maria Mendez. Based on these experiments, much was pulled together on what the box did and how it operated. As far as the box's internal functioning, they knew no more than that matter was probably converted to energy and back to matter. They suspected the box used some type of code to control what was converted to what.

From the full set of experiments, it was learned that the black box can convert any kind of object. More than one object can be converted at a time. The result of conversion is a second object, identical to the original object in every way measurable. This is true both for the objects' physical characteristics and their functions.

There are few limits to the black box's capabilities. During conversion, both objects are in effect frozen, that is they do not function in any way. Total mass is also limited. Only a total of 500 pounds of physical matter can be converted, whether this be the mass of one or of several objects. When the conversion process begins, the original object has to be immediately next to the box and is scanned by the box's generated

black box

beam. Objects can be moved during the process, but no more than one hundred yards away from the box. Objects can be placed behind walls or inside other objects. The black box ignores all objects except the original object it "records" and tracks. Once an object is "recorded", the box ignores all changes around or on the original object. The process terminates if the original object is changed; if, for example a piece of the original is cut off.

With respect to the second object, the converted object, the lessons are similar. The second object can also be placed anywhere. Placement must occur within the total time limit set by the black box -- one minute after pressing "e to m" and 30 seconds after pressing "verify." If the second object is scratched or otherwise damaged, the whole process terminates and the second object disappears.

Near the end of the experiments, one was run with a human subject, a soldier by the name of Sandy Hart. As in all previous experiments, the experiment was successful and the second Sandy, the converted one, was the same as the original Sandy in every way measurable.

After completing experimentation on the box's functions, experiments began on the box's internal mechanisms. Initially, the box proved impervious to all forms of scrutiny. Nothing was learned about the internal workings. When the final effort was made to open it, the box disappeared. Though neither the government nor the Smithsonian knew what happened, suspicion was that the box was made to disappear by a lab assistant now thought to be the box's keeper. The box's disappearance suggests other capabilities of the box. Either the box can act upon itself, or some other force, perhaps another black box, acted upon it.

Even with all the experiments, including the human experiment, it is uncertain what the black box actually accomplishes. Is the black box moving the original object? Is it creating an identical second object from the first? If the latter, does it use the mass of the original object or does it get mass from some other source? If from some other source, where does the mass of the original then go?

For Dr. Tarry, two further pieces of evidence, though not definitive, indicate other possibilities. The box's keeper visited Ti Ching. Her computer's memory, as well as her own, was wiped clean of any reference to the black box. Since the box's keeper visited her after the box disappeared, the black box may have been the tool.

Another piece of evidence is the mysterious movements and disappearance of the box's keeper. Using the box, there is good reason to believe the keeper is able to move anywhere. In spite of a massive international search effort, he was never found. This suggests more potential capabilities for the box.

As time dragged on, more and more questions were raised over the wisdom of continuing the laboratory investigation. Military and research scientists pressed for continuing research. Political people were happy this was going nowhere and wanted an excuse to finally bury this whole project.

Cleaning his glasses with a soft cloth from his desk, Dr. Tarry decides that it's time to go home. It's way after work hours. He sighs. There are so many potential capabilities for the box. Where does he even begin?

black box

Chapter 2. Note

Suburban Maryland; Wednesday, the next day.
South American jungle; Friday morning, two days later.
South American jungle; later that Friday afternoon.

    Sitting on the back patio eating breakfast with Jason, Taj complains about the last few months between bites of an English muffin and spun honey.
    "We were so close to something so terribly important," she says between mouthfuls "Then it was gone and we were left here alone."
    "I know," Jason says as he pours himself more coffee. "We were in the middle of a great historical event and yet both of us feel like overlooked footnotes. The government keeps us a secret in hope that the black box and its keeper will return to us. Of course, they are also still concerned about the law suit we threatened."
    "When we last talked to the box's keeper, he said that for now, we should just refer to him as a 'shepherd'," Taj reminds him.
    Jason nods. "Neither the black box nor its keeper, I mean the shepherd, has surfaced since our last talk with him. Conversionists might have discovered information about the South American jungle and the black box. I

know an expedition had gone there, but found nothing, but I'm betting that there's been more expeditions."

"It was better not to go public." Taj reassures him. "Between the conversionists and the anticonversionists, we would have no peace. I keep waiting for our story to get leaked to them."

"Nothing so far, but something has to happen soon," Jason cautions. "As the shepherd said during his final visit with us, be prepared for his return.

"We're ready," Taj exclaims. "The pets are ready. I say let's get this show on the road. I'm tired of waiting."

"Taj, you are always impatient," Jason says. "We have to wait." He smiles at her reassuringly. "It is clear that we were integral to his plan."

"He's said that in time, we would understand the indispensable role of shepherds, carefully guiding their charge to a desired goal," Taj replies, sighing. "I fear he's talking about months and not years." Taj and Jason's eyes meet. "But we're ready."

Off in another part of the house, Amber barks as mail drops through the front door slot. A single envelope falls to the floor.

Amber picks up the letter in her mouth and races over to Taj and Jason, wagging her tail as she waits for Jason to take it from her.

"This is an unusual letter," says Jason as he holds it up for Taj to see. "It's a hand-addressed envelope with no return address. I think this might be from our friend."

Before he can open it, Taj takes it out of his hands, tears open the envelope and reads the letter out loud.

"Dear Jason and Taj. Though you were unaware, periodically I observed the two of you during this past year. As I expected and hoped, I observed two patient, well-prepared people. For both of these characteristics, I am deeply appreciative. Finally, your time and mine has

black box

come. Meet me, as I instructed you, where this journey began. The map and instructions I gave you will guide you. When we meet, I will explain everything. You are both about to begin the second stage of your journey. Assuming you receive this by Wednesday, I'll see you Saturday. Take care."

He signed the note, "Another shepherd."

As dawn breaks, two middle-aged conversionists, Paul and Judy Cross, leave the staging camp and head out for the jungle. This is their first jungle trip and they are clearly apprehensive. Still, there is no turning back as far as they are concerned. They traveled thousands of miles for one reason. They wanted to go where "conversionism" began, the site where the engineer Ti Ching found the original black box.

Other than being strong believers in conversionism, Paul and Judy are just regular people. After meeting Christopher, the conversionists' national leader, they were impressed and inspired by his message. For them, conversionism is more secular and personal. While the black box is an intriguing element of conversionism, they are more impressed by the door it opened for their personal development. Their coming here is more to be touched by the experience than to actually find the black box or go through its conversion process. That's not to say they wouldn't go through conversion if they have the chance.

By going out in the jungle, they hope to find a sort of primeval environment in which to begin anew their own personal growth. They have become complacent. They need a challenge to face together.

Moving through the jungle is hard. They are not in great shape, the underbrush is thick, and the jungle air is hot and humid. Still they move purposefully. Here in the jungle, each time one of them confronts some jungle animal or plant testing their resolve, the other finds a way to extract them from the confrontation. Alone, the jungle might win. Together, the jungle slowly yields.

As the day wears on, Paul and Judy understand and appreciate the looks they received from their friends before they left on this trip. These were friends who found out they were not only going into the jungle, but that they intended to stay the night. Still they keep going. This is all part of the experience. This is all necessary.

Having take longer than expected, by late afternoon they reach a stream and a tree they figure is within a mile of the clearing. Exhausted, they turn to each other and face the decision to either go on or camp here for the night. As the spot they're in seems safe and dry enough to pitch their camp, they decide to sleep here and rise early in the morning. That way, they will reach the clearing shortly after dawn tomorrow.

The two conversionists set up camp, eat supper, and think about what they are doing and what tomorrow will be like.

As Paul lights the fire, Judy talks. "Conversionism is personal to me as it is to you. There was a time when I thought regular religion was for me, but I became increasingly distant from organized religion and disillusioned. Not that all religions are inherently flawed."

"Religion helps some people reach beyond their everyday existence and beyond their time here on Earth," she goes on. "As long as religion is a partner in that reach, it is extremely valuable. But for many, religion becomes an escape from one's own personal obligation and responsibility. Then religion is more harmful than good."

"That's what happened to me. I stopped thinking

black box

and was only 'believing'." Judy says tersely, throwing some more brush into the fire.

"You're right," Paul responds as he stirs the fire, gazing up into the trees. "Conversionism is different from most religions. There is no declaration of god's existence. There is no declaration to the contrary, either. Conversionism has no 'written word' to guide its followers. All we have is video."

"There is not even a human messenger from God. We have rumor of a bearded man being the box's 'keeper.' But, even if he really exists, he makes it clear he doesn't aspire to the limelight."

"We have something very simple. A physical object, the black box, which shows it can perform a miracle of sorts. To each person is left the nature and the meaning of that miracle and a personal religion."

"For us, the message is an important one and it is a message addressed to the two of us as partners," Judy says excitedly as she settles against Paul, resting on his shoulder. "What we are together is the foundation of what we together will become. The black box is symbolic of our ability to escape our physical pasts, rise above the constraints of our environment, and achieve a higher level of existence."

"Tomorrow, we'll reach the site of the black box's first known appearance," Paul reminds her. "From that place, we will draw more strength, not only for our return from the jungle but for our years ahead."

Amid the sounds of the jungle at night, extreme weariness takes hold of Paul and Judy. They quickly fall asleep dreaming of their future with the black box.

By the time Jason and Taj land in South America, it is shortly after lunchtime on Friday. So far, everything is on schedule. As they exit the plane, they look around the tarmac to see if anyone might be there to meet them. They don't notice anyone tailing them from the airport. To throw off government surveillance, they did not use their real names. Instead, they list their reservations under T. and J. Shepherd. Apparently, this little ploy worked because they knew they were still under surveillance back in the States. Fortunately, opening their mail was no longer one of the government's surveillance methods. Even so, Taj and Jason covered their tracks just in case.

Taj and Jason slip into the airport terminal and inquire after directions to the staging area for the jungle hike. They learn that Ti Ching's old base camp is now a small village. With a four-wheel drive vehicle, they will be able to drive that far. From there, they will have to walk to wherever else they want to go. With this information in hand, they rent an old jeep-like vehicle, but decide against getting a driver or guide. Their understanding is that once they are on the right road, the road only goes one place.

As Taj and Jason walk away from the garage where they rented their vehicle, the garage owner shakes his head and wonders if they are conversionists like the couple who was here yesterday. If more of them keep coming, he notes, he may just need to buy more vehicles.

black box

Chapter 3. Capture

South American jungle; Saturday morning, the next day.

Once again, the jungle animals suffer a slight disturbance. Again a human stands in the clearing. As they look over this human, it moves toward the earthen mound that so recently changed. Chewing their breakfast, the animals wonder if this creature has something to do with the earthen mound and whatever might be inside.

The sun is just barely rising when he once again appears at the clearing with the earthen mound. He scans the jungle around him. Other than this clearing, the jungle looks much as it did the first time he came. He's not sure how long it will stay this way, but it is truly a beautiful spot.

Moving through the clearing, he sees, sadly so, that nature has been invaded. No doubt that is his fault. Around the earthen mound, he sees telltale signs that people were here. It is good that he didn't wait too long to come here after the box arrived. Conversionists were here before and are likely to return before long. Not a bad people, but they are not the people he wants or needs to see right now. It will be good to see Jason and Taj in a few hours. But first he must prepare.

Down on his knees, he digs into the earthen mound. After a few moments of digging, he feels the object. Fortunately, no one has been here in these few days. He reaches in and retrieves the black box.

He shakes his head. He knows better. This is sloppy. He needs to be more careful. The last thing he needs right now is for someone else to gain possession of the box.

For him to be able to move around freely, he's going to need a different passport, some other identification, and more U.S. currency. He scoops up a couple handfuls of dirt from the earthen mound. The dirt should be adequate building material.

After piling the handfuls of dirt next to the black box, he places his hands on the black box and activates it. He hesitates for a moment and listens to his surroundings. Nothing. He goes back to work.

Back away from the clearing, but within sight of it, Paul and Judy crouch low. Ever since the bearded stranger arrived, they have been observing him. It is a stroke of luck that they decided to stay in the jungle that night and did not awaken until after dawn. They were just about to hike into the clearing when the man appeared. One moment there was the empty clearing; the next moment, there was a man there. Both of them quickly and quietly ducked down out of sight.

As they watch him, they see him retrieve the black box from the earthen mound. Judy motions to Paul.

black box

Each of them wants to move closer.

The bearded stranger seems to be in no hurry. In fact, it looks like he is planning to use the box to convert something. He takes handfuls of dirt and places them near the box. But why would he want to convert dirt into dirt?

Judy moves. A dry branch cracks beneath her foot.

When the man looks up, they duck even further down, laying down on the fertile jungle soil. After a few moments, Paul inches his way back up for a better view of the man and the box. The man may have heard them, but he did not see them.

The man touches the box. Paul and Judy watch his hands carefully. Both see him place the five fingers of each hand to the two top front corners of the black box.

With that combination, the box activates. Not being close enough to see what keys and lights appear, they try to watch the positions of his fingers and the sequence he follows in touching the keys. He touches more keys than they expected. So intent on memorizing the man's touch patterns, Paul and Judy fail to notice at first the box's conversion of the handfuls of dirt.

Near the right side of the black box is not another pile of dirt, but money, some papers, and what looks like a passport. Judy, just barely able to see behind Paul, pulls herself closer for a better view and causes both of them to crash into the brush.

The man looks directly towards the noise, towards them. Across an expanse of about a hundred feet, they stare at each other uneasily.

This is sloppy, the shepherd thinks. Where did they come from? How long have they been there? If it is when he heard that sound, they may have been there the whole time.

The shepherd looks the couple up and down. They are probably as scared as they are excited. Odds are they are conversionists. They're sure not government types. He has to find a way for everybody to exit out of this situation so that no one gets hurt.

Acting decisively, the shepherd stands up and calls over to the man and woman. "Can I be of some assistance?"

Stepping out from behind the bush they landed in, Paul calls back nervously that they are Paul and Judy Cross, conversionists.

"This is sort of a pilgrimage to a holy place," Paul calls a little more quietly. "Last night we camped just a short way away. We arrived here just as you did."

"Are you the man who is often referred to as the black box's keeper?" Judy asks from behind Paul. "If you are, we are extremely honored to meet you! We have so many questions. So very many questions."

"I guess so. I do serve as the box's keeper on occasion," replies the shepherd, picking up the money and documents from the ground and slipping them into his pockets.

"You have always been a mystery to all of us," says Judy. "No one is sure if you really existed."

, "No, I am real and obviously, alive." The shepherd says lightly, trying to keep the conversation friendly. "It was not my intention to create any great mystery about myself, only to stay out of the public eye. Today, I am not doing particularly well, as you can see." He smiles at them.

"We're sorry for interrupting your work," Paul says, moving further out into the clearing, now only a several feet from the shepherd. "It is not our intention. We're here on a sort of pilgrimage, a sort of search for

black box

the 'holy grail' and a search for personal growth. We could never conceive that we would actually get to see the black box, let alone meet the person who is its keeper. You can't imagine what this means to us."

"Who are you? Where did you come from?" Judy says enthusiastically, pushing past Paul. The shepherd feels his body tense as she is now at arms' length. "Why are you here?"

"That's all right," the shepherd responds, adjusting to block their view of the box. "I have some sense of how you must feel right now. If you didn't have strong beliefs, you wouldn't have traveled thousands of miles and risked miles and miles of jungle. Then comes the big surprise. Here, I stand in front of you with the black box at my side."

"In all honesty, I am not in a position to answer all your questions." The shepherd pauses before he goes on.

"Who am I? Well, in most ways, I am a human being. I am no god, as humans generally think of a god. As for where did I come from, that's a little more difficult to answer. I ask that you let me beg off on that question. Why am I here? I watch over your development, with or without the box, as a people."

"As many conversionists believe, the box is but a tool. No more than that. What is important is not the box, but all of you as people. The box's role is not to *make* you a better person, but to open up the path for you making yourself a better person. If you want to reach a higher level of existence, it lies within your own self to do so. The box's lesson is that you can break with your past, remove the restraints of your environment and control your own destinies. That is the vital lesson of the black box."

"Will you show us how the box works?" Paul asks, excited. "We've only seen videos of the experiments." He glances back at Judy and she shakes her head, clearly overjoyed by the idea.

"Yes, it's terribly important to us," she says, breathless.

"If I show you an actual conversion, will that be enough? Can we leave it at that?" the shepherd asks, sighing.

"Yes, yes, yes," they reply quickly, too quickly.

The shepherd is doubtful. Still, a demonstration will buy him time and develop greater empathy with them.

"Let me show you something." He motions for them to stand close.

The shepherd picks up a broken branch and places it to the top and left of the box. Following the usual pattern, he asks Judy to help by placing her two hands on the box's top. The shepherd also places his hands there. He asks them both to step back again and takes them through the steps. The result is a branch to the top and right of the box. Paul and Judy say nothing for awhile. Video is one thing; actually seeing the black box work with their own eyes is something quite different.

When Paul and Judy do start talking, they do so behind their hands, speaking softly to each other. Apparently, there is some minor disagreement.

"Are we right in thinking we saw what we saw?" Judy asks when both of them look up. "We think we saw you convert handfuls of dirt into money and paper. Is that what really happened? We didn't know the box could do any such thing. We doubt that anyone, except you of course, knows that the box can perform a miracle like that."

"That's something I can't go into," the shepherd says casually, throwing a leaf out of the way that has fallen onto the corner of the black box. These two people want to know more about the box's capabilities than he

black box

wants anyone other than Taj and Jason to know.

"Listen, I want to be a lot more helpful, but I really can't at this time," the shepherd tells them. "I have my own mission to fulfill while I am here. I'm just trying to make sure it is accomplished. As you know, life seldom goes as planned, even if you have something like this black box. Obviously, this is a classic example of how plans go awry," he notes, trying to ease the tension.

He looks at Paul and Judy. His thoughts turn to the box that is on the ground and still activated. He's not sure there is enough time for him to program and execute an escape. But he doesn't have too many other choices.

"Judy. Paul," he begins. "I know you have a thousand questions and its right that you should. As I tried to tell you before, you know that I probably can't answer them. Maybe at a later time, more can be revealed. You are obviously nice people who care deeply about conversion and I wish I could give you more now."

"Please stay and talk to us!" Paul pleads. "We need to see and touch the black box. We need to go through this conversion. So many of us need to go through it."

The shepherd scans his surroundings. Knowingly or not, the two conversionists are moving to block the two natural exits from the clearing.

"We have come so far," says Judy, her voice stronger, more demanding now. "Don't make us leave without going through personal conversion. We used to believe that that box's actual conversion was not essential to us. But to be this close! We must be converted!" Judy grabs hold of the shepherd's arms, gripping them tightly.

"I just can't, for reasons I can't fully explain to the two of you," he says as he tries to pry Judy's grip from his arms. "I'm sorry. But I can't. And I'm afraid that I must go now."

"We've searched so long," Paul cautions. "You have in your hands the whole foundation for what we believe. Even if we could justify the loss to ourselves, how could we face our fellow conversionists? Please. Just come back with us."

The shepherd must escape now. Paul and Judy have the natural exits blocked. He doesn't want this to end violently, so the box must be his escape route.

Breaking out of Judy's grip, the shepherd drops to the ground and presses the black box's keys. Behind him, Paul and Judy scream. He can feel them jump on him, tearing at his arms and back to try to get to the black box.

Seeing a large stone nearby, Paul picks it up. Heaving it high above his head, he brings it down on the shepherd's body.

He strikes him once, hard.

Seeing the shepherd lying there unconscious and badly bleeding, they are frightened. Both lean over the shepherd to try tof

There is no way that they will be able to carry him out of here in time to save him. No way can they get out and back with help in time.

Paul and Judy look at each other, sweat dripping down their faces.

"What have we done?" Paul asks.

They look at the shepherd. They look at the black box, now gone dormant.

A combination of fear and zeal temporarily replaces whatever rationality and human concern remains in the two of them. They grab the black box, pick up their camping gear, and run away.

They both know what they are doing is absolutely wrong, but they cannot stop. They do not stop.

black box

Chapter 4. Alive

South American jungle; minutes later that day.

"Stupid, stupid, stupid," is what the shepherd repeats to himself as he tries to keep conscious. "How did I let this happen? So much rides on my keeping this whole journey from getting too far off track. And here I go and get caught by an 'accident.' Sometimes, I wish I were the 'god' many think I am. No, I'm no god. I am stupid and dying."

He must stay conscious. His only hope is to hold on long enough for Taj and Jason to get to him.

If only he can get himself to move, there is the second box, the emergency box that gives him the ability to move at will, to even restore an unhealthy body.

But what good does it do if he can't get to it? The lower part of his body isn't responding. What he needs is the right someone to find him. He needs Taj and Jason and he needs them quickly. None of his fellow shepherds knew where he is.

Shortly after noon, Taj and Jason enter the clearing. As they look across the clearing, they see someone lying on the ground. Quickly, they run toward the clearing's center. In the distance, they see what looks like the shepherd lying on the ground.

"Oh no!" cries Jason. "That's blood!"

As Taj and Jason run to him, they are stunned by what they see. There is a deep wound on the back of his head covered with blood.

Taj makes it to the shepherd's side first and checks for a pulse. There is one, albeit a faint one.

"Jason, give me your water bottle and a long piece of cloth," Taj directs. "Let's try to get his wound cleansed and the bleeding stopped."

As Jason tears his extra t-shirt into strips, he notices for the first time that to one side of the shepherd's body there is a newly excavated earthen mound. Whatever was there is now gone. He suspects it was the original missing black box.

He hears Taj trying to talk the shepherd into consciousness, telling him that they're both there and that he will be all right.

"Jason, I think he's semi-conscious," Taj tells him quietly. "Let's keep trying to wake him. I suspect that he has a severe concussion at minimum, more likely, much worse. A large portion of his skull is crushed and I think there is serious brain damage. There is no movement in his lower body, not even the slightest twitch."

They work on him for some time. His periods of semi-consciousness increase in frequency. He tries to say something to them, something about a second box. They think they hear him say something about a tree with a rectangle on it.

Noticing that Jason keeps looking around the clearing, Taj suggests that he go check out what's there.

black box

If there is a second box, maybe there is some way they could use it to save the shepherd. They both know that they'll never be able to carry him out of the jungle without killing him.

Jason starts at the edge of the clearing and works his way around it. In his first couple of rounds, there is no sign of a tree with a rectangle on it. But on his third trip around, he sees a large old tree. It is hidden in a small grove of trees that had apparently been there for a long time. On the oldest tree is a rectangle. Jason starts checking around the roots. Around the backside of the tree, an area between two large roots is filled with dirt. With his knife, Jason starts clearing away the dirt. After clearing about six inches of dirt, his knife strikes a solid, dark object. Feverishly, he clears away enough dirt to reveal what appears to be a second black box.

As he pulls it from among the tree roots, he shouts to Taj, "I found it! I found a black box!"

"Hurry back!" she shouts. "I think he may be coming around."

Chapter 5. Restore

South American jungle; moments later.

"Who's there?"
The shepherd can't yet seem to focus his eyes on anything.
Taj gives Jason a look. He doesn't recognize them. "It's us, Taj and Jason," Taj assures him, unscrewing the top of her canteen and bringing it down to his mouth. "Here, drink up. And don't move too much. I'm keeping pressure on your wound."
The shepherd drinks a little with Taj's help, "I don't know how long I've been lying here, but it seems like a lifetime," he says weakly.
"If I can communicate to you about the second black box, I might have a chance," the shepherd murmurs.
"Relax for a few moments," Jason tells him, afraid the shepherd will slip into unconsciousness yet again. "We're here now and we're ready to do whatever we can to help you."
The shepherd's head jolts, racked by pain.

black box

Kneeling next to him, Taj leans down to speak to the shepherd again, "You must be in great pain, but we don't know what to do. Can you tell us what to do to help?

"Yes," he says. "I hear you. But it's hard to function."

"I'm having trouble moving my legs." The shepherd pauses for a second. "Am I paralyzed?"

Jason sighs, not relishing having to be the one to give the shepherd the news. "Since we've been here, we've seen no sign of movement below your neck. There's no way for us to tell how complete the paralysis is or how severe is the injury to your head. But it is bad. Very bad. It is amazing that you're still alive, let alone speaking to us."

"You've lost a tremendous amount of blood," cautions Taj. "More than you realize. We slowed down the bleeding, but we can't completely stop it. Unless we do something very quickly, I don't see how you will survive."

"Can the black box help in any way?" Jason asks. "I found it."

We can't move you; the distance is too great."

"Is there some way to use the black box that we don't know about? Can the box repair the injury somehow?"

Taj and Jason listen closely for a reply. Unless the box performs another miracle, the shepherd will die shortly.

The shepherd slowly opens his eyes. They can barely hear his response, but they both know it's a yes.

Though his voice is weak from the pain and blood loss, the shepherd's resolve to survive is strong.

"Lift my head up a little higher so I can see it and the two of you," the shepherd requests. "Very carefully, please."

"Is that okay?" Jason asks as he positions the shepherd's head.

"Yes." the shepherd replies weakly and gratefully. "Now listen to me and listen carefully." He takes a breath and speaks slowly, pausing often to let a wave of pain pass.

"The black box has more powers than those of which you are aware. Activating these powers requires different steps to activate the box and different steps to instruct the box."

"There is point in the process when my body will be frozen and I no longer can participate. I rely on the two of you to follow through at that point as I will have instructed you."

"Once the process begins, you will be on your own. Given how weak I am, I'm not sure how much time we have or whether or not we'll have a second chance if we fail," he tells them. "Activating the box for this process is a bit different than your experience and goes like this. Only two hands are needed. You can both participate in activating the box or just one of you can do it."

"We'll do it together," Taj says for both of them..

"Okay, then. I want the two of you to place five fingers on each of the top, front two corners of the box. Your thumb and smallest finger should touch the box's front and side panels. Your middle finger should touch the top. Your other two fingers should touch the box's top two edges. Try it."

Taj and Jason position the box and themselves for the activation process. The first two tries produce no result. Since the box has no features, there is a problem determining which surfaces are the top and bottom and

black box

the front and back. On the third try, the box activates.

"Excellent," says the shepherd. He smiles weakly. "Welcome to the black box's level two."

"Now," indicates the shepherd, "I'll give you the shorthand route. There are other ways, but this is fastest."

"Here's what you need to do. Press the 'record' key after you activate the box using the 'level two' activation method. Then, again as before, press the 'm to e' key followed by the 'e to m' key. The next step is new."

"Press the 'modify' key. This tells the box that you want something other than straight duplication."

"For a restoration, press the 'restore' key next. When the 'verify' key lights, press it. Then, the 'delete' key will light. Press it as well."

"Please. Move quickly." The shepherd entreats them as he feels himself slipping out of consciousness. "We don't have much time."

"Taj!" Jason shouts, snapping them both back to attention. "We need to concentrate. We've got to try to save him. We don't know if the box can bring him back if he is dead."

They activate the box to "level two." Just as instructed, they proceed through the steps. At each point, they check with each other before proceeding. They want to be sure the steps are correct. As they press the 'e to m' key, a second, apparently identical shepherd appears to the right of the black box.

Jason and Taj feel a sense of panic. In front of them are two shepherds, both gravely injured. Both are possibly dead by now. Knowing that time is working against them, they quickly move on. The 'modify' key is pressed. Nothing changes. The 'restore' key is then pressed.

In moments, a transformation takes place. The second shepherd, also severely injured, disappears. A few moments later, in his place appears an altered second shepherd. This one has no signs of injury. This one look very much like the shepherd they met nearly a year ago. But is he alive? He is still frozen in place by the box. They have no way of knowing.

"Jason," Taj says softly, "Press the 'verify and then 'delete' key now. This is the only chance we will have."

"Yes," Jason says. He pushes the keys.

They wait for some sign of life in the shepherd. Then they see it, a small movement of his boot.

"Hey you two, want to greet me?" comes his strong voice.

Elated, Jason and Taj embrace the shepherd. He embraces them back.

"I'm curious about one thing," Taj says later, hesitating as she speaks.

"Just one thing!" Jason laughs. "How about a whole boatload of things?"

"Yes, I suspect your 'curiosity' is about to step forward and want to know more." The shepherd smiles and gestures for them to gather around the box.

"Today, you saw some of what can be done at 'level two.'"

"When you pressed the 'modify' key after the 'e to m' key, you told the box you wanted to change the second object. The question is how. In this case, you indicated you wanted to 'restore' the original object. That implied that the original object in front of the box was somehow critically different from the original object. In my situation, the head injury was the critical difference."

"Restore can only work if the box has, in its memory, a personal code that guides the restoration process. This particular box always has my personal code

black box

as per my instruction. The original black box also has my personal code. It will also have my code if my 'person' went through the standard conversion process at an earlier time."

"Restoration' is a safety device to deal with situations just like today. Because of the roles you are about to take on, we need to give both boxes your personal codes. That way you will be protected as well."

"Were you dead?" Taj asks. "For a few minutes, it seemed like you were gone."

"Honestly," the shepherd replies. "I don't know. The box restores even in the case of death." He sighs and looks off into the jungle. "I myself have serious questions about what restoration does after one dies, especially after the body has fully decomposed. Fortunately, today's event seems to have skirted that."

"What about the other keys and lights?" Taj says. "What do they do?"

"What kind of 'stuff' did you see lit?" the shepherd asks. He wants to test their memory.

"As I remember, there was a keyboard and a display of some type located in the front and right portion of the black box's top surface," Jason responds, sketching the display in the air.

"What you saw is a keyboard and corresponding display that controls the modification process," the shepherd replies. "If you want to modify an object other than straight restoration, use the keyboard."

"With it you can enter a personal code. The black box uses this to guide any aspect of modification. If you want to change an object, you alter the object's personal code. If you want to modify it so drastically as to be a different object, you enter the personal code of that different object."

"But listen," he says. "It's late and we will lose sunlight shortly. Let's hike out of here quickly as we can.

I'll tell you more as we walk."

As they make their way through the jungle, Taj and Jason throw question after question the shepherd's way. In spite of their probing, he says he will not go beyond revealing more of the 'level two' capabilities, implying that there is more to 'level two' than revealed so far.

"When we received your letter, we were so excited," Jason tells him. "Our first experiments with the box opened up a whole new part of our lives. For a while, we weren't sure we would see you or the black box ever again. We were frustrated with waiting and feeling left out."

"Our aspirations are always pretty high, but this is a whole other level!" Taj interrupts, as impatient as ever. "The black box's capabilities imply that virtually anything is possible. We now believe that we, even though not extraordinary, can accomplish extraordinary things."

"At first, we thought it all tied back to the black box," Jason explains. "Our sense was that we were incapable without the box. That it was necessary. Then we realized that was foolish. Depending upon the box completely is to deny that humans can make something as powerful as the black box in the first place. Once we accepted that the black box itself is probably a human creation, we looked more for the potential we have within our selves."

"We know the government still watches our financial transactions," Jason continues. "Their mistake. We created alternate identities. Since then, every spare minute has gone into learning. We've studied philosophy and religion so we can better understand the thinking

black box

behind conversionist and anticonversionist movements and studied political science since government plays a serious role in this. And last, we've spent time learning applied science, too, trying to better understand the black box's technology."

"You must track down the missing original black box," the shepherd tells them. "As for the two conversionists who attacked me, I want no retribution. Only the box's recovery is important."

"So, what's the plan?" Jason asks.

"We're ready for this," Taj adds.

The shepherd nods. He thinks they're ready as well. He stops them for a moment so they can catch their breath and listen closely to his plan.

"In the first stage of the plan, I will take the second black box and meet you back in the U.S.," he says. "Return as if nothing has happened. Put your affairs in order. This will be the last time your life will have any semblance of normalcy."

Chapter 6. Modify

National office of the conversionists, Washington, D.C.;
three days later
Private laboratory, Washington, D.C.; two days later.

Christopher dreaded this late night meeting in his office. But he drowns in excitement as well. Tonight, he is to receive the black box itself, the source of his uncontrollable excitement. But how did they get it? From this unanswered question flows dread.

The phone rings. It's the security guard. There are two people to see him. Is it okay to send them up? Yes, he tells the guard: they are expected.

A few minutes later, there is a knock on the door to his outer office. He walks out and opens the door. In the doorway stand Paul and Judy Cross, the two conversionists who called earlier that day. One of them carries a package. He welcomes them and walks them back into his office.

"Please make yourselves comfortable," Christopher says. "Would you like some water or something else to drink?"

They thank him, but decline his offer.

Christopher sees that Paul and Judy are nervous.

black box

They fidget in Christopher's guest chairs and look everywhere but directly at him.

"Take your time and tell me the story from the beginning," Christopher says, sitting down casually, hoping that his calm demeanor will allow them to relax a little. "Tell it to me carefully as you know I have some concerns. You don't need to hurry."

"Our last name is Cross," Paul starts. "I'm Paul and this is my wife, Judy. You obviously don't know us, but we have been conversionists from the beginning of the movement. It has become a dominant force in our lives. We feel so strongly that we took it upon ourselves to make a pilgrimage to the South American jungle where the black box was first found."

"We didn't expect to find anything," Judy says when Paul pauses and glances at her, as if she could explain better. "We were only looking for inspiration. We thought the environment would help develop our philosophy."

"But there it was, the black box." Paul looks down at his hands. "And not only the black box, but also the box's keeper. We were," Paul stops, searching for the right words, clearing his throat, "excited beyond belief."

Together Paul and Judy patch together the story of what happened that day. When they get to the keeper's making of currency and paper, Christopher stops them.

"Are you absolutely sure you saw him convert plain dirt into money?" Christopher asks. He's skeptical. "No one ever saw the black box do anything but convert an object into its duplicate."

They assure him that was exactly what they saw.

As they near the part about striking the keeper with the stone, they talk faster, not knowing how Christopher will respond.

When they tell him, he is outraged.

"How in the name of conversionism could you

strike the man who is the keeper of the box?" Christopher shouts. "Other than Sandy, this man is as close as we have to a saint."

"I can't believe this." Christopher stands up. He angrily paces the length of his office.

"Okay. Okay," he calms himself. "Where is he now? Can I talk to him?"

"We were so upset," Judy starts, tears rolling from her eyes. "We had to leave him there. I'm pretty sure he's probably dead by now."

"You're pretty sure he is dead?" Christopher yells. "You mean you don't know? Did you try to help him? Did you get him out of the jungle and to medical care?"

"Dead! You mean you killed him and left him in the jungle. What kind of conversionists are you?" Christopher slams his fist into the back of his desk chair. "We don't believe in killing people! We worked hard when the box was lost to assure the world that our movement was nonviolent. Ours is a peaceful movement."

"Yet here in one brief moment of panic, you have undone all that."

"We panicked!" Paul cries, pleading for some understanding. "It was dumb. It was immoral. But we panicked. The prospect of losing the black box after coming so far and being so close made us lose control. After that, there was nothing we could do to save him."

"Unacceptable." Christopher knows that his tone is menacing, but he doesn't care. "You didn't try to save him. As conversionists, you had an obligation. As people, you had that obligation. I might even forgive your initial running away, but you didn't go back."

Christopher paces around the room again for a few minutes, trying to shake out some of his rage.

"You have the black box?" He asks, his rage

black box

barely in check.

Sheepishly, they nod and hand him the package. Christopher takes it out of their hands and slowly unwraps the package. He puts the black box down on his desk. He sits down in his chair and looks at it. As always, the box says nothing and gives no absolution.

"Did you do as I asked over the telephone and write down the process you saw used on the box?" Christopher asks impatiently.

They have and hand him their notes.

"Stay in Washington through the weekend," he tells them. "Give me a phone number where I can reach you over the next couple of days. I need to think this through. You two are in deep trouble and because of that, you have put the rest of us in deep trouble."

"In the meantime, I'll hold onto the box. I have a safe here where it will be very secure. Once I figure out what we need to do next, I'll call you and we'll meet again," he says, gesturing savagely towards the door. "Leave now!"

After they leave, Christopher leans back in his chair and stares at the black box. He can't believe this happened. The box's return should be a joyous occasion. Instead, it is a tragedy, the tragic death of a human being. Not just any human being, but the box's keeper.

He can already feel mighty forces tearing at him over what he should do next. The nature of conversionism demands a full accounting of what happened. But that will surely result in their losing the black box to who knows whom. How can he be part of giving away the black box, the very basis of conversionism?

To give it back likely means returning it to the government. Except for some military and research scientists, the government doesn't want the black box to exist at all. There was little true remorse when it was lost the first time. There will be little more this time when it is 'lost' a second time.

How could he return it? He doesn't even know where to return it. The government is not the owner. Neither is the Smithsonian. Of course, neither are the conversionists the real owner. The only real owner is dead now.

Could he keep it a secret? He doesn't see how. Paul and Judy are scared, but they are even more enthralled with their discovery. No way will he able to keep them from talking.

In many ways, he's trapped. He begins to have more empathy for Paul and Judy. Sure, this is different. He's not going to accidentally kill somebody. He's also not going to do the honorable thing and return the box.

He slumps down in his chair despondently. Conversionism's future as a movement depends on these decisions. The future of what conversionism seeks, personal growth, will feel the impact of his decisions. The future of the black box itself is now in his hands.

He notifies key conversionist leaders about a meeting at a private laboratory that they used for black-box related research. While not telling them what this is all about, he stresses that it is of the highest importance. The meeting is set for Monday morning at nine o'clock.

Christopher calls Paul and Judy and invites them to the meeting as well. He offers more compassion this time, stressing that he better understands what was going through their minds that day in the jungle. In preparation for the meeting, he lays out stringent rules for their involvement. They are more than happy to agree to the rules.

black box

After opening the meeting, Christopher introduces Paul and Judy. In his own way, he tells the story of what happened in the jungle. As he watches the people in the room, he feels the anticipation rising. People are scanning the room. They look for any sign of a black rectangular solid. Then he makes his recommendation.

"What to do with the black box is not a decision with a clear right or wrong answer. If we tell all, we will lose the black box and the movement itself will be in disgrace. If we don't, the box may still be taken away at some point and disgrace may still fall on the movement."

"For now, the box must be protected at all costs. It is our equivalent of the 'holy grail'. No one else will protect the box."

"There is another piece of information that further muddies the situation. On Saturday, I contacted a couple of people I worked with in the past. They live in the jungle village nearest to the black box's original sighting. At my request, they went to the site on Sunday to see what they could find. What they found was close to nothing. There was no sign of the box's keeper. There were signs of dried blood on a large stone. There were a few forgotten U.S coins under the stone."

"Upon returning to the village, they did further checking. Early Saturday morning, the same day that the incident occurred with Paul and Judy, another man and woman also went out to the clearing. Close to darkness, they returned about the same time that another man, with a beard, entered the village. When asked about the bearded man, the villagers indicated nothing remarkable. The bearded man appeared healthy and walked briskly past them. No one else saw that man. On the other hand, the couple was seen leaving by jeep and has since returned to the United States."

"What does this mean? It means that the box's keeper may not be dead. There is no clear evidence we can find other than the story from our two conversionists and the sketchy reports from the village. It also means that there may be other people involved in all this. We're still trying to find out who the couple is and what might be their interest. Remember, there are stories about a couple being involved the first time the box appeared. They may or may not be the same people. If they are, they may know more about the box and its keeper."

Murmurs move around the room as the conversionist leadership tries to make sense of all this.

"My recommendation, not without reservation, is that we keep the box and keep this whole episode a secret for as long as we can," Christopher continues. "When it becomes known, we'll proceed with damage control. I don't believe we can come out any worse. Besides, we will possess the box and have the opportunity to learn more about it."

"In fact, that's my other recommendation. I recommend we proceed immediately to experiment with the box. Who knows how long we will be able to retain it. We should learn as much from it as we possibly can."

Christopher watches the many conversations going on around the room, but he already knows their eventual decision. Who among them is going to vote to return the box to the government? No one.

The recommendations are put into the form of a motion, seconded, and passed within a few minutes. The vote is unanimous.

"We will now adjourn to the main lab. The black box awaits us," Christopher announces.

The room immediately empties as the conversionists move to the main lab. Already there are five conversionist scientists. As the conversionist leaders

black box

arrive they see a familiar image, a brightly lit table with a black object on it. The room is quiet. Before them in reality, not on video, is the black box, the symbol of conversionism.

Christopher and the conversionist scientists take center stage.

Following the notes prepared by the two conversionists, they activate the box just as Jason and Taj did. But after activating the box, the conversionists are stuck. While those who had captured the box knew how to reveal the box's "level two," including the "modify" key, the "restore" key, the keyboard and its display, they have no idea how to use "level two." They were only close enough to see the keeper use the keyboard and see the result.

Initially, they experiment with a combination of keys, but nothing works quite right. They do not understand the "restore" function so they have no way of knowing what to do and when. The "modify" function is even more confusing.

With strong urging from his fellow conversionists, Christopher has the scientists return to the basic conversion process. Already, the early indications of a queue are evident. People are beginning to a form a line in anticipation of being converted. It reminds him of lines formed for communion or mass baptism.

"We're here. The black box is here." Christopher says to the conversionists. "We all know for what each of us has waited so long. Is there risk involved? We believe not, as evidenced by the experience of Sandy. "

"Patience. Everyone here will have the opportunity to go through conversion. You already formed a sort of queue. I suggest we use that. I will be the last. After we are all done, the scientists will return to their work."

With that, the conversions begin. Each person is put through the basic conversion process just as was Sandy a year before. Every conversion is closely monitored. There are no physical signs of change.

But Christopher sees change in their voices and faces. He senses re-birth and renewal. He perceives the glow of people having gone through a true religious or mystical experience. He senses that their spirits have been uplifted.

As promised, Christopher is the last to go through conversion. He tries to critically assess his own changes, but with little success. After all this time and all this build-up, he cannot tell what is "real" or what is "purely psychological" or what is both. He is inclined to believe that changes are only facilitated by the black box. Real changes had to be made by the people themselves.

The conversions take many hours. By the time they are done, it is late afternoon.

Slowly, everyone except Christopher and the scientists drifts out of the lab. Everything vitally important to the conversionist leaders was accomplished today. What remains is diligent science. The scientists are tired as well. Christopher suggests they go home, get a good night's sleep, and start again tomorrow morning. They agree. Under watchful eyes, the black box is locked away in a large, walk-in safe. Several guards are posted and electronic surveillance is initiated.

Christopher leaves, also in need of a good night's sleep. But it will not be restful. His curiosity about the "modify" function is piqued. In his pocket, he fingers the coins his South American contacts found and air-expressed to him. These coins came from dirt, he thinks.

But the important questions are about the box's keeper. How did a man, supposedly dead, walk into a

black box

village a few hours later as healthy as can be? Was it the black box that saved him? But it wasn't this one apparently. Is there another black box? Modification as well as conversion?

As promised, the modification experiments begin the next morning.

In opening the session, Christopher makes it clear that this is to be a slow and deliberate process. Modification is a whole new area which none of them knew anything about.

There is some fear. Conversion is predictable and has circumscribed results, as best they can measure. Modification opens a whole new realm of possibilities with much greater risk of doing harm.

They try initially to use the "modify" and "restore" keys, but never get anything to work with that combination. They miss something. Since they don't use objects that went through conversion, there is nothing in the box's memory to use for restoration. In one run, they happen to use an object that did go through conversion. But because they made no modifications and the object itself had not changed, the restoration process produced the identical object. There were no wounds or cuts or any other changes to tell the scientists that, in fact, restoration actually occurred.

Not being able to "see" any successes, they abandon the "restore" key and turn their attention to the keyboard and screen.

Here they begin to get changes, but with no predictability. In most cases, nothing happens. What appears to be going on is that when the black box does not recognize a valid code, it does nothing at all. Trying different combinations of letters and numbers, the codes appear to be of two types.

One set of codes, always beginning with the number one, makes modifications in the original object, but the object stays essentially the same. At one point, they get a second object that is missing a small piece as compared to the original object. But that isn't quite right either. The mass of the two objects is identical. Apparently, the box just rearranges the mass and puts the missing piece, or at least its mass, somewhere else in the object.

At another point, they enter very complex codes. Most produce no concrete results. The box just rejects the code and does nothing. However, on one occasion, a cube of stone becomes an unidentifiable chunk. Several other unidentifiable masses are produced, but nothing they can use as the basis for producing something identifiable. While not learning a lot, they do learn that this result occurs when they start their complex codes with the number zero. They learn the second object always has the same mass as the first. Though only a suspicion, there are probably billions of codes representing all the objects that exist in the universe.

After several days of experiments, they put aside the "0" code method that makes wholly different objects and focus on the "1" code method that makes smaller changes. This strategy appears safer and potentially more controllable. Still, they need to be careful in the days ahead.

Chapter 7. Miscode

Private laboratory, Washington, D.C.; several days later.

As Christopher watches his scientists work on the black box experiments, he is troubled.

Right now his people experiment with the "1" code. Not much progress is made but they see a hint of positive results. Still, any potentially meaningful results, from the perspective of conversionists, appear far away or will occur only by accident. Whoever designed this black box made it incredibly complex. They will continue this line of experimentation for about another week; then, if there is no major progress, he will probably pull the plug, at least for a while. Some of his scientists will not be at all happy about that prospect. They really believe this box can be programmed to expand human capability.

But there are other considerations, other demands for the black box. When the conversionists first obtained the box, its leaders went through conversion. That's fine. Most of his fellow conversionists remain caught up in what they went through or, at least, what they believe they went through. After all, conversion is why his people and he wanted the black box in the first place. Now, the experiments interfere with that. The black box's conversion process is not accessible to rank and file conversionists. Only the leadership and these scientists experienced conversion.

Again, he finds himself on the horns of a dilemma. He's committed to making the black box accessible to all who want conversion, but he has yet to come up with a strategy for how to do so without a stampede of sorts. By the conversionist leadership's best estimates, millions of people worldwide will want conversion immediately. Access will need to be rationed. One potential strategy is setting up a lottery to decide who gets access when. But the box's conversion process is not very quick. They will only be able to average about one person every five minutes. At that rate and running twenty-four hours a day, it will take nearly a year to convert a hundred thousand people. If a million or more want conversion, it will take 10 years.

But the problem is even larger. He's observed those who went through conversion and he's noticed a range of responses. For several, there is little significant measurable change. Several seem to take a real step forward and are quite fascinating to watch. Others appear to make no progress and may even regress. He worries about these people and that this regression might result from conversion not living up to their high expectations. These are people who expect real miracles and have trouble finding miracles in themselves

A few conversionists think it does nothing at all. For that part of our conversionist movement, this is no surprise and not an issue.

Is he ready to set up a process for millions of people worldwide given what we know so far? But can he deny them access? Little, if any, harm appears to

black box

occur. On the other hand, maybe a little good occurs.

As he prepares to leave, Christopher walks over to Dr. Kulp, lead scientist on the project.

"Listen, I'm going out of town for a couple of days to settle down the West Coast. They're maybe too excited about our new discovery. I want them to get back on track," Christopher explains to the lead scientist. "When I get back, we will almost assuredly shift to making conversion available to our fellow conversionists. That doesn't mean research completely stops, but it will be slowed down for awhile. If we were to start up large scale conversions, the black box will be tied up for large portions of time."

This is not good news for Dr. Kulp. Though a conversionist, Dr. Kulp is also a scientist. She's already made it clear that experimentation should last longer. Conversionists must determine how to control the modification aspects of conversion.

"I want you to be extremely careful," Christopher cautions. "There's great temptation to take short cuts, but let me be very clear. I will not tolerate them. Too much is at stake. Too much risk remains. Somewhere down the road, we'll be able to control 'modification' and be able to direct the results that each of us wants. Again, that's later. You're authorized for more animal and inanimate object experiments, but nothing that puts our people at risk."

Christopher makes sure to look directly at Dr. Kulp as he tells her this. He wants to be sure that she understands that he's serious about the restrictions he's laid out for her.

Dr. Kulp agrees, but not with as much conviction as Christopher would like. Still, he's not that worried. The research team is not making much progress and it is unlikely that they will accomplish much while he is gone.

Sam Blanc helps the scientists with the black box experiments. In turn, they help him achieve a greater sense of self-worth. For most of his life, he was an aggressive and a sometimes violent person. As a child, his parents, both now dead, abused him. His aggression helped him survive that experience as well as the life that followed. He has already served two prison terms for assault. He is trying to change but believes he will fail. More violent behavior will send him back to jail or kill him.

In conversionism, he finds people who believe that you can rise above the human failings. Christopher is a particular source of inspiration. After being paroled from a prison term for assault, Sam participated in a conversionist rally and became a conversionist volunteer. Over the course of this, he met Christopher.

Sam was honest from the beginning about who he is and what he seeks, that is, a way to break free from all the forces that feed his aggressive nature. As a first step, Christopher gave Sam a job in their lab. Stability in his life and considerate people around him has helped, but he still gets into trouble periodically.

A few days earlier, Sam went through the basic conversion process. While he feels better, it hasn't solved his problem. Just last night, he went to a new bar and got into a fight with someone he didn't know. He broke the person's nose. Sam slipped out a side door before anyone stopped him and before the police arrived. No, basic conversion is not enough. He needs something more.

Almost immediately after Christopher leaves the lab, Dr. Kulp lays out the situation, "We only have a few days before we will lose much of our access to the black

black box

box."

"This is unacceptable!" one of the other scientists shouts. "You have to do something!"

"Fair enough," Dr. Kulp sighs. "But I challenge you to make the best use of these next few days. Maybe we will get lucky. We must push harder for concrete and usable results. If we get them, maybe I can convince Christopher to give us more time."

"We'll charge ahead, but we have to be careful," she warns all of them. "Only inanimate object and animal experiments. No major mistakes."

They nod, thinking more of her admonition to push hard than her warning. At they get to work, their pace quickens and the range of experimentation widens.

They focus on experimentation with the "1" code. As they determined early, this set of codes starts with the original object and then makes limited modifications to it during the conversion process. With "1" codes, the black box recognizes the object to the left and front of it, envelops it in the beam, and can then modify the original object. From what the researchers understand, the box "recognizes" what type of object it is, e.g., a living organism. The box actually goes further to recognize the object all the way to it being a unique individual, like a specific individual person. The black box's memory holds that recognition, as well as the object's personal code, during the conversion process.

Within this code, they believe there are groupings of codes. For example, there are likely to be groups of codes that relate to certain parts and characteristics of objects. This explains how their one experiment moved a piece of the object to somewhere else in the object. Also, it is consistent with another experiment, in this case with the "0" codes, that made a near totally different object. If they understand and control this code, they can change objects in a more predictable way.

For their next rounds of experiments, they decide to focus on animals. In animals, they are that much closer to a human model, their ultimate goal. The one restriction is to not harm the animals.

More and more, they jump around with the number codes they use. All begin with the number "1," but vary widely after that. Every so often, they see some recognizable changes in the objects, but nothing predictable or useful.

As the days pass, they make almost no progress. When Friday arrives, they all know they are near the end of their experimentation. Christopher will return that afternoon and will phase down their research effort.

In frustration, one scientist enters "1" plus all nines after that. Something happens. The animal, a fairly aggressive white rat, behaves differently, but they can't be sure in what way. The white rat still functions as an animal, but it isn't as "wild;" it seems calm and affectionate. The research team is enthusiastic. At last, they have a positive result.

Dr. Kulp, realizing that their time is almost up, asks one of the researchers to go get one of the more aggressive animals. The researcher returns with a monkey that has been causing problems for them. The monkey is aggressive and violent, apparently due to former abuse by the staff at a small private zoo.

As before with animals that have been hard to handle, they place the monkey in a large cage. Following the same procedure as with the white rat, the research team uses the "1" code followed by all nines. Then there is the duplicate monkey, but without any of the aggressive behavior of the original. When approached and touched by one of the researchers, the monkey responds in much the same way that a baby monkey responds to its mother, sweetly clinging to the researcher. They have success.

black box

All along, they hoped to find some way to have conversion directly and measurably "improve" creatures. Their hope is to rid the creatures, and ultimately humans, of negative characteristics. The black box "cleansed" the animal, ridding it of its aggression.

But would this breakthrough be enough? Would Christopher allow the experiments to continue for more time? Dr. Kulp is doubtful. She sees how many conversionist leaders show a distinct lack of interest in any thing beyond basic conversion. Even now, they might see these new results as little more than what humans already accomplish in basic conversion. Why risk anything further, they will challenge.

"I don't think we have enough to change the course," she says to her team. "This looks promising, but I don't think it's enough for Christopher and the leadership. Without being able to show that this goes beyond basic conversion, Christopher will have no choice."

Off from the side of the room where he has been watching the latest experiment, Sam Blanc interrupts Dr. Kulp. "Suppose we could show that this '1' code process goes significantly and positively beyond basic conversion?"

"Then, maybe we could convince them to give us more time," she responds cautiously. "But there's no way. The animals don't give us a definitive result."

"What if a human were to go through this process?" Sam asks. "What if a human with a history of aggression and, in fact, still plagued with anger, were to go through the process and be 'improved? Would that change their minds?"

"No way can we do that," Dr. Kulp crosses her arms. "Christopher was adamant. We don't have the authority to do human experimentation. Even if we did, we're still not really sure what happens here."

"Listen, Dr. Kulp," Sam says. "What I see happened here is special. I went through the basic conversion and I know my rage is still with me. There's a man nursing a broken nose this morning who can tell you that. I'm not trying to take anything away from basic conversion, but it didn't do what I needed it to."

Sam clears his throat. "I have no family. I'm all alone, except for all of you. I'm asking for your help. If I don't find an effective treatment, I'm going to be back in prison for hurting someone I don't want to really hurt."

"Let me go through the process. Some time ago, a woman named Sandy made her own choice, volunteered for the first experiment with the black box, and a whole positive world opened up. With me, there's little to be lost."

Dr. Kulp uncrosses her arms. She looks around the silent room.

They are scared by the prospect of putting a human being through this process. Sam is probably their only chance and he is as close to an ideal candidate as they could have found.

"Sam, are you absolutely sure that you want to do this?" she asks, placing her hands on Sam's shoulders. She wants him to do this, but she wants him to be sure. "We can't promise anything. You may even die in the process."

"I understand the risk," Sam snaps back. "I have nothing to lose. But I do have an awful lot to gain, if we are successful. Can we proceed? Now? I'm begging you."

Dr. Kulp looks at her fellow scientists and asks for their sentiments. To a person, they want to proceed.

"Then proceed we will," she says.

Just as with the monkey before him, they place

black box

Sam to the front and left of the box and initiate the modification process. After pressing the "modify" key, they entered the code "1" followed by all nines. They look at Sam and see no visible change. They press "verify" and "delete." At this point, the original Sam disappears, leaving only the second Sam. Sam moves, just barely. It is clear that he is alive. But is he okay?

"Sam," Dr. Kulp asks. "Can you hear me? Can you understand me?"

Off in another room where the animals are kept, the animal keeper returns from the scientists' deliberations. He examines the monkey. Something is not right with the monkey. Not only is the wildness gone, but something else is missing as well. The keeper knows that this was an abused animal and that its aggressive behavior was probably a learned behavior. Then the keeper recognizes what he is seeing. The monkey has lost more than just his aggressive behavior.

Dr. Kulp observes Sam's face. A very different expression is on his face than just a few minutes ago. He responds to her voice, but more as a baby responding to a sound or movement than as an adult responding to another adult's voice. She reaches over and shakes him gently.

Sam cries, but it's not the kind with tears. No. It's an infant's cry.

"Sam, can you speak?" Dr. Kulp asks. There is no real response.

Over the next few minutes, the more Dr. Kulp watches the more it is clear what happened. What she sees is an adult body with a baby's mind. All the behavior is that of a newborn baby just beginning to discover the world around it. The sounds are all pre-language. The understanding is pre-learning. The movements are pre-development. There is no sign of the adult named Sam Blanc.

Terror is on the researchers' faces.

"Apparently, the code '1' and all nines is targeted at cognitive and memory functions of the brain," Dr. Kulp explains to her team as her anger begins to mount. "By our actions, the black box completely wiped clean all the learning, good and bad, that Sam ever had. All that he has is his autonomic response system and his basic bodily functions. The mind is clear for 'new' programming which of course we are not smart enough to know how to do. Sam is an infant, at most, in an adult's body. His mind is a blank slate, thanks to us."

"We screwed up royally and Sam paid the price for our stupidity," Dr. Kulp angrily throws down her observation notes.

"If only we had known before we hit the 'delete' key," one of the other scientists shakes his head.

"No way we could have," Dr. Kulp responds, her anger subsiding. "The black box freezes the object in place during conversion. There was no way for us to recognize that he no longer functioned as an adult."

"What happened here?" Christopher asks from the doorway. He spots Sam on the floor, gurgling; the research team is gathered in a conference circle at one of the lab tables. Christopher walks over and kneels next to him.

"What the hell happened here? What's wrong with Sam?"

Dr. Kulp straightens her lab coat and tells Christopher what happened since he left.

When Christopher asks for Sam's status, she tells him that she doesn't know whether his learning is gone

black box

forever or only temporarily. She suspects that his learning is gone unless they can find some way to reverse the process.

"Everyone out of here," Christopher shouts after a long period of shocked silence. "This lab and this experimentation are shut down, period. Leave phone numbers where all of you can all be reached and I'll contact you when I'm good and ready. Think about what happened here and what we all may have done to another human being and to the conversionist movement. Until you hear from me, you will say nothing to anybody about what has happened here today."

With their heads down, the researchers quickly leave the lab.

"Don't leave yet, doctor," Christopher says as he turns to Dr. Kulp, "the black box is going to be locked up in the main safe which cannot be opened without my part of the combination. Nothing is to be said to anybody about these events until I can figure out what we do next. Is that perfectly clear?"

"Christopher," she pauses, "I'm so sorry. I'm so angry with myself."

"Me as well," he tells her.

With that, they lock away the black box.

"I'm taking Sam with me now," Christopher tells Dr. Kulp as she leaves. "He and I are going out to the conversionist retreat facility in the mountains. I'm going to see if we can bring him back."

For the conversionists who know about Sam, his "modification" is interpreted in different ways. Some conversionists see Sam's modification as rebirth, a rebirth without sin or the negatives he picked up in this world, as very positive. For some, Sam is the symbol of a sin committed and of people and a movement that reached too far. For others, including Christopher, it is personal. Sam is a human being and they are going to try to bring him back.

Chapter 8. Devil's Hand

Washington, D.C.; the next day.
Washington, D.C.; a week later.

As she sits in her darkened den on this cloudy Saturday morning, L.O. Moses goes over in her mind where the anticonversionist stands. Almost a year has passed and they have had little real progress. This realization hits her even as she sits in her den, relaxing on a weekend morning.

Their whole purpose as the anticonversionist movement is to remove those forces that prevent them from returning to Eden. The promise that a world without the black box is a better world is not fulfilled. Removing the 'devil's hand' had no measurable impact. Either they were wrong or they didn't do it right. The possibility exists that the black box is still out there somewhere. While this is troubling, this thought brings some comfort. At least then, the failures of the past year are less theirs.

Honestly, they are better at fighting against something, the black box, than fighting for something. As a movement, they started to tackle crime, disease, drugs, illiteracy, poverty, and homelessness. But they made little progress. Even a movement as big as theirs appears to make such a small dent. As time passed, the anticonversionist movement became increasingly frustrated. Without the devil's hand, it should be at least a bit easier.

In the past few months, the movement is more settled. People, though still wishing for a miracle, see that some progress is being made. A few more people are literate. A few more are healthier. A few more escape poverty. Some now have shelter. There is a little more food on some tables.

Maybe they are better off that the 'good people' are mostly what remains of the anticonversionist movement today. The real 'crackpots' left. Moses was not sorry to see them go. Maybe every movement should face this situation. This way it weeds out those people it would do better without in the first place. She suspects Christopher feels the same way.

"We are a long way from Eden, but we aren't finished yet," she tells herself as she turns to the computer and preparation of her sermon.

Word of the miscoded conversion spread quickly among the conversionists. The stories that circulated are seldom complete. As a result, the story varies widely. Often people hear what confirms their own beliefs.

For some conversionists, Sam's experience is the total cleansing, back to baptism. While many religions tout being reborn, the black box brings a whole new perspective to that concept. The Sam prior to conversion symbolizes all the evil that the world can put upon a human being. The Sam after conversion is the true "born again" person. Even Christopher is built into the story. As it is told, Sam is learning again at the feet of

black box

Christopher. This time he learns all that is good about the world. The black box gives Sam a second chance. Some conversionists beg for that same opportunity, a second chance, in spite of knowing that they will start over with the mind of an infant.

For other conversionists who view the black box more as a tool to facilitate personal growth, the tragedy of Sam's experience is a great personal loss. They mourn the loss of person that was Sam. They also speak of the danger of relying upon the black box for salvation. The loss of Sam's self confirms that danger. For these people, the black box was and still is a symbol of how humans aspire to move closer to perfection. But they believe it is still up to people themselves to do major work. The black box's purpose is not to serve as a short cut or as an easy way to a higher level of existence.

For still other conversionists and many other people who hear the story, there is great curiosity as to what Sam is going through. From all they hear, Sam's mind was a complete blank after conversion: no memories, no knowledge and no learned behavior. To him, the whole world is new. Many people express a certain wonderment about what it would be like to see the world's images for the first time as an adult. Is Sam's mind like a baby's seeing the first images? Or is his mind more like an adult's trying to process all the colors, shapes, sounds, smells and feels?

Inevitably, the story spreads beyond the conversionists. Some conversionists and almost all anticonversionists see the experiment confirming the black box is indeed the "devil's hand," snatching the soul away from Sam Blanc.

However, the biggest news for anticonversionists is not Sam's conversion. The biggest news is that the black box still exists.

"Video, video," Reverend Moses mutters as she enters her church. "Where would the world be today without people's insatiable desire to record everything for posterity?"

Two hours before her church service begins, a former conversionist will slip into the back of the church. In this person's hand will be a package. Its contents include video of the conversionists' experiment with Sam.

Over the past year, Reverend Moses has had the opportunity to get to know Christopher fairly well. Sure, their first few encounters were true fire and brimstone. But that settled down as they got to know each other as people. They have their differences, huge differences. But they also have common ground. They both believe they are doing what is best not only for their followers, but for everyone as well.

She's truly sorry to see this happen to Christopher and is surprised to hear that it even happened. Moses, too, fears that her follower's, like Christopher's, will get out of hand. She even telephoned Christopher to tell him she is aware of the experiment and offered her sympathies. They only spoke for a few minutes as the connection from the retreat house was bad and Christopher was distracted.

While she feels compassion for Christopher and Sam, she's not displeased that Christopher will be preoccupied for some time. If this video is what she is told it is, she is going to be very busy. The conversionists had just handed the anticonversionists a massive opportunity to neutralize the conversionist movement and go after both the box and the conversion process.

Now at the back of the church, a conversionist passes her the video. She quickly goes to her office,

black box

loads the video and watches.

"This video should do it," she thinks.

There is Sam Blanc, the person, standing in front of a bunch of white-coated scientists. To some extent, he comes off as a misguided 'believer' that offers himself as a sacrifice to the conversionist religion and its evil symbol, the black box. It is a useful touch when the camera pans over to the black box a couple of times. The black box looks ominous, just waiting to receive the sacrifice.

Then there is the result. The images of Sam are devastating. From a fully functioning adult to an adult-sized infant. He gurgles. He tries to crawl. But the images of his face hit the hardest. In his face, there's nothing but 'blankness.' Until now, the conversionist had the 'sainted' image of Sandy working for them. Now, the anticonversionists have the counter-image, the 'empty' Sam.

She knows it is nearly time to enter the pulpit and go on the air. She clicks off the VCR and calls for her assistant to deliver the video to the control booth.

The anticonversionist message is about to gain pre-eminence.

"People," she calls out to her congregation. "Let me tell you. The black box still exists. As we feared, the 'devil's hand' has been at work all this time. As we fear, the 'devil's hand' remains a threat to us all."

The video plays for her worldwide audience.

"The 'devil's hand' is revealed for the terrible force it is. Look at the robust Sam Blanc. Look at Sam Blanc pleading for help. Then look at Sam Blanc after the black box extracts its sacrifice. Look at Sam Blanc's body crawling on the floor. Look at Sam Blanc's face, empty of any human memory and empty of any human thought."

"Yes, the 'devil's hand' is back. But fear not,

because we, the anticonversionists, are back as well. Fear not, because we will not rest until the black box is destroyed and the 'devil's hand' is no longer a threat."

black box

Chapter 9. Banned

Washington, D.C.; days later.
Private laboratory in Washington, D.C.; six months later.
Government laboratory in Washington, D.C.; later that evening.

As a result of video's release and the anticonversionists' push, the public once again debates a conversion ban.

At the federal level, Congressional committees hold a number of hearings. Christopher and other conversionist leaders are subpoenaed, although Christopher is in hiding, having left the conversionist retreat. The federal government, citing national security, calls for the conversionists to hand over the black box immediately.

The black box's fate remains tied up in the courts. The government's ownership claim holds sway with some courts, but not in others. Collectively, the courts have yet to take a definitive stand. All this is going to take time and probably a ruling by the Supreme Court. The courts refuse to force conversionists to give up the black box, as long as conversionist leadership provides assurance that the box is safe and secure. The conversionist leadership is able to provide the assurance and protect the black box, at least for now.

While the courts have yet to issue a final ruling on who owns the black box, Congress and the White House begin their move to ban conversion. Reverend Moses and her anticonversionist movement are greatly strengthened by the miscoded conversion and the video "vacant" images of Sam. Without Christopher, the conversionist movement is in complete disarray. Different subgroups in the conversionist movement take contrary positions. Though not discarding the philosophy behind conversionism, some conversionists argue against "black box" conversions as well.

When the final vote is taken, the ban on personal conversion, using the black box, passes by a wide margin in both houses of Congress. The President signs it.

Late at night, the conversionist laboratory alarm system is disabled and the back door slips open. An intruder moves down the hallways, bypassing the guards at each key point. Overhead, the surveillance cameras keep watch. At just the right moment, the intruder slides under the cameras at the point when the intruder will be least likely to be seen. The intruder enters the room where the black box is kept. The safe is opened and the black box taken out. The safe is closed and the intruder exits with the black box and again evades surveillance. The alarm system is re-activated.

An hour later and miles away in a darkened entrance to a building, the black box is handed to another person. No words are exchanged.

With the black box wrapped in dark cloth, Dr.

black box

Tarry enters the darkened building alone and proceeds to his well-equipped laboratory. Moving carefully to an office perched overlooking the lab, he turns on a small light. After all this time, it feels good to have it back.

Once again, he has the black box. This time he will learn all of its secrets; he will not lose it again.

As he looks down on the darkened lab, he laments the story about the box's keeper, the one person who knew what this is all about. They came so close to capturing him when he worked in their lab as an assistant. But, just as they were about to catch him and the black box, he disappeared yet again.

Still, there is no confirming evidence that the box's keeper is gone forever. As did the conversionists, his people went back to the jungle and found no signs of the bearded stranger, the box's keeper. There are stories that he survived. He hopes they are true.

As he sits back in his chair and thinks over what happened, new questions emerge in his mind about the Maryland couple, Jason and Taj. Apparently, from what his people have learned, the couple was in the jungle at about the same time and have not been seen or heard from since shortly after the incident. They flew back to the U.S. immediately after the incident. They were back at their home only for a few hours and have not been back since. They and their pets just vanished.

All this makes him very uneasy.

On the other hand, he has the box. Tomorrow, his people, along with Joseph and Maria, will begin again their efforts to reveal the box's secrets. But he also had a promise to keep, a condition of his receiving the box in the first place. This is not going to be the relatively loose research of his last experiments with the box. Instead, now, he has made a promise; he must find a way to restore Sam Blanc. For many reasons, he intends to keep that promise.

Chapter 10. Personal Code

Private research lab in suburban Washington, D.C.;
Monday, the next morning.

      This morning feels different as Joseph and Maria enter the grounds of the private research lab that Dr. Tarry and they use. They pass the guards at the entrance to the lab. For some reason, the guards seem more uneasy and cautious this morning than on past mornings.

      "Did you notice the guards?" Maria asks quietly as they continue toward the main lab. "I haven't seen a group of guards behaving like that since that time when the black box was in our hands. I suspect this has something to do with our late night call from Tarry."

      "I suspect you're right," agrees Joseph. "Tarry was excited and secretive. He wouldn't say what it was, just that we should be here first thing this morning. You don't suppose that he's gotten some line on the black box again?"

      "Last we heard, the box was still tied up in the courts," Maria says, looking out over the lab's grounds as they make their way to the lab. "The conversionists have it locked away in their laboratory. But you never know

black box

with Tarry. He's no longer the military scientist that he was when we all first met. Now he's quite the politician."

"He doesn't have much choice about being a politician if he wants to keep this whole effort alive and under some reasonable control," Joseph mutters wryly as they enter the main lab; Dr. Tarry's personal office overlooks the floor of the lab. "Well, we'll find out soon because there he is."

"Maria. Joseph. So good to see you this morning." Dr. Tarry greets them cheerfully and guides them into his upstairs office. "I think I've got something that you just might be interested in."

"Go ahead, take a look," says Dr. Tarry as he points to his conference table, partly covered by a white cloth.

"Big secrecy this morning?" Maria laughs as she walks over to the table and lifts the cloth.

"No, I think 'great big surprise' is the right term," exclaims Joseph as he sees the black object on the table. " This wasn't exactly on the planned schedule for this morning as far as I know."

"You're right," Dr. Tarry nods. "I received a surprise call yesterday morning from an interesting source. The caller informed me that the black box might become available if there were certain assurances and promises. The terms were eminently reasonable and I said yes."

"Last night, the black box was taken out of the conversionist lab and handed over to me here. Once again, the black box is our responsibility."

"Who all knows about this?" Maria asks.

"Just a few people," Dr. Tarry answers, lowering his voice. "And that's the way it's going to be for now. Look out into the lab. You'll notice it's mostly empty. Everyone is being reassigned even as we speak.. The lab staff is being told that money is limited and we're going with just a skeleton staff for a while. The three of us are that skeleton staff. Even the guards don't know anything except that there is increased concern about a terrorist attack on this lab

"Won't the conversionists scream when they find the box missing?" Joseph asks, tossing the cloth cover for the black box back over top of it.. "What about the courts and the politicians?"

"If we're lucky, they won't find out, at least not for a while," Tarry responds. "Only about five people know the black box is not still locked up in that safe. No one is allowed to access it. Both conversionist and government security teams are preventing any access to the safe in which it is kept."

"With all that, how did someone get it out?" Maria asks, incredulous as she glances at the cloth and knows that the black box is beneath it.. "This would require the perfect thief or collusion between the conversionists and the government. Which is it?"

"I can't say right now." Dr. Tarry replies. "It's one of the promises I had to make."

"So, when you get down to it," says Joseph as he watches Maria settle into one of Dr. Tarry's office chairs, "the black box is like a nuclear reactor, functioning like a limitless battery of stored energy."

"That's right," responds Tarry as he leans against his desk. "But unlike a nuclear reactor, the box can easily pick out what mass it wants to convert. And it can handle any type of material. Then there's the by-product issue. As far as we can tell, the black box produces no by-products."

"We're not sure," Tarry continues, "how to reverse the process, how to put the proverbial 'energy

black box

genie' back into the bottle. It might not even be possible. But modification suggests that just maybe we might be able to convert energy into mass."

Joseph thinks for a moment or two before responding. "You're talking about the last round of experiments with the "1" code process and the "0" process?"

Dr. Tarry nods.

Joseph shakes his head. "Somewhere in there is all the capabilities of our entire world of electronics plus the capabilities of a reactor. Still, are we any farther on whether or not there's a remote device that activates the black box?"

"No," replies Dr. Tarry. "There have been no signs of communication between the black box and any other object. The only exceptions to that are the objects that go through conversion and the box's operator. Other than that, there seems to be no communication whatsoever."

"So," Maria says from her chair, "we have yet to know anything about the internal workings of the box. And, from what I gather, there are no breakthroughs on the horizon?" Maria looks pointedly at Dr. Tarry.

Tarry sighs, a little defeated. "No, there aren't any looming breakthroughs. It still remains the proverbial 'black box'."

Maria eyes both of them. "Then let's get started."

As Joseph and Maria leave the room, Dr. Tarry flicks the cloth that covers the black box again. Even he has to reassure himself that it's here.

This time he has more to work with, more than just the black box itself. Earlier, in exchange for the government's being less aggressive in regaining the black box, the conversionists offered a deal which the government accepted while waiting for the courts to wrestle through the legal issues. The conversionists turned over documentation and videos of their experiments, under the condition they be used only for further government research. As a result, Dr. Tarry and his team had all the information learned by the conversionists with respect to "modification." For as far the conversionists went, they had complete records of what was done with what result, including the final experiment -- the modification of Sam.

For two days, Maria, Joseph and Dr. Tarry pour over the documents and videos from the conversionists' experiments. The conversionist scientists were thorough and careful, with one large exception: the experiment with Sam.

Today, the three of them plan to shift from a review of previous experiments and to their own experiments.

Maria leans back in her chair and sips her coffee. "Okay," she asks Tarry, "just how did you get the box from the conversionists? We've been pretty patient on that one these last couple of days."

"I know you've been patient," he replies. "But you can see why this is tricky and that there are people to protect. It isn't that I don't trust the two of you. You know that I do or you wouldn't be here. But the other party to this arrangement doesn't know you."

The phone on Dr. Tarry's desk rings. He picks it up and speaks to the guards at the rear entrance. He asks one of the guards to escort today's guests to the main lab area. He will meet them there.

"What is that all about?" Joseph says, his voice rising. "Who's coming and what do they have to do with all this?"

black box

"My source and our new collaborators," Dr. Tarry responds as he walks over to the main lab door and opens it.

As Maria and Joseph see the two guests enter, it is all amazingly clear as to how the box was obtained and why it was given to them. In the door stand Christopher Carey and Sam Blanc. Sam looks serene. With bleary eyes and an unshaven face, Christopher looks desperate and resolute.

"Let me introduce everyone here, though I doubt if it's totally necessary," Dr. Tarry says as he leads the two guests forward.
"Probably not," says Christopher softly. "But let me introduce Sam to you all since he is why we are partners in this research effort."

With a nod from Christopher, Sam steps forward and puts out his hand to Dr. Tarry.

"Hello, my name is Sam. It is a pleasure to meet you."

He then moves a step to the left extends his hand to Maria. "You must be Maria." He moves another step. "And you must be Joseph."

Joseph, Maria and Dr. Tarry are astonished. Here is a person who behaves like an adult, though they all sense a certain lack of depth to Sam.

"Christopher tells me about your willingness to help me," Sam continues. "I thank you."

"As you can see," Christopher says, picking up the conversation, "Sam has come a long way in the six months since the experiment. Sam lost all he learned, but, fortunately, not his ability to learn." Christopher smiles warmly at Sam. "I'm not sure why, but Sam learns at a pretty rapid pace. He has had good teachers and I've spent almost my whole time with him."

A soft, sad tone returns to Christopher's voice as he continues. "But there's so much that is missing. All of his memory is lost. All his learned behaviors and his personality are essentially lost. Losing some of his learned behaviors was not all bad. The old Sam would be the first to agree." Christopher stops the conversation for a moment to look over at Sam standing beside Joseph, serenely staring out at the lab. Christopher sighs. "The new Sam was a virtual blank slate when I took him out of the lab that day. He behaved like a baby in an adult body."

"Since no one knows much about Sam's background and his family is dead, there is very little that we can reconstruct from his past."

"We also faced the dilemma of how to handle those things that Sam was trying to get beyond when he volunteered for the experiment. The greatest tragedy will be for him to go through all this and still end up with the negatives that he was trying to escape."

"Why come to us?" Joseph asks. "I don't quite understand. You're making good progress. In fact, you're making amazing progress. And why, if you've been able to stay hidden all this time, why would you risk getting caught?"

Joseph shakes his head. "What I really don't understand is why you would risk giving the black box to us."

"Why do it?" Christopher grimaces slightly before he continues talking. "The primary reason is Sam. Sam is making progress. There is no doubt about that. Eventually, he will be a fully functioning adult. But the more Sam develops, the more he asks for and seems to need to recover his past. His past is critical to what he is to become."

"We must find a way to restore the original Sam

black box

that was lost that day. If we can restore Sam and deal with the 'aggression' problem, so much the better."

"There's a new branch to the conversionist movement. For them, 'modification' is the power to re-shape people and the world in which people live. They argue for renewal of the 'modification' experiments. As days pass, they enlist more and more allies who just want access to basic conversion. Within two weeks, a vote will be taken at the national conversionist convention. By that time, they will have the votes."

"Am I right in understanding that we have only two weeks to learn what we can learn?" Maria interrupts. "That in two weeks, conversionists will re-open the conversion work, the first step being taking the black box out of the safe?"

"You got it exactly right," Christopher says, rubbing his eyes. "They'll defy court orders and start this whole thing up again. If we don't make real progress that I can use at the convention, I face either returning the box to the safe or risking a massive blow-up when the box is found missing."

"In the meantime, I will leave Sam here with you during this time. He might even be helpful to you. He lacks much of the clutter that sometimes limits thinking. His reasoning skills are quite first rate. His curiosity borders on being obnoxious. But you will get to like him. He is a very kind and caring person just trying to find his self."

With only two weeks with which to work and with Sam standing there as a symbol of what they must accomplish, Dr. Tarry, Joseph and Maria bury themselves in trying to unravel the black box mystery. Cots are brought in as they commit themselves to living at the lab for this period. It is also a good way to take care of Sam and keep him protected.

Focusing their attention on the "restore" function, they go back over the conversionist experiments and why they decided to drop this line of inquiry. For one thing, they never made any real progress with "restore." But they never spent much time on it. Also, they had no real incentive or interest in that area. Quite the contrary is the case here. This is the current research team's primary interest. They need only look across the room to see the incentive—Sam.

Quickly, they see a flaw in the conversionist experiments. The conversionists never restored an object that was modified in some measurable way. So for the current experiments, they will modify an object and then try to restore it. [9]

---

[9] The inquiry and the experiments focus on two strategies. The first is the "1" code process that changes an object to a greater or lesser extent. This is what turned Sam into an "infant" of sorts. While it is very clear from the conversionists' experiments how Sam's brain was "erased," there is no clue as to how to reverse the process. "Erasing the brain contents is the straightforward "1 plus all nines" process. They try it on a few animals and see exactly what it does.

Given the way the black box works, they will either have to add his memories and learned behavior back one element at a time or extract all this from the box's memory, assuming his memories and learned behavior are even there. The former strategy is out of the question. After all, the reason why Sam can't just learn all this using his quickly developing brain is that no one has the information. Without that information, there is no way to tell the black box what to add back in. That approach is clearly a dead end.

But did the black box still somehow hold the contents of Sam's brain before "modification?" Nothing in the previous experiments indicated a way to access the black box's memory to, in effect, re-establish Sam's memory. They see only two routes to pursue. The first is to discover the code for Sam's previous memory and learned behaviors and have the black box add it to Sam using the "1" code process. This creates close to the same problem as does

black box

With a solid wood cube, they put together a string of experiments. As had the conversionists, they use a particular "1" code to move a piece of the cube to some other place in it. The experiment works and the cube had one corner of it "moved" within the cube. Moving the modified cube to the box's front and left, they then go for the "restore" function. Following notes from the conversionists' experiments, they hit the following

---

trying to reconstruct his memory a piece at a time. They don't know the codes. None of the previous experiments really figured out how to use the codes, only that they are the key to controlling the box's process.

The second route, about which they also have very little information, is the "restore" function. Intuitively, this one holds the most promise. Everything they know about the black box suggests that it was very carefully designed. In that design, there seem to be a number of precautions, "safety features," to ensure that major mistakes are not made by those not fully understanding the black box. Maybe that is part of what the "restore" function is all about. Maybe "restore" is a way to recover an object that is somehow lost or messed up during "modification." Sam's situation fits that scenario exactly.

In reviewing the black box's history, there is another reason why "restore" might hold promise. That reasoning goes back to what they know and suspect about the box's keeper. They remember the story Christopher told them about the bearded stranger. He was seen leaving the jungle after the incident with the two conversionists. Given that person's apparent lack of any major physical damage, there is reason to believe that he was restored. How the box's keeper was restored is a mystery. The box would have to be capable of restoring a person badly injured and near death.

But that brings up another troubling issue. For this to happen to the box's keeper, there needed to be a second black box. Dr. Tarry always suspected that there is one. The box's keeper seems fully capable of operating even when the black box is in someone else's hands. Either he does it by remote or there is a second box. The second box theory is the more likely scenario.

sequence of keys— "record" then "modify" then "m to e" then "e to m." To the left side of the box is now a duplicate of the first cube with the corner having been moved. They press the "restore" key. The second cube changes. In the seconds they have, they quickly examine it. They hit the "verify" and then "delete" keys. The conversion process ends.

"Do we agree that we have what we have?" Joseph asks looking around the room. "The new cube is the same as the original cube. The moved corner is restored and we once again have a perfect cube."

They try the same experiment using lab animals. Ethical concerns are raised about modifying a living animal's body in a substantial way, but these concerns are dismissed given the urgency of the experiments and their relative comfort with using the restore function.

A part of the lab animal is "moved" by the black box, a leg, an arm, or a head. Subsequently, the black box restores that which was moved. The results are identical to the inanimate object experiments.

To be sure, they then split the experiments. They don't immediately restore the object but do several modifications and restorations of other objects in the interim. They put a previously modified lab animal, with only minor alterations, back into position and do a "restore." The restore process works perfectly.

Apparently, the black box keeps a converted object's code in its memory. If it is like a computer, what it keeps is at least the code for the latest version of the object. This suggests that Sam's former self, including his original memory, is probably still in the box's memory. All they have to do is restore it.

They run one more test with a somewhat aggressive monkey in which they used the "1 and all nines" code. They erase the brain's memory and learned behavior, therefore changing the monkey into an "infant"

black box

monkey. They then follow the same "restore" process as previously. The result is restoration of the original monkey, adult, but as aggressive as before.

Christopher rejoins them for the last round of experiments

Tomorrow afternoon, the conversionists will vote on whether or not to re-activate the black box experiments and conversions. There is no doubt they will vote for re-activation. Already, research and conversion teams are being assembled. They will open the safe the morning after the vote and begin their work immediately. Once the vote is taken, it will be impossible to get access to the safe to return the black box.

Christopher is not sure he wants to return the box even if he has the chance.

Chapter 11. Redemption

Private research lab in suburban Washington, D.C.; an hour later.

With the hours slipping away, they face the decision of whether or not to proceed. Sam is to be a full partner in that decision. Though much is still missing for him, his reasoning skills are strong. He goes over the previous experiments, both documents and video. While a lot of the "science" makes no sense to him, the essence of what is going on is understood. He watches his videoed statement before his modification to gain a better sense of what the old Sam might do under these circumstances.

"These last six months are a major factor in my decision," Sam explains. "From what I saw, the old Sam was trying to find a way out of what he saw as an unacceptable situation. He had to rid himself of his aggression. In his mind, black box conversion was the only hope. Christopher and I both know now there are many other options. What I can't do without the black box is recover all of my past self that was lost in conversion. That is why I must take the risk. That's why I

black box

ask for your help now."

The group decides to proceed. The vote is unanimous.

Everyone moves over toward the black box sitting on the white lab table in the center of the room. Christopher guides Sam to the black box's front and right and then steps out of the way. Dr. Tarry and Joseph jointly operate the black box to make sure there are no mistakes. The risk is great and no one speaks

Dr. Tarry and Joseph activate the box. They start the sequence—"record."

A telephone rings, echoing through the quiet laboratory. The sound shakes them all. Dr. Tarry starts to proceed again and then stops.

"Let's stop the sequence," he says. "Christopher, please watch after Sam for a few moments; see if there's anything he needs in the meantime."

Dr. Tarry picks up the phone. He says very little, mostly listening and responding yes to a series of questions. The last thing the group hears Tarry say into the phone is that yes, he will stop the experiment.

Tarry hangs up the phone and turns to the rest of them. "I've agreed to the conditions of the caller and have notified the lab's security. We will wait here in the lab for our guests to arrive." With a nod, Tarry walks up to his office, leaving the rest of them alone, wondering who the newest set of guests will be.

In his office, he slumps down in his chair. His face still reflects shock, but there are also signs of relief.

About fifteen minutes later, Maria hears the

knock at the lab door.

As Dr. Tarry rushes down from his office and escorts the three guests to the lab's center, he calls to Joseph, Maria, Christopher and Sam, "Come here, you need to meet some people. Somehow, this is a meeting that I expected would never happen. Let me introduce our guests. On my left is the so-called 'Maryland couple,' Taj Curie and Jason Kalder. On my right is the person around whom much of our recent lives revolve. Some of you refer to him as the bearded man and some as the 'box's keeper'."

"In turn, let me introduce our team. I suspect you will recognize them all. This man is Dr. Joseph Form, a scientist on leave from the Smithsonian Institution. Next to him is Maria Mendez, a government troubleshooter who was with the project from the beginning, as was Joseph. Over there is Christopher Carey, the national leader of the conversionist movement. Next to him is Sam Blanc, the person whom we are all here to help. Finally, there is me, Martin Tarry, the government's and the Pentagon's lead scientist on this."

"If you will permit me," the shepherd interrupts gently. "I don't generally go by a name. People that I know well, like Taj and Jason, tend to think of me as a sort of shepherd. Use it if you like."

The shepherd smiles reassuringly at the group before continuing. "We would not be meeting today if not for Sam here. As the primary shepherd, it is not my role to stop conversionists from experimentation. Learning and personal growth are things that I try to facilitate. But sometimes, things go awry. Most times, the world goes on, people make their own course corrections, and, out of the whole experience, people gain come greater wisdom. In this case, one problem, Sam's modification, is not completely correctable without my knowledge and the black box."

black box

"Could we have used the 'restore' function to get Sam back to where he was originally?" Joseph asks. "That's what we were about to do."

"The answer to question is 'yes,'" replies the shepherd. "The process you were following will restore Sam to exactly what he was just before the initial modification occurred. Nothing that happened during or after modification will have taken effect. But that's not what you all want. I'm quite sure that's not what Sam wants."

The shepherd steps closer to Sam, guiding him away from the group so that they can talk privately.

"Sam, I am able to offer you options. Only you can make the choice. Trust me. You are fully capable of making that choice."

"If you want," the shepherd says more loudly, addressing Sam, but also announcing it to the rest of the group as well, "you can be as you are now and grow from there. A total and complete second shot at life from the beginning. That is a choice people do not get. A second option is for you to go back to the 'old Sam,' a person with aggressive characteristics you so hated. You will not retain the experience of your last six months with Christopher. A third option is a combination. This is the one that only I can offer you. If you wish, I can give you back the memories and learning of the 'old Sam,' take away the learned 'aggressiveness,' and allow you to retain the experience of the past six months."

"You can do that?" Sam asks.

"Yes," replies the shepherd, moving them both back to the center of the room. "As you always suspected," he says, indicating the scientists, "the black box has many capabilities, many of which you are not and will never be aware. The 'level 2' capabilities were not exactly meant to be revealed when they were."

"We understand the desire to help Sam, but you

take a huge risk," cautions Maria. "How do you know you can trust us? You know us some, but not that well. At least, I don't think you do. Is your only reason for coming your concern for Sam?"

"Not exactly," the shepherd replies. "These two people by my side are no small factor in my decision. Taj and Jason argue quite persuasively that Sam needs and deserves our help. They argue that the right thing to do is to offer Sam these options and let him choose what he wants his life to be. As you will no doubt learn, these two new friends of mine are two quite extraordinary people."

"Do I really have the option of recovering my old memories and learning, discarding the aggressive characteristics, and retaining my experiences with Christopher since modification? Are you really saying that you can and, if I so choose, will make that happen?" asks Sam, awed by the prospect.

"Yes," the shepherd replies reassuringly. "Is that the option you want?"

"Are you absolutely sure?"

"Yes, that's what I want," answers Sam. "I am as sure as I believe a person can be."

The shepherd places his hands on Sam's shoulders. "If that is what you want, then that is what we shall do." The shepherd looks around the room. "Anyone here want to say anything to convince Sam one way or the other? Please feel free to speak."

No one speaks.

Dr. Tarry lays down the ground rules for Joseph and Maria. "I gave my personal assurances that the shepherd has complete control over what happens next. I will tolerate no interference. I expect there will be no interference."

black box

"Once the process is complete, the three of them will leave immediately. Again, no interference."

"On his side, the shepherd understands that we will not relinquish the black box and that he will not be allowed to carry out the box when he leaves."

Tarry, Joseph, and Maria re-join Sam, Taj and Jason, and the shepherd. "With all that taken care of, I'd say the rest lies in the shepherd's hands. Proceed in any way that you choose. We are here to help if you need us. Otherwise, we will watch with deep interest."

"Thank you, Dr. Tarry, we will proceed quickly," says the shepherd. "But first, a little bit of housekeeping. Jason and Taj, please go with Dr. Tarry and make sure that all the recording equipment for documenting the conversion process is turned off. I suspect it is still running from earlier work."

"Yes, of course," Dr. Tarry nods in agreement as Taj and Jason and he go over to the recording equipment and turn it all off.

"My reason for turning off the recording equipment is that I don't want a permanent record of what I do here," the shepherd tells Tarry, Joseph and Maria. "In fact, I will ask all, except Taj and Jason, to turn away when I get to the modification codes."

They all move to area where the box sits. Sam takes up the position to the black box's front and left.

"Very good," the shepherd says to Sam. "Sam, for you, the process I use will be similar as what you were about to go through. The difference is that I will make two modifications to the 'old Sam.' Though you will not be aware of it, these modifications will be given to the black box just before I press the 'restore' key. Both are what are referred to as '1' code modifications. Neither is an issue of changing mass so we won't have to deal with any complications there. Essentially, I will be instructing the black box to delete the learned aggression from your distant past and add the learning acquired since the modification."

"Is everyone ready?" the shepherd asks. "Sam, are you ready?"

"I am," Sam replies quietly.

"Then we proceed," says the shepherd as he begins the process.

Just as in the jungle, he activates "level 2" of the black box. He goes through the sequence -- "record" then "modify" then "m to e" then "e to m." At that point, two Sams stand before them. The shepherd motions for everyone to turn away. All, except Taj and Jason, turn away, though reluctant to do so.

The shepherd proceeds to enter the first "1" code series that retains the memories and learning from the last six months. Then he proceeds to enter the second "1" code series that deletes the learned aggressive behavior. This is more complicated since it requires separating out one piece of learning from all the other learning of the "old Sam." The shepherd queries the box by entering certain key sequences. The black box responds with certain information on the display helpful to constructing the correct codes. Finally, the shepherd has the right codes to do just what is needed. He enters the code sequences.

But before completing the process, he takes one additional step. He reaches under the box with both hands and touches the box in a certain way. For a moment, the underside of the box glows faintly.

As the shepherd looks up, he glances at Taj and Jason. They nod back. Everything is taken care of.

"Okay, please turn around. The secret stuff is done," the shepherd says warmly.

The shepherd completes the process, pressing "restore." Everyone is shocked to see a different Sam appear. This is obviously the Sam that was modified

black box

some six months ago and is even dressed like the earlier Sam. Everything about him, except the two modifications in memory and learning, is that of the pre-modification Sam. The shepherd presses "verify" and "delete" to complete the process.

Sam checks himself over before moving and speaking.

"It worked!" He shouts. "It really worked! I remember everything from childhood to what happened as I began today's 'modification'. The memories of my aggressive behavior are all there, but the feeling is different. I don't feel trapped by those memories." Sam beams happily at all of them.

"Don't worry Sam," the shepherd assures him. "Your learned aggression is gone. From here on, it's up to you. If you're not careful, you can slip back. If you work hard at it, your overly aggressive behavior will remain a part of your past only."

After everyone has congratulated Sam, Maria finds champagne in the lab refrigerator and passes out paper cups.

The shepherd first toasts Sam and then toasts Christopher for all that he tried to do with the conversionist movement.

"Your movement can accomplish much good," the shepherd tells them. "But it has to learn to deal with its destructive qualities. But in spite of all that, I applaud you for your "black box" philosophy, that the box is only a tool."

A toast also goes to the team of Dr. Tarry, Joseph and Maria, "I thank you for infusing conscience and caring in government and science's work with the black box. I wish you well as you try to uncover the black box's secrets. But, don't get too involved with the box's mechanics. The black box's real importance is its relationship with and symbolism for people."

Reluctantly, Dr. Tarry allows the shepherd to leave after it is clear there would be no more conversation. As he walks back across the lab with Maria and Joseph, he says to them, "I still don't fully trust the three of them. I like them, but I don't fully trust them. Why were they being so nice? Why take this risk? How can they be sure that I will keep my promise? I easily could break my word. What would they have done if I had?"

"Oh no," he groans. "Something else is going on here. There *is* a second box."

Dr. Tarry looks frantically at the door through which the shepherd, Taj, and Jason left and then back at the box. "That is how the shepherd is whole after being injured and left for dead. They could have contacted Christopher and saved Sam with that second box at any time. They came here to help Sam, but they also came for another reason. The box. They came to recover the original black box."

He rushes to the black box and tightly grabs hold of it. Maybe, he can stop it from disappearing this time.

While everyone looks on in amazement, the box briefly glows before it disappears, leaving Dr. Tarry with two arms full of empty air and a mouth full of curses.

Chapter 12. Conveyance

A remote, primitive cabin in the Blue Ridge Mountains in Virginia; later that day.

Today was a long and difficult day for the three of them. The events at the laboratory were a bit tricky but ultimately satisfying. As they unlock the cabin door and make their way in, they are relieved to be away from the rest of the world for a few more hours. They know this luxury will not last and they are deeply appreciative of its value.

Once inside, they find matches and light the lamps. As more and more of the room lightens, they can see the table near the center of the room. Two dark shapes are sitting on the table.

"What do you think is going through Dr. Tarry's mind right now?" asks Taj mischievously. "That's the second time he's lost the black box back to you. He's must be wondering if he is ever meant to learn its secrets."

"I suspect he's frustrated at this moment," the shepherd says. "But he will recover. In time, he will have other opportunities."

Taj interrupts, "Somehow, I think he's going to listen a bit more carefully to your choice of words in future encounters. Saying that you will not carry the black box away does not mean that you will not 'spirit' the box away. The black box's 'return' capability is quite something else."

"Yes, it proves quite useful," the shepherd agrees. "I suspect Dr. Tarry now realizes that there is an activation and keying sequence that causes the box to return to its 'home.' I gather he suspected it from our first encounter. This time I'm sure he is convinced. Fortunately, he lacks clear information on how to make it happen. He suspects that the 'return' function requires a second black box."

"All in all Tarry is not a bad sort of person. He's grown. Maria and Joseph will also be allies to us in the work ahead."

Lying in his bed, the shepherd thinks about Taj and Jason. Reflecting back on the past six months again, he thinks of all that Jason and Taj learned and how fast they have learned it. They are now fully conversant with the box's "level 1 and 2" functions, all the way from initial activation to controlling the modification process. Most of it is relatively straightforward.

The hardest part is learning how to use the personal codes system that governs the black box's functioning. As the conversionists learned, the "1" codes and the "0" codes are the initial parts of any modification. They tell the box how much and what kind of modification. While the conversionists assume they have to discover individual personal codes or sets of them, they missed what makes the black box, "user friendly." The box's interactive mode allows the box's operator to

black box

query the box in helping determine which codes accomplish what purpose.

Through this query process, he taught Taj and Jason how to access and use the box's transportation capability. This capability was essential for them being able to move around freely. Using just one box, he can program the box to send him anywhere. Even the "100 yard" limit, apparent in Dr. Tarry's, Joseph's and Maria experiments, can be bypassed. All they need is a set of geographical coordinates for the box to reference. Without coordinates, the box's default position is to not move an object, other than find a safe place for it. In transporting over any distance, the box verifies the transportation can be completed without harming the transported person or object. If programmed, the box automatically returns the person, but only if the box knows where to look to for the transported person.

Over the past six months, Taj and Jason have constructed a safety system as well, with only a small amount of guidance from him. The idea is that once their mission is known publicly, the couple will need places and resources to access at a moment's notice.

Using a combination of black box transportation capability and public transportation, Taj and Jason set up a system of safe houses at key points around the world. In several cases, the safe houses are buried in large urban areas where two ordinary people can easily lose themselves. In other cases, the safe houses are like this cabin, remote from the rest of the world. All safe houses are set up so that large periods of vacancy or the sudden arrival of two people will not create problems.

As the two conversionists discovered that day in the jungle, the black box is quite convenient for making the things required to function in the day-to-day world. In each safe house, Taj and Jason made and stored several types of currency as well as items useful in barter. Travel documents of many kinds, permitting them to travel virtually anywhere, were constructed and stored there. While the black box can always produce what they need from something as available as plain dirt, wisdom dictates that they prepare in advance. The jungle incident is a sobering reminder.

The safety system's final piece is alternative identities. The black box can make any alteration in the human body necessary to produce an unrecognizable alternative identity. Taj and Jason did just that. Stored in the two black boxes are the "1" code modifications that would change them into one of many alternative identities.

Earlier, as they put themselves through that experience, they find, just as he had, that this is an uncomfortable process. Neither of them really wants to relinquish their original selves even for a short time. Sure, it may only be external body features, but these external body features are an integral part of who they are. Of who he is.

Just a few days ago, they put into place the complex safety system's last component. It had to be before they took the risk taken in the lab earlier today.

Before they went to the lab, he sat them down and told them they were ready for the journey that lay ahead. Tomorrow, the full extent of that journey will be revealed to them.

Shortly after dawn the next morning, the shepherd wakes up, dresses and goes out onto the cabin's wooden front porch. Jason and Taj are already sitting out there drinking coffee and going over the black box's operations one more time.

"Good morning," Taj and Jason greet him.

black box

"Good morning to you, too," the shepherd responds groggily. "I can see the two of you did better on sleep than I did. Somehow, that doesn't seem quite right. I'm the old hand at all this. You're the rookies."

"We're just good at disguising it," Taj laughs. "Actually, we used the black box to give ourselves an extra dose of chipperness. We'll be intolerable all day."

"I wouldn't worry too much if I were you," Jason smiles. "It won't last. Our underlying anxiety will wear us down before too long."

"So, what's this you've got planned for us today?" he asks the shepherd.

"Transition," the shepherd responds. "Time to transition from planning for your journey and mission to actually beginning them."

He looks steadily at Jason and Taj. They both set down their coffee cups. The shepherd goes on. "All our roles are about to change."

"Okay. Just what do you mean?" Taj asks.

"For a very, very long time, my role was as Earth's shepherd," he explains. "That meant many things over the years, but it was all designed to come to this moment and to this transition. My time has come to step back and turn much of Earth's shepherding role over to new shepherds. Guess who the lucky people are?"

"Why do I suspect that we're somehow involved?" quips Taj.

"Because you are smart, good people and you're right," says the shepherd. "No big surprise."

He pauses. "Well, maybe some of what I say will be a big surprise." He smiles at them. "You two will jointly assume the roles as Earth's shepherds."

"Us? Only us?" Jason asks, incredulous. "We're it? For the whole planet?"

"Except for a little help from me once in a while, yes, you two are it." The shepherd gives them both hugs, trying to reassure them. "Congratulations. That's the way it is meant to be. Two people, working together as a team, will be Earth's shepherds."

"But, you obviously have one other little bit of help, the black box," he reminds them. "One black box is now yours. I retain the other one."

"Beyond the safety systems you installed, my black box and I will always be another. If you are in a situation requiring my help, my black box and I will always be there to support you. But a cautionary note: I may not always choose to intervene."

"Give us that again," Jason interrupts. "You might not always respond to our call for help?"

"That's right," says the shepherd. "Ideally, you will never want or need to use my help. Ideally, our only interaction will be to get together once in a while, sharing a conversation on a morning like this. That's the way it should be. However, I suspect that the 'ideal' will not be reached, at least not for some time."

"You are to grow. Earth is to grow. Growth does not occur without negatives like pain and risk. You two will bear a disproportionate share of those negatives and of this responsibility." The shepherd's expression is more serious now. "Welcome to the consequences of being chosen and having accepted."

"But don't worry," he says in response to their uneasy glances. "I will never let you down when you truly need me. That's my commitment to you and to Earth. That remains the primary shepherds' role and responsibility, one that I can't relinquish even if I wanted to.

"However, as I am now *the* primary shepherd, I now have to assume roles and responsibilities beyond Earth. You and Earth are growing up."

----

black box

Later that morning, the shepherd sits them down with the black box and says, "Let me show you how to install a security code. With this code in place, the box will physically go to a pre-specified place if someone other than the two of you or I attempts to activate the box."

Using the black box's keyboard and query function, he shows them how to activate the security feature, install a security code, and set a geographical "home" to which the box will return.

"Why didn't you do this before?" asks Taj, surprised at this capability. "Wouldn't that have prevented an awful lot of the problems from happening?"

"I didn't want to prevent these things from happening," responds the shepherd. "I needed to see how people respond to the black box's first coming. But now we enter a new phase where this is no longer the preferred route."

"Now is the time for me to complete the transition," says the shepherd. "You know you are to be Earth's shepherds."

"Though you might prefer it, there is no strategic plan and no detailed blueprint. Much depends on how the two of you and the black box interact with the world and the world with you. Most particulars are up to the two of you acting as a team. To ensure that 'acting as a team' is always the rule, I made one adjustment to the black box this morning. It now requires the two of you together to activate the box for either 'level 1' or 'level 2.'"

"While I have great faith in you, you are still human beings and you have been given something that is as close to absolute power as any human being will ever have. Requiring you two to function as a team in order to use the box is a safety valve."

"Though lacking a plan or blueprint, you have a

mission," the shepherd continues. "On the surface, it seems fairly simple and straightforward. It is not."

"Very simply, your mission is to 'do the good that must be done'."

"We are literally to 'do good' using the black box as a tool?" asks Taj.

"That's right," replies the shepherd. "You are to be the ultimate 'do-gooders."

"But listen carefully. To even start, you will have to figure out what is 'good'. Not an easy task."

"Further, you can't do all the good that people want done or even that need<u>s</u> to be done. You have to decide what is the good that must be done, a higher bar," the Shepherd tells them, speaking so his voice emphasizes the good that *must* be done. "Together you must decide how to allocate the box and yourselves as a scarce resource. That's your mission."

"Why did we as shepherds chose to install the black box here and the two of you as Earth's shepherds? Because we believe Earth is at a point in its development where human beings are ready to pursue much higher level of existences than all except a few species have ever aspired to."

"For my mission to succeed, Earth's people will have to achieve that higher level on their own. Not right for me to make it happen using something like the black box. Then, human beings would not have reached that higher level themselves. The journey is part of the destination."

"As for the future, you and the rest of earth's people must pull it off yourselves. The black box just provides a little nudge."

The shepherd looks at Taj and Jason. He senses the frightening weight falling heavily on their human shoulders.

Much more they will discover once they are on

black box

their journey. In time, more might be revealed to them depending on how well they do.

    In a , a message will go out to the world on these two people and their mission. At that point, the black box will have been fully "installed."

Chapter 13. Mission

Private research lab in suburban Washington, D.C., one week later.
Washington, D.C.; one month later.

Shortly after noon, everyone assembles at the private laboratory that is the site of government's most recent research on the black box and the fateful meeting with the shepherd and his two colleagues. It is also the site from which the black box was lost.

Two days earlier, the shepherd made the original call to Dr. Tarry. He politely apologized for his spiriting away the box and indicated he will explain more shortly.

The shepherd's request was straightforward. He asked Dr. Tarry bring together many of the people who were involved at one point or another with the black box, including Joseph Form and Maria Mendez, Reverend Moses, Christopher Carey, Sam, and Sandy. Sometime around 12:30 in the afternoon, the shepherd directed that a messenger will arrive with an envelope. Dr. Tarry should then distribute the envelope's contents to these key people. The message inside will be self-explanatory.

At 12:45, just as Dr. Tarry turns back towards the assembled group to announce his suspicion that the

black box

message is not coming, he hears the sound of a side door opening. Two people are walking toward the group. As they emerge from the dark edges of the lab into the heavily lighted center, Tarry recognizes the pair from their last visit here.

Dr. Tarry clears his throat. "I think our messengers just arrived."

Dr. Tarry sees, in Taj's hands, a letter-sized envelope, probably containing the message to which the shepherd referred. He sees, in Jason's hands, a large package with what looked like the familiar dimensions of the black box.

"Hello, Dr. Tarry," Taj says. "We'd like to thank you for forgiving our transgression from the last time we were together and to thank you for pulling all these people together on such short notice."

She addresses the rest of the group. "And thanks to the rest of you for coming here today."

"The shepherd was a little unclear to Dr. Tarry about who would be the messenger. The three of us agreed that it would be best if it were Jason and me that came."

"Before we start," Jason adds, "we want to caution you from the urge you must be having."

"Please don't attempt to hold us or to try to take away the object in the package I'm carrying. If you try, you will not succeed." Jason shakes his head. "You would just be creating an unpleasant atmosphere for us all. The shepherd has the second black box and will take us and this box out of here instantaneously if there is any interference."

Suddenly Jason's expression turns from dour to cheerful. "Good that we got that out of the way. Let's move on to pleasanter things. Let's distribute the shepherd's message. Very shortly, this same message will be distributed to all major news organizations across the world."

Copies of the shepherd's message are distributed to the group. The message reads as follows:

> What I have to say to all of you is of the greatest importance. It has to do with the future of the people who live on this magnificent place called Earth.
>
> While I don't really have a name, most who know of my work or me refer to me as the shepherd. That's appropriate, because that is my role. Now, for Earth, it is also the role of two people whom you will get to know better. Their names are Taj Curie and Jason Kalder. They are people born and raised on Earth. I have come to know them well and believe their selection as Earth's shepherds is a good decision.
>
> This is about your Earth and its long and complex history. It is about you, the people who inhabit it. It is about shepherds, like me, helping human beings achieve much higher levels of existence than they normally aspire to.
>
> Our main tool is a black box, now familiar to most of you. A black box is very powerful and capable of many things. But it is still only a tool. It does nothing unless people instruct it to do so. In a certain way, a black box is now to become a tool for you. We, as shepherds, choose to formally install a black box on

black box

Earth.

Obviously not everyone can or should have access to such a tool. Just the recognition of its existence accomplishes part of what we hope for. The knowledge of what it can do and of its making by people much like you should be a source of inspiration. A black box symbolizes what people can achieve.

Who will have and control this black box? That will be Jason and Taj. They will not be totally alone. I will never be too far away. But they and you together are on your own, essentially. You should not want it any other way. Whatever greatness you achieve is your responsibility and is to your credit.

Taj and Jason's mission is simple on the surface and complex beneath the surface. They are to 'do the good that must be done.' That has always been a black box's intended purpose.

There will always be more good needed and wanted than these two caring people can do with the black box. They will have to sort that out. You all can help them. If we primary shepherds determine they are seriously abusing this power, we will take the box away from them and from Earth. Jason and Taj are the only option that is being afforded Earth at this time and, possibly, at any time.

Now, be aware that precautions are in place to protect the box and protect these shepherds. Their work will be done in relative secrecy and they have the tools, through the box, for protecting their privacy. Any attempt to harm them will be countered definitively. Any attempt to take the box will be impossible and counterproductive. The black box now only works for them and only when they work it together. Lest you fear their power, be assured they will be watched to make sure they do no great harm.

Like all people, they will make mistakes, they will have differences, and they will grow. Their commitment to do what is right is deep and their capacity to grow is great. The capacity to grow is why they and Earth were selected at this time.

As shepherds, our overall mission for Earth is about how far human beings evolve and develop. It is about how far human beings, both as individuals and as a species, take themselves. Our mission, as shepherds, is not to make you better, but to provide a small nudge so that you better your selves.

To help you understand all this, a small number of people receiving this message were much more deeply involved with the black box during its first coming on Earth. Look to them to help address the many questions this message will raise but cannot answer.

I wish you all well.

Jason and Taj wait for everyone to finish reading

black box

the message and absorb its significance. They have more to say to the people here.

"Seeing that you all finished reading the message," Taj starts, "please allow Jason and me to talk with you for a few moments. You who were deeply involved with the black box's first coming here on Earth know what this black box can do. You know what weighty responsibility falls on Jason's and my shoulders. We freely accept that responsibility, but that doesn't make us any less anxious."

"Like you, we read, hear and think about 'absolute power' as a corrupting influence," Jason says. "In our hands, a black box is very close to absolute power. The shepherd and we took careful steps to reduce the influence and the risk, but it will always be there. We ask for your help."

Jason continues speaking, as he moves face-to-face with Reverend Moses and puts his hand on her shoulder. "We understand how anticonversionists feel about all this. Their feelings are as legitimate as any others. We do not ask that you and your people do a 180-degree turn and embrace the black box and us. That's not fair or reasonable. You cannot be sure whether or not this is just another disguise for the 'devil's hand' here on Earth. There's no way for us to be absolutely sure either."

"You may decide that you will fight against us and continue to call for the box's destruction. By our deeds, we will show you why the box's destruction serves no one well. We ask that you watch what we do and, to the extent you can, keep an open mind on the issue of whether what we do is good or evil. If you permit us, we would like to call upon you at times to gain your perspective and advice."

Taj then approaches Dr. Tarry, speaking at the same time to Maria and Joseph. Taj clears her throat. "Via the three of you lies access to government and scientific worlds. You know well that they will ask many questions. Government will voice many concerns. We need you to serve as our intermediary now and in the times to come. Sometimes, people will pose questions that we can answer and, as a result, we may be helpful. This may allay some of their fears. Other times, we will have questions that can help us in our work."

"As Jason asks of Reverend Moses, we would like to continue our dialogue with the three of you. Your knowledge is a valuable resource to us as we deal with both the scientific and political aspects of the world. Your feedback can help us as we strive to fulfill our mission."

"Christopher," Jason speaks now to him, "We know that the conversionists will be much more positive about what they hear today. For many of them, it will confirm many of their beliefs. Others will find themselves in much the same place as before today. Let us assure you that the message you try to get across to your fellow conversionists is a very valuable message. You will hear it from us many times in the years to come."

"We also ask for your help in the difficult times ahead. Besides the ongoing dialogue we have asked of the others, we will need your assistance in one area unique to conversionists. Many of them will believe that our mission should include using the black box for carrying out massive personal conversions. That is not what the box is to be used for. From the shepherd, we know this much. Human beings can do it on their own. To the extent you are willing, we do request that you transmit that message on our behalf."

Taj and Jason now take Sam and Sandy aside. "The two of you," Taj says softly, her voice more gentle than before, "in many ways, are as unique as are we. Each in your own way had an experience with the black box that no other human being will ever appreciate. We think there is much to be gained by a greater interaction between the two of you and in sharing that experience with others. Both of you have grown greatly as a result of your experience with the box. In neither case is the box responsible for most of that growth. You are responsible and you deserve virtually all of the credit. Sandy, if you wish, we will petition the government for a relaxation of the restrictions on your movement."

"Also, if you two are willing, Jason and I want to maintain contact with the two of you to see how you do, learn from you and share some of our own experiences."

Dr. Tarry is impressed with the humanity expressed in Jason and Taj's actions and words. The shepherd made a good choice in choosing the two of them.

When Taj and Jason are done talking to Sam and Sandy, Dr. Tarry looks at Maria and Joseph before speaking. They nod back. Dr. Tarry clears his throat. "I believe that I can speak for myself and Maria and Joseph when I say that it would be an honor for us to assist you."

"We completely concur with Dr. Tarry. We're honored by your request and ready to help," says Maria.

"It is much easier for me than it is for Reverend Moses," says Christopher, stepping forward. "We have all been through a lot together and we share that common experience. The world's problems are far too great for any of us to tackle alone. Working together, we can do a lot more. As for getting the message to conversionists, not a problem."

"Christopher is right that my situation is more problematic," agrees Reverend Moses. "I see the two of you and I admit that I am impressed. But I am not convinced as to who is right. I see no convincing evidence, one way or the other, as to whether or not the black box is the proverbial 'devil's hand.' I'd be irresponsible to abandon our movement without further evidence. I can't and won't do that."

"But you already understood and expected that. You're asking only for dialogue and some degree of openness. You ask that I watch your deeds. That you will get. I have no interest in leading my people down the wrong path. I remain open to being convinced that mine is the wrong path."

"As we discovered in these few minutes, there is much that draws Sam and I together," Sandy says. "We suspect that others in this room are also drawn closer together in one way or another as well."

She looks at Taj and Jason. "I accept your offer and will join in petitioning the government for greater freedom of movement and association for myself. There are risks, but I can survive as long as I have friends willing to help me. Sam offers his help as well."

"Thanks to all of you from both of us," Jason responds. "We recognize that none of you really knows us or has any reason to trust us. Over time and through deeds, we hope that will change. We are prepared to do this alone if we have to. We'll do it better if we're not alone."

"I agree," Taj says. "There are many times when the shepherd and we feel very alone in all this. This, we can assure you all, is not one of those times."

From the Dr. Tarry's darkened office above the lab comes an unusual sound. Dr. Tarry recognizes it as the gentle clapping of a person's hands with a now familiar voice behind it.

"I congratulate all of you. All of you," says the shepherd. "And I emphasize 'all of you', make we 'primary' shepherds very proud at this moment. Who says that human beings are an intractable lot?" The shepherd chuckles lightly to himself.

black box

Coming out and down from the office above the lab, the shepherd is cheerfully apologetic. "You'll all have to forgive me for eavesdropping on this dialogue, but it is very important to me to see how this first meeting went, not only for how the group responded but how Taj and Jason did."

He beams at the couple standing in the center of the group. "Taj. Jason. I continue to be greatly pleased with your work. I promise that I will not be running this close of surveillance on your work in the future."

"In many ways, today was just like that day back in Dulles Airport a long time ago. I had to meet the two of you before I could hand over the black box; otherwise, I wouldn't have been sure that you were the right ones. As was the case then, I deeply regret the inconvenience I cause, but I highly value the comfort it brings me. Our thanks to what you have said today and for what we hope you will achieve tomorrow."

"This has been an affirmation for me," says the shepherd, "and, I think, for all of you. From now on I am content to step back and take on my role as observer as Taj and Jason become Earth's primary shepherds and, like the rest of you, wait and see."

As the months pass after the shepherd's message about the black box and about Taj and Jason, the world community is cautious in their response and deliberately slow in sorting out what the message means. The group that was assembled in the lab that day works hard to validate the shepherd's message and to relay to people how high are the stakes.

The conversionists, as expected, respond positively to the message though there continue to be rumblings about being denied access to personal conversion. Some newly emerging leaders threaten to challenge Christopher's position and authority on this. For now, the majority remains with Christopher.

The first response of anticonversionists is negative, though leaving some room to maneuver. In the immediate months following the announcement, anticonversionist rhetoric is a bit softer. The lack of personal conversions using the black box reduces the potential for direct confrontation. The term "anticonversionism" is used less and less. Reverend Moses is committing more and more resources to the "return to Eden" movement, a movement for people to take control of their lives and join in making their communities better places to live.

The scientific community, with guidance from Dr. Tarry and Joseph, engages in lines of "black box technology" research suggested by the black box's existence. At the same time, the field of philosophy finds new life and enthusiasm. Not only is the field dealing with the questions raised by the existence of the black box and the human potential for achieving higher level of existence, but they try to develop practical theories for helping Taj and Jason deal with their given mission.

Not achieving any sense of consensus and hearing no great outcry from the public, government officials hold their collective "political" breath. Maria assumes the federal government's monitoring post and put out the little political "brush fires" that occur from time to time.

Sandy and Sam are virtually inseparable friends and start a movement, within the overall conversionist movement, to assist persons who, through their own personal resources, try to grow and reach higher levels of existence.

All in all, "wait and see" are the watchwords for the early days of the black box's second coming, the so-called "black box era."

black box

Epilogue

Washington, D.C.; later that day.

    Taj and Jason sit in a different house than their original Maryland house. This home, at least temporarily, is more secure and more private than the previous one. Easy enough to slip in and out of. In time, they will have to move on. Through the use of the box, they can change their looks to avoid scrutiny, but they decide against that. As a group or individually, they and the pets, Amber and G, can now move through space at will. That will be their way of dealing with public exposure.

    Time is a whole other, but fascinating matter to them. The box might be capable of time travel. The shepherd leaves the question open. He does not deny it when asked. He also does not reveal if it is so or, if so, how to use it.

    They have other questions that go unanswered for now. Can it add or subtract matter? Can it hold, obtain or make more energy than the unit contained therein? Can it convert matter into energy or energy into matter directly? As much as they know, they always worked in converting matter ultimately to matter.

Many other large questions remain for them. The "soul" question still lurks out there. Who is right? The conversionists? The anticonversionists? Maybe the two of them would learn the answer. Maybe it is a question that cannot be answered definitively.

The dilemma of how they should use this scarce and powerful resource is almost overwhelming. It is almost the proverbial "Solomon's" dilemma. This resource can fix anything or anybody. It cures people and keeps them alive, possibly forever. There still is the capacity limit. Why 500 pounds? Why a limit? Is it really the limit? They need to think that through and how that limit might constrain their work.

Again, the primary challenge faces them. The real dilemma for them is not to do good, but to decide what good to do. More and more, they realize that there is much more good to do than they and the box have the capacity to do. According to the shepherd, their mission is "to do the good that *must* be done." Not necessarily what needs to be done and not necessarily what is wanted to be done; they struggle with an almost categorical imperative -- the good that *must* be done.

As the shepherd told them, the box's passing to Jason and Taj has to do with new shepherds being appointed at a certain point in a world's development. A world's shepherd, usually two people together, ultimately have to be indigenous to that world.

What about other worlds? The shepherds were there as well, providing a small "nudge" at critical points in a particular world's equivalent of "human" development. There is always the bearded shepherd, or someone else like him, who oversees a particular world's indigenous shepherds. There is always, at the right moment, a black box.

Taj and Jason, with the help of the black box, are

black box

now the Earth's shepherds. Their friend, the primary shepherd, is never too far away.

Later than night, as Taj and Jason and the pets sleep, the morning Washington Post hits the driveway. Inside the plastic sleeve and on the folded sheets of newsprint is headline after headline: tsunamis, earthquakes, volcanoes, war, hunger, epidemics, slave trade in children, organized crime, government corruption, homeless people, genocide, and more.

For Taj and Jason, so much lies ahead. "Saving the world" will be complex and no small task.

BLACK BOX -- INSTRUCTIONS
Level One

ACTIVATION

Using four hands, touch the box's top four corners simultaneously.
> **Response:** Illuminates (1) the "e" light, (2) the "record" key/light. If no activity for 10 minutes, box shuts down.

OPERATION

Place original object to the left and front of the box and press the "record" key.
> **Response:** Illuminates original object by scanner beam. Illuminates the "m to e" key/light. If no activity for 1 minute, process terminates.

Press the "m to e" key.
> **Response:** Illuminates the "e to m" key/light. If no activity for 1 minute, process terminates.

Press the "m to e" light. Within a few moments, the "e" light flickers. Seconds later, the "e to m" light brightens. Press the "e to m" key.
> **Response:** Illuminates the blinking "verify" key/light. Box's object appears to right and front of box. Original and box's object inert. If no activity for 1 minute, process terminates.

If box's object is acceptable, press the "verify" key.
> **Response:** Illuminates the flashing "delete" key/light. If no activity for 30 seconds, process terminates.

If black box process and outcome are acceptable, press the "delete" key.
> **Response:** Original object is gone. Box's object remains. Box shuts down.

black box

BLACK BOX -- INSTRUCTIONS
Level Two – For Restoration Only

ACTIVATION

Using two hands, touch the box's top and front two corners simultaneously. Touch fingers 1 and 5 to sides, finger 3 to top, and fingers 2 and 4 to edges. (Alternative activation method to be used when this default activation method not feasible.)

> **Response:** Illuminates (1) the "e" light, (2) all key/lights for level one, and (3) the "modify" and "restore" key/lights. Activates the keyboard and screen. If no activity for 10 minutes, box shuts down.

OPERATION (For Restoration Only)

Place original object to the left and front of the box and press the "record" key. If available, enter or retrieve personal code for original object.

> **Response:** Illuminates original object by scanner beam. Brightens the "m to e" key/light. If no activity for 1 minute, process terminates.

Press the "m to e" key.

> **Response:** Brightens the "e to m" key/light. If no activity for 1 minute, process terminates.

Press the "e to m" key.

> **Response:** Box's object appears to right and front of box. Original and box's object inert. If no activity for 1 minute, process terminates.

Press the "modify" key then the "restore" key.

> **Response:** Searches memory for personal code. Modified box's object, restored original object, appears to right and front of box. Original and box's object inert. If no activity for 1 minute,

process terminates.

If box's restored original object is acceptable, press the "verify" key.

> **Response:** Illuminates the flashing "delete" key/light. If no activity for 30 seconds, process terminates.

If black box process and outcome are acceptable, press the "delete" key.

> **Response:** Original object is gone. Box's restored original object remains. Box shuts down.

black box

BLACK BOX -- INSTRUCTIONS
Level Two – For Basic Modification Only

ACTIVATION

Using two hands, touch the box's top and front two corners simultaneously. Touch fingers 1 and 5 to sides, finger 3 to top, and fingers 2 and 4 to edges. (Alternative activation method to be used when this default activation method not feasible.)
> **Response:** Illuminates (1) the "e" light, (2) all key/lights for level one, and (3) the "modify" and "restore" key/lights. Activates the keyboard and screen. If no activity for 10 minutes, box shuts down.

OPERATION (For Basic Modification Only)

Place original object to the left and front of the box and press the "record" key. If available, enter or retrieve personal code for original object.
> **Response:** Illuminates original object by scanner beam. Brightens the "m to e" key/light. If no activity for 1 minute, process terminates.

Press the "m to e" key.
> **Response:** Brightens the "e to m" key/light. If no activity for 1 minute, process terminates.

Press the "e to m" key.
> **Response:** Box's object appears to right and front of box. Original and box's object inert. If no activity for 1 minute, process terminates.

Press the "modify" key, then enter the appropriate code for the desired modification. If needed, access the box's interactive mode for assistance with coding. Use "1" codes for minor modification and "0" codes for major modification. Special care is needed when using "erasure" codes, codes ending in all nines.

> **Response:** Modifies box's object according to modification code. The modified original appears to right and front of box. Original and box's object inert. If no activity for 1 minute, process terminates.

If box's modified object is acceptable, press the "verify" key.

> **Response:** Illuminates the flashing "delete" key/light. If no activity for 30 seconds, process terminates.

If black box process and outcome are acceptable, press the "delete" key.

> **Response:** Original object is gone. Box's modified original object remains. Box shuts down.

black box

Made in the USA
San Bernardino, CA
07 November 2013